a
little
sisterly
advice

a little sisterly advice

Jennifer Stewart Griffith

spring creek
BOOK COMPANY
Provo, Utah

ISBN 13: 978-1-932898-54-5
ISBN 10: 1-932898-54-9
e. 1

Published by:
Spring Creek Book Company
P.O. Box 50355
Provo, Utah 84605-0355

www.springcreekbooks.com

Cover design © Spring Creek Book Company
Cover design by Nicole Cunningham

Printed in the United States of America
10 9 8 7 6 5 4 3 2 1
Printed on acid-free paper

Library of Congress Cataloging-in-Publication Data
Griffith, Jennifer Stewart, 1971
  A little sisterly advice / Jennifer Stewart Griffith.
     p. cm.
  ISBN-13: 978-1-932898-54-5 (pbk. : alk. paper)
  ISBN-10: 1-932898-54-9 (pbk. : alk. paper)
  1. Dating (Social customs)--Fiction. 2. Women college students--Fiction. 3. Sisters--Ogden--Utah--Fiction. I. Title.

PS3607.R5487L58 2006
813'.6--dc22
                          2006007704

DEDICATION

For Ginny
and all the other beautiful redheads in my life

ACKNOWLEDGEMENTS

With grateful thanks to my sweet and boundlessly talented mother, Tina Stewart. And thanks to Adrienne, Colleen, Louise, and Mary for their encouragement and help.

SEASON ONE: AUTUMN

CHAPTER ONE

※

"So, what do you think it is, Bee? Why am I so undatable?"

Julia pushed a jumble of her red hair behind her ear, checked her side mirror for traffic and looked over at Bianca. She'd pondered the question about herself so many times, especially lately as college loomed—and still no dates, and no answers why. Maybe it was this red hair.

"Sorry. What? This car is so stinking loud. Why didn't Ted put a muffler on this heap before he sold it to me? Some people's brothers. I should have negotiated. It's not like there's a muffler shop at The Store," by which Bianca meant the Dillard's where she worked at the perfume counter. "Employee discounts. Gotta love them 'cause you can't hardly live without them."

"So, I was saying," Julia called over the Karmann Ghia's noisy engine, "why am I undatable? Do I emit some kind of high-pitched beeping that keeps guys away?"

"Like only dogs can hear? Ha. You're so hilarious." Bianca rolled up her window and smoothed her blonde hair. Even though it was hot Julia took the cue and closed her window, too. "Definitely not undatable." Julia breathed a sigh of relief at this reassurance.

"You know what I think, Jules?" Bianca dropped her emery board in her lap and shifted to face her younger sister. "I think potentially you're a totally datable guy-catching spider lady." Really? Hmm. Did she want that? "I've been watching you this summer, and you have a pretty face and a cute figure and stuff. You just haven't figured out how to make the most of them." Julia had been watching Bianca this summer, too, and noted she frequently

3

made the most of her own generous figure. "What you need is a little confidence."

That was for sure. Julia could barely hold a conversation with her sister, let alone the scads of older guys and girls who spent every Saturday night at the two sisters' apartment in Ogden playing cards and watching movies. Even after three months of total social immersion in Bianca's world, chitchat still pained her, especially with guys. What was she supposed to say to them? Julia had studied Bianca's every easy, peppy move as she flitted among the crowd of mall-salesmen in their employee-discounted latest styles lounging on that icky brown couch. But if there was a formula, it eluded her.

"Is there some secret to this I'm missing?"

"Yes! Ooh. Downshift here on this hill. Really punch the clutch so the gears don't grind." Julia did her best. "There's a secret to the game, sis. Things every woman needs to know about how to snare her man. Wiles. Feminine wiles. They're inside you if you let them out." Inside Julia? Hard to believe.

"You poor little thing." Bianca shook her head piteously. "You were stuck at that weird arts high school all those years—when you should have been young and having fun. Just you and your piano. You probably never even had a chance to relax and hang out. Bless your heart. How many hours a day were you plunking away at those black and whites? Six?" She rolled her eyes, so Julia didn't want to admit it was more like seven or eight.

But now it had been three months in their apartment in Ogden, living together as roommates—three months of sister to sister fun, going to movies, grocery shopping at midnight, eating truckloads of Doritos and bean dip—but three months in a place with no piano. It was the longest time in memory that she'd gone without Liszt, Hoffmann, or Mendelssohn. Her fingers gripped the steering wheel, longing to play.

"Thanks for letting me drive."

"Sure. Actually, I needed time to fix my nails. The girls at Le Nails gave me this french manicure for free during my lunch break, but they didn't exactly file them straight." She started sawing with the emery board again. "I hate to admit it, but I love the smell of fresh acrylic. I'll take it over that new Elizabeth Arden scent any day. It just smells fresh, don't you think?"

Julia had never grown—or applied—long nails in her life. It just wouldn't work with all the key pounding she had to do. As they got closer to Huntsville, a Grieg melody, the mountain theme from Peer Gynt, grew louder in her mind. It was going to be great to sit down at her old piano again, even if it was just for a couple of days.

Holy cow. Was this really the last weekend before she had to start college? How could summer be over? It didn't feel like fall at all yet. None of the trees in this canyon had changed yet to fall colors. Still hot, still green and summery everywhere. Her first summer in Utah, but her last weekend of summer before starting school at Utah State. There had been so many firsts and lasts all happening within a short period of a few months: her first time ever to move—ripped from her childhood home in Alexandria, Virginia, and plunked down in the very un-metropolitan Huntsville, Utah; her first time to live away from her parents—at the summer apartment in Ogden with Bianca (as well as all those *other* people who never seemed to leave); and now her last day of her first job—at the (horrors!) Texaco in a not-so-good part of Ogden. It was tough on a girl who preferred a smooth and steady life with no waves of change.

"You're starting school, and I've been thinking about how you must be feeling. I mean, I remember how it was two years ago when I started school at Northern Virginia. Rrrare." Bianca made a scared cat sound. "I'm thinking that if you can go in there with the right attitude and a big ol' chunk of confidence, you can totally rule the social scene. I mean, how big is Utah State going to be, anyway?" Big. The catalog said something like 20,000 students. The thought made Julia kind of cringe. Her high school class at Duke Ellington had been so small and exclusive.

"So, part of what I'm saying, Jules, is the right outfit—it can dredge up confidence from the bottom of your soul that you never even thought was there. Ooh. Maybe we should streak your hair. We could pick up that new Loréal Bold as Brass highlighting kit at Albertson's on the way home. We used to do it to each other's hair all the time back when I was in cheer. No, never mind. I've got to work tomorrow morning. I forgot. Then Nina needs me to help with decorations for her apartment-warming in the afternoon. Ooh. That's my cell." She flipped it open. "Hey, Clint. What's up?" Bianca switched into her bubbly talking-to-a-guy voice. "Sorry. Can't. I'm heading for the hills. . . . No. . . .Gosh! Not the Jordanelle Dam, honey. But those were fun times, weren't they?"

Julia always felt weird listening in on other people's phone conversations, but as there was no way to politely excuse herself from a moving vehicle, she cracked her window and resigned herself to her position as a semi-professional eavesdropper.

"What, do you think my sister and I spend every daylight hour on some beach? Don't I wish!" Bianca's giggle was like a fountain of trickling water.

Over the drubbing wind noise Julia could just hear the hwa-hwa-hwa of Clint's voice on the other end of the phone. She remembered him from that weekend at Willard Bay on his roommate Dave's boat. Why hadn't she worn a T-shirt cover up that day? It still pained her to think of it.

"No. Really, sweetpea. Jules is driving, and we're going to visit the parentals at their Dream House. Yeah, Huntsville. Laundry beckons, you know. Hey. You're breaking up. Have fun without us, if you can. Bye." She shouted the last word and hung up.

"That was Clint. He and Dave are heading over to Bear Lake with the boat again. Too bad we can't go, eh? They're so . . . rich! I need more of that kind of guy in my life."

Julia figured she needed even *one* guy in her own life. How would it be if she were like Bianca with tons of them calling and inviting her places? Wanting her around to keep the conversation sparkly? Julia was so far from that person she could barely imagine it.

"Julia! I've got an idea." All the shining beams of Bianca's pretty face lit up. They seemed reflected and doubly luminescent in the strands of her blonde hair.

"What is it?"

"How many days until you have to move up to school?"

"It starts Monday. I'm leaving Sunday night. So, like two days."

"Great. That should give me enough time. I'm going to make you this super funnest thing. I'll get going on it tonight, but not until after you and I have done a little shopping trip in my closet. Are you ready for a fashion makeover? And remember, I don't care *who* insists gaucho pants are in this season. You should only wear them if they're right for you!"

Makeover. At the word, a wave of relief washed over Julia. That was exactly what she needed! A fashion, makeup, hair, personality, and confidence makeover. Thank goodness for older sisters. Fairy godmother glitter dust seemed to be shimmering in the summer sunbeams, whispering, "Cinderella, it's time!" Wow. Could Julia shed her nerdy, undatable exterior and emerge as the socially non-retarded person she always dreamed of being? Or, heaven forbid, would she just be the pumpkin? Her orangish hair might be a bad omen.

"Okay. That's settled. Now. Let's talk about my career. I think I can see myself in advertising. And I have to tell you, I'm so sick of dating Josh. He thinks he's all important just because his dad is the mayor of Ogden. Shah! As if that makes him Cream O' Weber royalty or something. Do you know he got bit by six dogs while campaigning for his dad's reelection so far this year? So glad I wasn't knocking those doors with him. Dogs! If I wasn't starting to look at political journalism as a serious career possibility, I think I'd tell Josh *bye*. But I need to hang onto my contacts. Keep all my options open."

The canyon opened up into a lovely valley, with the Pineview Reservoir glinting in the fading light, the fading light of Julia's last Friday of summer.

CHAPTER TWO

❖

"Hi, Mom. It's Julia." She ran her fingertip across the kitchen wall of Old Farm apartment #3-C. The paint was glossy and clean.

"Hello, sweetheart." It had only been ninety-eight minutes since she left Huntsville, but it was really good to hear her mom's happy voice—like Logan wasn't actually the million miles away that it felt. "You got there safely."

"Yeah. It wasn't bad, and I'm all unloaded and everything, but not unpacked." She could picture Mrs. Cronquist doing her Sunday night routine at the kitchen island of the Dream House, wiping down the polished granite countertops, and starting the stainless steel dishwasher before bed. She was probably in her blue striped housecoat or her flannel plaid pajamas and her stocking feet by now. She didn't look anything like a fifty year-old mother of four.

"Are your roommates there yet? Have you met them? Cathy wants to know." Julia could hear Cathy's muffled voice in the background asking something about whether any of them looked like they were Julia's same size so she could borrow their clothes.

"No one has been home while I've been here, but all their stuff is around." Mostly clothes on the floor of both bedrooms. That was okay. She didn't expect anybody to be a super neat freak. Actually, it took the neatness pressure off Julia. "They'll probably be home soon. Did I tell you their names all start with K?"

While Julia talked she was busily unloading the three grocery sacks her mom had tossed into the back seat of the family's old Buick

8

Century at the last second, just after her dad, Rex Cronquist, had checked the oil and windshield wipers a second time. In the second sack Julia discovered a loaf of her mom's best three grain bread with the recipe taped to the top and what looked like a peach pie. Mmm. Jan Cronquist had a way with baking of all kinds, although other forms of cooking—boiling, frying, poaching, toasting, etc.—escaped her.

"Oh, Mom! I just found it. The pie! Thanks so much. You're the best."

"I'm glad you could move out and finally realize that, dear."

Julia heard Cathy's voice in the background holler, "I *already* know it, ma." Cathy was still sixteen and living at home as a precocious parent-appreciator. It was time to sign off.

"Better not use up all the minutes on my phone card here. Thanks again. Wish me luck tomorrow." She took a deep breath. She didn't want to hang up.

"Good luck, sweetie. I just know you're going to knock the socks off all those piano professors. I'm so proud of you. Your dad says hi. We love you." They said good-bye, and Julia finished putting away her kitchen things.

Oh, look. How nice of her mother to include a cute little tin recipe box. It was probably filled with all the best baking secrets of Jan Cronquist. Wait. She opened it, and a piece of pink, scented stationery fell out. Julia unfolded it. There was Bianca's scrapbooking handwriting.

Dear Jules,

You're totally starting college! Congrats! So, I made you this box. It's all the little tidbits of wisdom I've gathered thru dating about how to beguile the guys. Feminine wiles, remember? I totally hope you take this advice to heart because it will take you really far this year. Be good! Have tons of fun, freshman girl!

Lots of love, B.

She'd drawn a little bumblebee with a smiley face next to her initial.

The box was filled with pastel colored recipe cards, sectioned off into "Basics," "Do's," "Don'ts," and "Just for Co-eds." Oh, this must be what Bianca had promised to work on for her. How sweet! Julia extracted them one at a time, starting with the "Basics" section.

"First off: You need to know about women so you can understand men," the cards began. "Cardinal rule is: women are women." That did ring somewhat profound in Julia's mind's ear. Perhaps it was because she'd been brought up in an age and a city where women weren't women. . . . although they weren't men either. It was all so confusing. Women were expected to be men and women at the same time, or so it seemed. Strong and assertive women, dominating women, coarse women, defiant and bold women—they were everywhere Julia looked. But Bianca said that wasn't the way to be? Interesting. She wondered why and read on.

The next one read, "Women must be feminine." Julia imagined Bianca speaking the phrase with a flutter of eyelashes and her chin cocked at an angle. "Then they can use their femininity to great advantage. A man wants a real woman, just like a woman wants a real man." Did Julia want a real man? She'd never given it much thought, but when she did think, she agreed Bianca was right.

There was more. "Throw out all those 20th Century can-do, working-in-a-man's-world ideas. We are women—don't 'hear us roar.' Hear us giggle while we curl our hair and run our bubble baths. Hear us gossip on the phone with our girlfriends. Hear us sing to little babies. Hear us slide our credit cards at Godiva Chocolate outlets everywhere." Hear us crunch greasy corn chips when no one is looking, thought Julia as she pulled a bag of summer-nostalgia Doritos from the grocery bag and wandered toward her new bedroom with the chips and the advice box.

When she'd sunk into the pile of unmade bedding atop her new bunk, she took out the next card. "Toss out all those current Hollywood skinny girls! Think *Jayne Mansfield*. Think *Marilyn*

Monroe. Whenever you are deciding whether to eat another mozzarella stick, think Jayne and Marilyn and tell yourself yes. I try to tell myself yes to tasty edibles several times a day." Good idea. She ate two Doritos in one bite then wiped her cheesy fingers on the knee of her jeans. Jayne Mansfield was Bianca's favorite movie star from Hollywood's golden days. Together they'd watched *The Girl Can't Help It* about twenty times over the summer.

On the back of the card there was further explanation: "Voluptuous is the key word. Remember where most women put on weight first." The key word described both Jayne and Marilyn. And Bianca, for that matter. With that in mind, Julia downed another little pile of chips, wishing for that odd but delicious complement of a little tin of Fritos bean dip to go with it.

There were a few more anti-feminista cards along those lines. The last entry in the "Basics" section read, "Work the 'damsel in distress' angle. If you look both pretty *and* helpless, almost any guy will leap to your rescue. They can't stop themselves. It's hardwired into their genetic makeup. Just be sure you've remembered *your* makeup that day. The prettier the damsel, the greater the hero instinct." Good point. Bianca was probably right about that—knights in shining armor seldom ride up to rescue the self-sufficient why-are-you-here-anyway damsel. Julia filed that one into her memory. Now she moved on to the simpler, more direct do's and don'ts.

"Tanned thighs of any size." "Be shorter than your date." "Always be out on Saturday night." "Never date someone younger— social suicide." "Never wear floral to a dance—screams *wallflower*." There were other succinct cards with simple no-nos: riding a bus, dressing outside your color season, dark roots, unbleached teeth. Some of them were obvious; others were surprises to Julia, things she'd never considered as having a cool factor before.

The "Just for Co-eds" section was even more specific. "Never wear both straps of your backpack at the same time." "Don't choose an all-girl major—how will you meet guys in class?" The Music Department might not qualify, but it was too late at this point. She'd accepted the scholarship and declared her major and started her classes now. Thank goodness she'd at least signed up for Chemistry after discussing her class load with Bianca over the summer.

There were quite a few in this group. "No living in the dorms. Ever." Why not? She'd heard it was a good way to meet people. On the other side was a clear explanation. "Why not? For one, no guy can directly pick a girl up for a date in the dorm. For another, while he's waiting for you he might see something he likes more. Finally, and most importantly, no possible doorstep scene." Okay. Good enough reasons.

The next card read, "No hanging around the foreign students," and, checking the back, Julia found the clarification, "Except for people with stylish accents." Lucky for Julia, her own definition of stylish accents was pretty broad.

The final one was written in black marker and triple underlined. "No, no, no going home for the weekends." Julia flipped it over to see if there was a reason why. "If you're gone on the weekends, you look unavailable for dating, and there are some fear boundaries an average guy will not cross."

Was Julia looking for an average guy? She wasn't sure. But she did know she was looking. Marriage was a top priority. You marry who you date. The corollary question then was, what if you don't date? The other corollary question was, is it *who* you date, or *whom* you date? Everyone said it incorrectly. Either way, when it came to dating, Bianca had much more experience than she did. Julia could hardly remember a weekend since Bianca turned sixteen four years ago when some guy didn't whisk her away on a Friday night to a dance or a ball game or a show.

This was a treasure trove of info, if she could implement it. Could she? Bianca's sequined "Go Team!" T-shirt echoed the words of Julia's inner cheerleader. She could try. She would definitely try. This was her year. Julia placed the box carefully in her sock drawer and decided she'd better get some sleep so she'd be all bright eyed and bushy haired (as she had no choice in the matter) for her new life that would start in the morning.

CHAPTER THREE

―――――✦―――――

"So, I've definitely decided on journalism." The apartment phone cord twisted and made Bianca's voice crackle through the receiver. It had been almost two weeks since Julia had visited with her sister. It felt like a year.

"As a major? Are you starting school again?"

"No. I'm talking a career."

"Sounds great."

"Doesn't it? I like the idea of meeting the public and getting to be on TV and stuff—plus asking questions to important people. Hey, I almost declared it as my major, though. Back at Northern Virginia. But just before I got around to it, I got that callback from Nieman Marcus at the Tyson's Corner Mall, remember? They made me an offer I couldn't refuse. Jewelry counter. Those were the days! Do you know I earned commission?" Julia had forgotten the exact reason why Bianca left school after the first semester of her sophomore year. Jewelry.

"Being the perfume girl isn't always as easy as you might think. After spraying little cardstock squares with Diana Fortuna's latest scent for six hours, it can start to give you a killer headache. The fumes, and all. Maybe Amanda will quit, and I can move up to the slot at the make-up counter. I'd like to get into professional makeovers someday. It's such a service to people, and I hear you can make a boatload of money."

Julia was glad she caught Bianca at home between work and helping Josh's dad with the campaign. She'd been really into politicking lately, and the primary election was coming up, so

Bianca didn't often have time for idle jabbering with her sister.

"I'm so totally pumped that you're all moved in with those cute girls I met at Dillard's last summer. Wasn't that such a perfect coincidence? I could just tell they were going to be so fun. Being on the dance team and all, they'll know tons of people. I bet you'll meet loads of athletes because of them. Work it, Jules. USU has some very fine basketball players, I hear. Oh, gotta go. Call waiting. Thanks for calling. Wear the red shirt to the class you have with the cutest guys. It looks great on you."

Julia hung up and wandered back to her Music Theory and Trig homework. Things were too quiet here. Kimmy, Kistie, and Kendra were off kicking their legs somewhere to the beat of some band Julia had most likely never heard of. It wasn't exactly the fun group of soul mates Bianca had predicted. The phone rang. No one else was home, and Julia was sure it would be for one of the K girls as usual, but she dutifully trudged back to the kitchen to answer it anyway.

"Julia! It's me Cathy." Chatty Cathy—hooray!

"Hi, Cathy. How's life at Huntsville High?"

"Fine. The usual. But you! How's your college world a-spinning? Have you applied for that weekend pianist job at the Radisson yet? I can just see you looking all glam in a flowing black dress collecting tip money in a big crystal bowl on top of some grand black Stradivarius." Julia knew Cathy meant Steinway.

"Sorry to disappoint you. There isn't a Radisson in Logan, just Ogden. And no, no job yet. Campus jobs are a lot harder to find than I thought." And the pay was practically nil. It was barely worth going, as it would only feed a person on a strict diet of ramen noodles, the lunch of champions.

"Darn. Well, I'm sure something will pop up soon. Definitely. Man, I can't believe you're up there, and I'm still here. Can I move in with you or something? I'd sleep in a closet and eat practically nothing." That was probably true—Cathy had less meat on her bones than most . . . bones.

"Now why would you want to do that? Aren't you the heart of

your school's activity roster? In charge of absolutely everything?"

"Not. What I am is the full time babysitter for Sister Flinders while serving as Mom and Dad's only go-to girl most of the time. I almost wish I'd never gotten my driver's licence. But, hey, now this is going to sound dumb, but I wondered if you could help me, uh, with a school activity." She snickered at herself, and Julia smiled, too. "Any chance you're coming home for the weekend?"

CHAPTER FOUR

───────────✦───────────

A butter yellow sun dawned on the next day of classes at Utah State. It was as if Earth knew school had started because Logan got its first frost the night before, and the tips of the maple leaves woke up red.

The roommates were already up and gone to their morning workout. She was starting to get used to them now, but they weren't exactly her idea of close friends. She'd always pictured roommates baking cookies together and gossiping about the guys next door, but the K's were always busy with drill team practice and away games and hanging out with their Ogden pals. It didn't give them much time at home, so it wasn't long before Julia realized she wouldn't be able to lean on Kimmy-Kistie-Kendra for getting to know people. She had to branch out. Maybe classes could be a resource.

Her Chemistry class had two labs. Well, a lab and a recitation. She added it at the last minute as a physical science credit and as a way to meet datable guys, as directed by Bianca. Unfortunately, she ended up in the pre-nursing section, filled entirely with prospective nurses. All female. Not even one budding male nurse broke the barrier, and, if he had, compared to all the perky Florence Nightingales in there, Julia knew she would have been the dimmest Bunsen burner in the lab.

The one good thing about the class was her lab partner, True— a fun pre-nursing student from Wyoming who marched to the beat of her own drum that was emanating from her iPod headset full time. It made her talk a little too loudly in the lab, but no one seemed to care. Her frilly clothing in floral prints made Julia nervous—the ruffled sleeves, though pretty, seemed to be ideal for soaking up chemical spills. Hazard.

"My parents named me Gertrude. Can you believe it? What planet were they from? Planet Duh? And with *this* nose! At least I wasn't my sister. They named her Kimara. Like they didn't know the similar sounding word, chimera, was some goat-headed dragon symbolizing doom. Imbeciles. So, call me True."

True, a natural mousy brunette with unnatural blonde highlights that streaked back to her scrunchie-bound ponytail, lived at Valley View Towers and already knew most of the girls on her floor by the time their Thursday night lab rolled around when she and Julia met for he first time. Her own dormmate hadn't shown up, so True considered the entire building her roomies.

"There are some really great gals up there. You could come visit this weekend—I'll introduce you around." It sounded like great fun to Julia, even though it went against Bianca's "no dorm" rule. There was no specific instruction, she reasoned, against entering the dorm—or being friends with people in the dorm—just no living there. So, she agreed.

That was last weekend. Julia met quite a few nice girls and had a great time. Of course, a studious student like Julia who cared about her grades and keeping a scholarship didn't have too much time for fun and games on top of nineteen credits. Two weeks into school, and she could tell she'd bitten off more than she could chew.

Julia was making the long walk home from the Fine Arts building on Thursday afternoon so she could get some dinner before she had to be back at the chemistry lab at six. She took a different route from usual and passed the Nelson Gym.

Just as she was going past the doors, a pack of athletic-types emerged, nearly knocking her backpack off her right shoulder. As she steadied herself, her nasal cavity flooded with the freshest smell her nose had ever encountered. It nearly made her swoon. She looked for the source, and there was a just-washed, well built, rock solid guy in a light grey T-shirt at her side. He brushed against her, apologized, and walked on. Julia stood there in a funk. It was like her olfactory nerves shut down her brain. He turned back, and she saw his face. Cut jaw, dark brows, kind blue eyes. He slicked his short cropped fair hair a bit and turned back to his friends. He noticed her! Who was he? That smell! That look! That everything! How could anything that good be real?

She walked the rest of the way down the hill, filled with *him*—whoever he was. She recreated that scent in her mind. Then she memorized it, or tried to, for future reference. It was pure heaven. It was divine breath. It was—what was it? She *must* see—and smell—him again.

As soon as she got home, she checked the clock and then rummaged around for her worn fall schedule. She flipped to the Physical Education section and tried to figure out which class might meet in the Nelson Gym ending at 4:30 on Thursday.

There were Tuesday-Thursday 3:30 sections of volleyball, aerobics, and rock climbing. It had to be the rock climbing. Well, she knew right where she was going to be next Tuesday at 4:30. Without fail.

A few minutes later, she sat at the table eating her grilled cheese sandwich, telling herself yes to a second, when her three roommates came in. They were all giggling as usual. One of them, she wasn't sure quite which "K" was which yet, got a glass of water and a candy bar from the fridge.

"I am such a pig. I had one of these yesterday, too."

"There's no way you're going to fit in your *new* room!"

New room? Was there a room switch happening? Julia barely got her stuff on her shelf all arranged.

"Forest Gate is the only place to live. I can't believe we didn't know before we signed up here. I'm so *mortified*."

The K's had talked about visiting their Ogden friends at Forest Gate a few times before, and Julia had overheard. But strange things were afoot here.

"Um, I guess we'd better tell her." One of them pointed a thumb at Julia.

"Okay. Julia. Like, we hate to break it to you, but we're moving."

She had her hand on her hip and was spinning her dance shoe in front of her by the shoelace.

"Oh, really? Where are we going?" She caught herself before she added the final "to" to the sentence.

"We? Oh, sorry. Not *we*." She drew an air circle around all four of them. "*We*." She drew another air circle around just the three of them.

"Oh." It all came together: the K's were moving to Forest Gate. Without her. She almost started to have hurt feelings, but then she remembered to take a step back, assess the situation, and realized it wasn't necessarily something about which to have hurt feelings. Instead, she asked business questions.

"So, who is moving in here? Anyone?"

"We talked it over with the managers. They said if we found someone to take our contracts, we could get out. And we did."

"Yeah, but tell her the other part."

"Oh. Yeah. There's a *little* problem." Julia instantly recognized the false underestimation. "You see, the people who bought our contracts? There are four of them. And so we told the managers here you were getting out, too. The deal is all signed. The new tenants even picked up our September rent, so we each made a hundred and fifty dollars on the deal. Sweet, huh? Here's your share."

Julia didn't count the cash, even though she doubted its completeness. How could they do this to her? And how could the managers take their word for it? Bad. This was what came of having married student managers. Bad, bad, bad. Now what was she going to do?

"When is the big move taking place?" She had to know when her homelessness was slated to begin. Anger started to swell in her, and she lost her appetite for her first grilled cheese sandwich, let alone a second.

"They're moving in Saturday morning, so the place has to be empty by then. We," she drew a circle around the three K's, "are out of here tonight. There was a whole apartment vacant at the coolest place to live, and we're headed out now. Each person gets their own room and bathroom, no sharing. It's really fly. We couldn't pass it up. Hope this doesn't inconvenience you," she said as she washed out the frypan with her initials on it and put it in an obvious moving box. It was the frypan Julia used to make the grilled cheese.

If there was a whole place empty, why wasn't there room for Julia? She started to ask the question, then stopped herself. She didn't want to be there. But now where was she going to go? Homeless at eighteen. A sad violin played strains of Mahler in her head. Or almost eighteen. Her birthday wasn't until Tuesday. Tuesday—the day she would see *him* again. How would she bathe? How would she get her hair done as a homeless person? Would she be making the nook in front of the Nelson Gym door her permanent abode?

It was almost time for her Chemistry lab, and she needed to get out of that toxic environment before she said something she would regret. Then her mind hit on a positive thought, and she grasped hold of it: True was in her Chem lab. She'd know what to do.

CHAPTER FIVE

Julia rolled up at the dratted Dream House just as the sun was setting behind the nearby hills. It was only about 4:00 on Friday afternoon, but the mountainous area made for an early sunset. Cathy, who zipped out when Julia's tires rattled on the gravel drive, greeted her sister with a huge hug.

"You're finally back. It felt like you'd never get here! But I knew you'd come, even though I just realized there was probably something super planned with your roomies for tonight. So, this is, like, a social sacrifice, isn't it? I totally appreciate your help."

"It's no problem, really, Cathy." She returned the sister hug and hoped Cathy wouldn't notice that everything Julia owned was crammed in the back of the car which was riding a bit low under the weight of all Julia's books in the trunk. But no such luck.

"How come you never unpacked? What's up with that?"

"Oh, that. Let's just say I'll be calling you with my new address next week."

"I see. Should I ask?" Cathy looked at her intently, but Julia shook her head. "Okay. You can tell me some other time. Anyway, the kids are getting together over at the gym at nine after the football game. First I need some help loading the stuff—Jed will be here with his truck at 8:45."

"Who's he?"

"The S.B.P.—student body pres. He's in the other ward, so you probably haven't met him. Anyway, Jed's not in charge of this activity, but he's the only one on student council with a truck."

The two girls passed through the double doors into the stone entryway and headed for the kitchen. "Mom has some cake saved in the fridge for you. Pineapple upside-down." That felt like home, even in the Dream House.

"So," Julia lifted another bite of pineapple, "tell me. How exactly did you get to be junior class president? Yeah, it's a totally small school, but you only lived here two months before your sophomore year ended. What's with that?"

"I don't know. Like you say, the mystique of the new girl, I guess." Cathy shrugged. "Not very many people ran for office."

Cathy was so humble about her charms—which only added to them—that Julia didn't really need to ask why Cathy was in school office. It was obvious. But she did wish she knew her younger sister's secret. She always seemed nonchalant about her popularity and was friendly to everyone, no matter where they could get her on the social ladder.

In fact, sometimes it sounded like Cathy was intentionally trying not to be popular. She said something like, *Don't peak too soon because you don't want to be a glory-days person, so keep all your coolest days ahead of you.* And another thing: Cathy never once seemed to analyze who was in and who wasn't. At least not that Julia ever heard aloud. Perhaps Cathy, too, had a secret confidential formula for popularity she always used, like Bianca did. If so, it was well hidden—under layers of pretending not to be trying. Someday Julia would ask her.

Cathy twiddled a fallen leaf in her hand, which she'd picked up while they were outside.

"Summer's gone now, isn't it. Totally. I was wondering, what was it like living with Bianca? What did you two do every day?" Cathy dropped the leaf in the garbage. She snitched the maraschino cherry from the side of Julia's plate and popped it into her mouth. Julia was glad to talk about the summer roommate situation rather than the current, nonexistent one.

"Oh, fun. We weren't too creative. It's kind of weird. For the first time in my life I was watching hours of TV every day."

"You're morphing into *me*. Who knew Julia would move in with

Bianca and become Cathy?" Julia motioned for Cathy to follow her to the sitting area, and they sprawled on the leather sectional. Cathy pulled a knobby throw over her legs. She was always cold—probably a function of having no body fat. The sisters talked about jobs and school for a few more minutes until Cathy stretched and stood to go.

"I'm off to the game. I'll see you around nine, right?" Julia nodded and waved good-bye to her little sister.

Julia needed to talk to her father about employment matters (i.e., money for food). There were no jobs to be had. At least none she could unearth. Unfortunately, he wouldn't be home for another hour, so she sat down at the piano. The pianos in the practice rooms at college didn't have the same feel as her parents' long used and beloved piano, and she dreaded going into them, so she hadn't done it much. Pressing these keys felt like home.

She started in on her favorite Gershwin piece, "Rhapsody in Blue," which she spent nearly the entire previous year memorizing and perfecting. Duke Ellington High School planned a jazz-themed concert for that spring, and Julia was to be the featured artist with a selection from that piece. Of course, it was scheduled for just after the move. Nothing could be done about that now. She began the familiar chords. She didn't even have to imagine the sheet music in her mind—it just flowed out her fingers. What a comfort it was! She didn't realize how much she'd missed it, or how much it relieved her stress. It made her so happy—until the third movement. There she began to stumble. If she could get the first chord, passages came easily, but there were a lot of rough places. She switched songs to a Bach piece she'd done at a recital years before. It was her tryout piece for Duke Ellington. A standby. The first part was easy, but the second half presented the same roughness as the Gershwin piece. It scared her.

"Your talent is like a knife. It must be sharpened often, or it will not cut. You must continue improving, or you will regress." Her teacher Mr. Johnson's words suddenly took on full meaning and filled her with horror. For the next two and a half hours, Julia pushed herself to renew that sharpness—a sharpness she'd need if she was going to keep her piano scholarship.

The doorbell finally broke her concentration. Cathy was still at the game, and their parents hadn't answered the door themselves for years.

"Hi. Is Cathy here?" A boy about Julia's age stood on the stoop. It was dark now, and Julia had forgotten to flip on the porch light. She did so now and saw a very nice-looking, if a bit gangly, boy. She motioned for him to come in. "I didn't mean to make you turn off the music." Turn off? He must have heard her practicing.

"Oh, no. Um, Cathy isn't back from the game. I'm Julia."

"Julia. I'm Jed. You're Cathy's older sister?" She nodded and realized this was the "S.B.P." who Cathy mentioned. It must be time to decorate. She hardly looked ready to go out, still wearing her moving-out clothes and her hair in a giant red ponytail. Jed plopped down on the living room sofa, acting as comfortable as could be in the Dream House—and his family didn't even live there.

"You can put that music on again, if you want to. I really like Chopin." When he arrived, she'd been in the middle of one of her tougher pieces, a Nocturne, assigned by her piano teacher at Duke Ellington—a challenge piece, which she mastered. It was one of the only ones she'd tried this evening without getting a block partway through, at least not before the doorbell rang.

"Oh, that was just me."

"You were playing that?" He looked shocked. Then deeply impressed. "How old are you?"

"Eighteen," she fibbed. Almost eighteen.

"And you can play that? Amazing."

It wasn't that big of a deal. Everyone who practiced as much as she did could play it. And lots of people she knew started out with more inborn talent than she had and were far more advanced pianists than she. There was no way she'd ever get into Columbia's piano program, even if she'd aced the audition she was supposed to have last spring. That seemed like forever ago.

"Give me a few more bars of that, just until Cathy gets here, okay?"

Julia hesitated to perform, especially considering her earlier mental blocks today, but Jed seemed so nonthreatening and such a genuine fan of the composer, that she gave in.

The Nocturne was four and a half minutes long, and she played it with hardly a missed note. In fact, she was so intent on it she forgot she had an audience. When she played the final chords in resolution of the minor piece, Jed gave enthusiastic applause.

"Amazing. Ama-a-zing."

She smiled and bowed her concert bow, ignoring the fact that her dirty jeans and T-shirt were a poor substitute for her black recital dress.

"How do you know so much about Chopin?" Julia sat down on the love seat across the living room from him. He put his feet on the coffee table. Jan might not like that in her Dream House. But Julia wanted to make him feel at home, so she put her feet up, too. She looked at the lanky guy again and saw he had a serious cowlick on the left side of his dark hairline that made his bangs stick up in little prickles. His nose was covered in faded freckles that must have been pretty fierce when he was seven or eight. But despite those oddities, something, probably from inside—a charisma—made him quite good looking. She could see why he was S.B.P.—girls tended to vote for the "cutest" candidate.

"My parents are music buffs. They like everything from Mozart to Coldplay, and they indoctrinated me young. For a couple of years, I tried to get my own different music, but they assimilated that, too, so I just gave up. They're good." Strange to hear a kid who seemed to like his parents. None of her friends, past or present, ever acted like their parents were even from Earth. Jed tugged down his Huntsville High School sweatshirt and scratched his ankle under his wool socks.

"So, how come you're not at the game? Don't you have any school spirit?" Julia, who never went to a regular high school, found the strange ritual of team sport fanaticism to be a mystery.

"None. Just kidding. The game got over a while ago. I guess Cathy had to take some kids home." Did Cathy have wheels? That reminded her—she never talked to her dad about the employment situation. She'd better do that. Jed was still looking at her and then at the piano. "I still can't believe how well you play. Eighteen, huh?" Her birthday wasn't until after Labor Day. He didn't need to know. "You ought to give lessons. This town is seriously short of piano teachers. I bet I could round up ten piano students for you inside of an hour."

"I've never thought about giving lessons—I've always been so busy taking them." And practicing. Plus, there was no way any kid in Alexandria, Virginia, would take lessons from some high school girl. There were so many true pros to choose from there.

"You could make loads of money doing it. Ten dollars for a half-hour lesson. That's twenty dollars an hour. Where else are you going to get that?" She didn't know. She had no marketable skills, other than her cash register abilities from the Texaco era. And it was pretty late in the game to be getting a campus job, that was for sure. Plus, it would save her from having to hit up her dad for cash, a task she didn't relish in the least.

"I'll think about it," she said, even though her mind was already grabbing hold of the thought. Would her parents let her use their Dream House for her job? That was uncertain. But twenty dollars an hour! Ten students. Five hours. A hundred dollars a week. No sweat. No Texaco smock. No brainer.

"You could even get more students if you wanted. I can get you as many as you need."

"That's completely nice of you. Like I say, I'll think about it, and I'll let you know."

Cathy came in just then, and the three of them loaded the huge papier mâché globe into the back of Jed's truck.

"It's a world service theme. All proceeds from the dance and social are going toward the Africa relief fund. Cathy thinks the kids need to get the idea of giving. Your sister's cool. There's a lot more to her than meets the eye."

Jed was right. Cathy was always trying to change people's way of thinking.

And there's a lot less of me, Julia thought with a sigh.

Chapter Six

❦

"Happy birthday to you, happy birthday to you!" True sang, waking up her new dormmate before her early run. Julia responded with a groggy thanks. "Do these sweats make me look fat?"

"No one can see you at this hour. It's still dark."

"So, they *do* make me look fat!"

"No. Not at all." It was only her second day as True's roommate, and already she'd received ten times as much consideration as in the two weeks off campus. And a hundred times as much conversation. It turned out she was only homeless from Friday to Monday afternoon, which made almost no difference since Monday was the Labor Day holiday, and she was at the Dream House all that time.

"Tell me. How do you do it?"

"What?"

"Get up so early? It's not even six."

"I know. But I have a secret weapon." She picked up a little tin can from her nightstand and shook it. "Altoids mints. They're like smelling salts. One deep whiff in the morning, and my brain couldn't possibly stay asleep." Curiously strong indeed. "Okay. Well, sleeping beauty, see ya in an hour." True popped half a stick of Doublemint in her mouth and headed out.

Julia had told True her predicament during lab right after the eviction notice. "I felt like a J in a sea of K's." She also described her secret relief at getting out before things got ugly.

"That's okay, I'll be a J with you." True, who sympathized immediately and suggested she move into the empty dorm space with her, arranged all the details the next morning with the Resident

Assistant. It couldn't have been smoother.

"Thanks, Jrue."

Luckily, Bianca was too busy to come to Huntsville for the weekend, so Julia didn't have to fess up about the dorm move; however, Bianca she must have located her somehow because she called Julia at her new place a little later that morning.

"Happy birthday, sister. How do you feel now you've reached the ripe old age?"

"Fine. How are things at The Store?"

"Same ole. Did I tell you? Ugh! The guy running against Mayor George, that's Josh's dad, I call him Mayor George. He thinks it's cute. Anyway, the guy running against him is so fake! I heard he even got arrested for stealing a car in the 1970s. And he talks all big about integrity. Someone could really do a makeover on that guy's personality. Do you know he even was accused of doing favors for his brother-in-law's construction company while he was on the city council? I can't believe he has the gall to even put his name in for mayor."

"Did Josh's dad tell you all this?"

"No, Josh has been doing his research. That's what I love about journalism. The background checks. It seems, like, so James Bond. But anyway, someone should totally call Dirksen, that's the challenger, on his lies. If only I were already a journalist, I'd go to his press conference and ask the tough questions. But, hey. Birthday! We need to celebrate. How's next Friday? A few days late, but you can never celebrate too long, right? What kind of cake do you want?"

"That's so nice of you, Bianca. Chocolate, of course. It goes without being said."

"Chocolate, of course! It does go without being said! And, I know, I know. I did tell you not to go home every weekend and stuff, but this is for a good social cause. In fact, it's for a very good social cause, Jules."

"What do you mean?" Oh. That was another thing she didn't want to mention to Bianca—the weekend factor. Every Saturday morning from here on out she had piano students at the Dream House. Jed was true to his word. He rounded up not ten, but eleven pre-teens for her to teach, one of whom was his little sister Amanda. Her first teaching day was this upcoming Saturday, and she was as nervous as could be. There were a million things she didn't know how to do, like assessing their beginning skill level, helping them choose which books to buy, assigning pieces. Her mind swirled, but Bianca brought her back to earth.

"Well, part of my present to you, okay the whole present, sorry, is that I'm going to invite your tall, dark destiny on Friday. You can't say no. He's so chic."

Chic? Julia wasn't quite sure what that meant, but tall and dark didn't sound bad.

"Julia, you have to meet him. I've only known him a few days, but he's totally impressive. Every time I talk to him I think he's totally perfect for you. Trust me. Besides, if you just remember some of those little tips I gave you, he'll be butter in your hands." Butter? In her hands? And how would that be good? Whatever. Anyway—could this be her chance?

"What's his name?"

"Scott. So, you'll be there? Great! We'll shop at five when I get off work, and the party's at 7:30. I found you a fabulous new outfit at a bargain price, and Charmaine said she'd hold it for you until then, so plan to buy, okay?" Finally, something stylish of her very own. What would it look like? And on the same night as meeting Scott The Chic. Oh, eighteen was already so much better than seventeen. Truly better, as she wouldn't have to tell people at college she was still seventeen anymore—she always got the stare for that. There was even a birthday card from Ted that came yesterday. She tore it open to read it before she studied her scriptures.

Hey, Sis!

Eighteen, huh? Jail bait no more. Way to go on gaining another year.

Love, Ted.

It didn't say much, but it was a nice thought from a big brother, who by rights should be too busy for his fam and old friends, just like all other madly in love people. From what their mom said, he was still ga-ga over the engineer-essa and should be proposing to Becca any day.

Although she still seethed about the house and the move (which were basically Ted's fault since he found the land for the Dream House, and because he was the first of the toppling dominoes to move out West to Utah from Virginia), she still admired him. Ted, for all his computer obsessiveness, wasn't a complete geek, as Bianca often said. Yeah, the shortish, square-faced four-eyes couldn't crack a joke to save his life, but he could describe an attack vehicle from Robot Wars and make it sound interesting even to arts-entrenched Julia. Plus, somehow she knew she could count on him in a pinch— not that she'd ever really needed to, but it was comforting to think of him as being there. And to get birthday cards from him.

Julia peeled the tooth-bleaching strips from her teeth and then waxed the tips of her hair for frizz control that birthday morn. Wait. This was Tuesday morning! The morning of the Nelson Gym stakeout! Would she see him again? Would he be there? Was he even real? Thursday was such a weird day and seemed so long ago, she wasn't sure if that part was just a daydream. But then she tried to recreate his smell in her mind, and there it was. Her mind could not have invented that amazing sensation. After five days of analysis, she concluded it was a perfect blend of Irish Spring and Aqua Velva. There might have been some Fab detergent thrown in there, too, but the Irish Spring was a certainty. Mmm.

What should she wear? Aha! It was the perfect day for her makeover outfit. She pulled it from her new closet and put it on.

A few minutes later, Julia stood in front of her bedroom mirror, frowning. Something wasn't quite right. The outfit that had looked so good in front of Bianca's closet mirror the other night wasn't working this morning for some reason. Maybe if she were going out dancing, and not trekking across the wilds of the USU campus it would have looked good, but there was altogether too much sparkly stuff for comfort. And she didn't have time to put her hair up to match it, or to show off the chandelier earrings, and it would have looked dumb, anyway. USU was a ponytail kind of a place, not a twist-with-a-fancy-clip place. The black pants were too tight for comfort, and the platform flip flops looked like a sprain waiting to happen. She couldn't do it.

Julia felt her whole new look disintegrating like Cinderella's stroke of midnight. Now the only thing left of the makeover was the T-shirt with the rhinestone studded words "Go Team" and the earrings, which she chucked after putting her gobs of red hair into an enormous ponytail. Finally, she grabbed her old jeans and her Doc Martens and clomped comfortably off to class.

Her 3:30 class dragged on until she thought she would scream. It was at least a fifteen minute walk to the Nelson Gym from the Fine Arts building, and she had to figure out for sure what class he had at that time, so she cut out of women's choir half an hour early. She made it to the west side of campus in seven minutes flat, back aching with the pounding it took from her flopping back pack.

It was her first time in the gym, and she didn't know quite where she was going, but the waiting area was glassed in, and when her eyes re-focused to the dimmer indoor light, she could see all three of the scheduled classes in progress in the same large sporting area: volleyball on the right, a huge aerobics group in the center, and insect-like rock climbers around the periphery on the old brick walls. Some were wearing climbing gear, others simply had gloves and running shoes, trying to get a hand-hold. It looked pretty slow to Julia—not the most heart-pumping of sports, although the climbers looked fit enough.

Where was he? There were several climbers in all grey, but none looked quite right. Would she have to smell him to recognize him? That wouldn't be good, especially in a long-term relationship. A few minutes passed, and a coach-type person blew a whistle. Like locusts in a wheat field they dropped to the ground and made for the locker room. Julia found a seat on the bench near the door.

Presently, towel-dried heads began to appear, and she opened her nostrils wide. Then she realized she must look like Miss Piggy and just began to breathe deeply. Even before her nose could locate him, his exquisite face emerged from the locker, and her eyes knew him. Her heart responded with an explosive pound.

"Hey, Danny Boy," one of the herd called. "Daniel!" Adonis turned his head and said yeah. Daniel! His name was Daniel! Not only did she see his face, she knew his name!

The crowd of boys bustled by with her *objet d'amour* on the far side. Nary a whiff of him reached her, but it didn't matter. She saw his face, she heard his name—and his voice. That *yeah* resonated in her ears still. She determined to commit its tones to the chambers of her heart and then call on it in times of loneliness. *Yeah. Yeah. It echoed there still.*

She fancied that as he turned his head to reply to his friend, his eyes met hers. Or, at least he saw her face. Was there a momentary pause then? Did he sense her eyes on his? The weight of her stare— could he feel it? He couldn't have missed it entirely. Maybe now as he walked down the sidewalk with his friends he wondered what that odd feeling he had a moment ago could have been. Ah. Bliss. Her birthday was complete.

"So, how did you find out his name?"

Julia explained, in great detail, the incident to True, who gave it all the enthusiasm it deserved as she lay in a pile of lavender and green pillows on her floral print bedspread. A sienna wash photo poster of a cowboy boot with roses spilling out the top was pasted to the cinderblock wall behind her, flanked by strips of colored paper with perky sayings and goals written on them.

"That is so great. Now what you have to do is find out his last name."

"How can I do that?" Julia hugged her red pillow closer and smoothed the ripples on her black and white comforter decorated with musical notes, clefs and roses. Her mom gave it to her as a going away to college gift.

"Easy. Just go get the class roll off the registration computer, and then it's the process of elimination."

"You can do that?"

"Sure. Why not? Then it will be easy to figure out the rest of his schedule. Plus, then you can call student information and find out where he lives and stuff. I'll show you, if you want." True eased off her pillows, pulled a pair of clean socks from one of the built-in drawers under her bed, and started putting them on.

"That would be great. Where are you headed now?" Julia wanted to get going on it as soon as possible. This burning to know all about him had to be a sign that they were supposed to be together. It was meant to be, even if he didn't know it yet. He'd be her boyfriend before the quarter was over. Yes. Her first boyfriend. And perhaps her last and only boyfriend, as well. *If you get it right the first time, why keep changing?* She had to know all about him so she could figure out the best way to get him to notice her.

"I'm going to try to get in a few hours of study over at the library. Want to stop by the Student Center on the way? We can check the class roll on the computer there. And the student information desk is right there, too."

"Great. Let's go!"

As the two girls walked across the campus in the autumn afternoon sun, bright yellow gingko leaves twirled down on them and swirled in the eddies of the breeze. A scent at once musty and fresh wafted through Julia's olfactories. It made her think of the spectacular colors she used to know every autumn along the Potomac River—plush reds, burning oranges, browns, golds. Would she always feel homesick at this time of year?

"So, I know you really like this Daniel guy." True kicked a fallen chestnut along the sidewalk. "And I know you say he's so gorgeous. I just hope he's not one of the Beautiful People."

Julia's attention returned to the task at hand.

"I hate to say it, but I'm sure he's one of the most beautiful people you'll ever see. I hope that doesn't disappoint you, True."

"No. You don't get what I'm saying. I know he's beautiful, but I'm talking about the Beautiful People."

Julia was perplexed.

"The core of good-looking people who have declared themselves popular on campus here just like they did in high school as jocks and cheerleaders—the ones who try to run everything simply because of their looks. It's the group that wannabes are always wanting to be part of. The Beautiful People stick with people of their own level of good-lookingness and shun others who try to infiltrate without the prerequisite brand-name clothing and styling products."

"It sounds like high school," Julia commented absently and thought about how different popularity circles had run in the arts prep school she'd attended. There, the popular people were the outgoing drama boys and girls who had nary a shred of inhibition. Or else they were the top musicians who were also nice. It was kind of the inverse of what she understood "real" high school to be.

"Yeah, only it's worse because we're supposed to be beyond that by now. And so should they. We shouldn't be expected to keep worshiping these vapid impostors just because they drive cars their daddies bought them." True had a few more choice words about the politics of popularity, but mostly they bounced off Julia's eardrums, which were occupied with listening to a Schumann piece playing inside her mind. It was the piece she'd been working on for college scholarship auditions. It was the piece she'd ultimately only played for Professor Kitano and had won him over. It was the piece that was the reason she was walking across this campus this very moment—perhaps to discover the identity of . . . her destiny.

Within half an hour, she knew his name was either Daniel Chitwood, age twenty-three, Business major, residing in Providence, a town south of Logan, or else his name was Daniel Dorame, age nineteen, Agriculture major, living near the college on Fourth North in Logan. The only other Daniel—Daniel Flake—registered for that class was thirty-something, and that didn't look right. Her Daniel was so young and fresh. Dorame? Chitwood? Flake? She was pulling for Dorame.

"So. Chitwood or Dorame. How are we going to figure out which one is yours?"

"How do you think it's pronounced? Door-aim? Dora Mae? Do-re-mi?"

"Hard to say. I prefer the Do-re-mi one. Then we can pretend he's a music afficionado."

The two girls passed the Hub restaurant in the basement of the Student Center on their way out. It was a dim cafeteria littered with copies of *The Utah Statesman* and flyers for campus clubs and events. Students seldom entered it singly, usually in pairs or trios instead. The orange vinyl booths brimmed with pseudo-intellectual chitchat and cheap coffee, and Julia had yet to venture into its depths to view the fare. Somehow the requirement of walking past legions of diners to even get near the food intimidated her.

"I'm never going in there." True pointed a thumb over her shoulder at the Hub as they left the building.

"Why not?"

"It's exactly what I was talking about—about the Beautiful People. They've made it their lair, so none of the rest of us can dine there comfortably. We're all looking around to see if we've been seen. The student government geeks all schedule their study groups in there and scowl at anyone walking past. It's so fake." True's gait sped up as she voiced her disgust for the Hub, another place Julia had never considered as having a cool factor. It was funny how different True and Bianca were—one scorning things that weren't cool enough, the other scorning things that were too cool. It was like the too hot porridge and Goldilocks.

Which porridge is just right?

They tramped across campus, kicking drifts of fallen leaves as they passed the brown brick buildings, the yellow brick buildings, and the yellow and brown brick buildings. The mature trees towered above them, and off to the west, the veritable forest of

Old Main Hill sloping toward downtown Logan gave Julia a sense of security. Those prickles of longing for Virginia could only be cured by peering over the edge of that hill. There she felt the warm protection of the tall trees. It felt like home there.

"Hey, here's a possible solution." True's ponytail swung side to side, and her step triggered the automatic sliding door at the concrete and glass Merrill Library. She lowered her voice to library level as they entered and climbed the stairs to the second floor study tables. "Just get the schedules for both young Daniels and hang out at the end of class times for each of them until you figure out which is which."

"You're a genius."

True dumped her book bag on a table, and they sat down. "I know. Happy birthday."

"I'm crossing my fingers for Do-re-mi!"

"Fa so la ti."

So, first thing the next morning, Julia snarfed a quick bagel then, registrar printouts in hand, began her investigation into both possible Daniels. Her first class didn't begin until 9:30, so she had an hour for spy work. Looking at the printouts, she found they had three classes together, so they must be friends. That would make it harder to figure out which was which. Then again, she didn't have to wait outside those classes. She could just try the classes they took independently of each other. She looked at the clock. Nine-sixteen. Chitwood had an 8:30 Economics class in the Business building— without Dorame. Where was the Business building? She checked the campus map on the wall near the registrar's office. Jackpot! It was on the other side of the library, not too far out of her way to the Ag building for her 9:30 Trig class. There was just enough time. She grabbed her backpack, slung it over one shoulder and made a run for the Business building.

Huffing and puffing, she arrived at the outer doors of the six story brown and yellow brick building just as classes let out. Swarms of students spewed forth from the double doors. Julia was headed the wrong way on a one-way street. Her only defense was to climb up onto one of the concrete benches that bordered the sidewalk. Standing atop it, she had a bird's eye view of all the people coming down the front steps and out onto the Quad. She scanned the crowd nervously, not knowing if this was a complete waste of time—time she didn't have much of, as her Trig class began in less than ten minutes.

Then, pushing his way through the open door, a familiar, stomach-flipping face appeared. Yes! It was Daniel Chitwood, age twenty-three, Providence resident. She'd found him on the first try! *Danny Boy Chitwood! Here I am!* She wanted to shout it to the whole world. But reason got the better of her, and then a passerby's massive backpack jostled her knee, and she lost her balance. She tumbled backward into the hedge, which, luckily, broke her fall. Several people stopped to help her, and as they extracted her from the bush, she saw his form pass by in the crowd. In slow motion, he turned his head toward her. She grinned with her newly bleached chompers, almost fiercely. *Yes, Daniel! It's me! Your true love.* His eye rested on her smile, and then he turned back toward the sidewalk ahead of him and walked on. Was that a grin tugging at his mouth? Could he feel the magic, too? She wasn't sure. The helping hands lifted her to safety, and she murmured her thanks. The main body of the bottlenecked crowd dispersed, and she was left standing nearly alone on the sidewalk. Ah, fate had smiled on her today.

The first chimes of the Old Main clock began to strike the half-hour song. She was late! As she unglued herself from her spot on the walk and began loping for the Ag building, she had a wide, goofy, gaping smile for everyone who passed. But then, a stranger stopped her.

"Excuse me, uh—"

"Yeah?" Julia didn't have time to visit now. Trig was starting, and if she missed the first part of the discussion, she could be lost for a week.

"You should know, um, there's a, a something in your—" He made a little itching motion between his front teeth.

Something? What something? She clapped her hand over her

mouth. Oh, no! Blueberry bagel remnant! And Daniel had been the target of the world's biggest grin. Please say he hadn't noticed! But, she recalled his look and knew he had. That lingering glance at her mouth told her everything she needed to know. Somehow she didn't think that was the way Bianca would have recommended the damsel in distress thing happening. "Gunk on tooth" had totally trumped the "lovely and helpless" part of the damsel requirement. No wonder he hadn't lent his own hand to her in heroic fashion! *Pah!* She exhaled audibly then made one last swipe of her pearlies and stomped off to class.

CHAPTER SEVEN

True consumed a celery stick in the slowest fashion imaginable—
by peeling each strand of celery string individually and nibbling
them one by one.

"So, I can't believe you went to that awesome arts high school.
I didn't even know there was such a thing. What was it called
again?"

"Duke Ellington School for the Performing Arts. It's in
downtown Washington, D.C. And, yeah. It was a fun place. But
of all the kids who went there, I bet I'm the only one at USU."
Julia's Music Theory books were draped open and face down across
her stomach as she stared at the dorm's textured ceiling. She was
looking for cowboy hats in the spackle today.

"Lucky you. Where did everyone else go?"

"Columbia, Julliard, other good music schools."

"Why didn't you do that? You're good enough. I've heard you
play. You could have gone to any of those places."

"Lots of reasons. Mostly because we moved." Moved. Yeah. In
the spring. Right before scholarship auditions for those schools.
Right before the concert season—which forced Julia to ditch out
as lead pianist on both the orchestra and the jazz band. Right
before graduation, which meant she had to forfeit the satisfaction
of saying she graduated from Duke Ellington High School for
the Performing Arts in Washington, D.C., in exchange for the
title "Julia Cronquist, graduate of Huntsville High, Huntsville,
Utah." No one would believe she'd even attended that awesome
arts school. They'd see her Huntsville diploma and think she was

40

delusional. And maybe she was delusional. It all seemed like long, long ago in a galaxy far, far away—like it might have never really happened.

She sighed. "Lots of reasons."

True peeled another celery strand and started in on it.

"Don't you like it here? I thought your parents had some fabuloso mansion in the hills now. You've got some castle to go home to with a grand piano there and glamorous parents."

"Glamorous parents? My dad is a mortician."

"Oh, well. You know what I mean. In that house. How many bedrooms did you say it has?"

"Five. And a two-acre lot. And breathtaking views of Pineview Reservoir. And an 'ideal proximity' to Snowbasin Ski Resort. I don't ski. And winding staircases, and a secret door behind a bookcase, and three fireplaces, and a turret." She rolled her eyes. Real estate. Her whole life plan was skewed all because of real estate.

"Tell me. Is there something wrong with you?"

"Probably." Julia sniffed and smiled. Yeah, she did sound like a spoiled brat at this point, like nothing was good enough for her. But the truth was, something far, far less was just fine for her— their little brick ranch home in Alexandria would have suited her just fine. At least through her high school graduation.

We Cronquists do things as a family, rotten timing or not. And we all have to sacrifice sometimes. Yeah, a huge raise and promotion to manager of the funeral home conglomerate's corporate headquarters for the Western States Division was such a sacrifice for their dad. Being able to pretty much set his hours and duties—such a hardship. Such a sacrifice for their mom to get away from her seven-year calling as Relief Society president of their ward and live somewhere that she never had to drive in traffic if she didn't want to.

And her siblings? Ted was already working in Utah. Bianca? It didn't matter where Bianca lived. The outdoors was irrelevant to her life. Any mall in the civilized world was fine with her. And Cathy was still just a sophomore then. Moving to a new school in March gave her a leg-up on the next year's social scene.

"Don't get me wrong, True. USU is great. It's so great. I love it. They have a very well respected piano performance program. My professors are awesome. And it's beautiful here. And it's fun living by my grandparents on my dad's side. And I have the world's best roommate, of course." True chuckled and waved her off. "And, yeah, the house, is, well, the Dream House. It's just the timing kind of stunk."

"What happened?"

"My dad had a job transfer, and our house in Virginia sold, and it wasn't really a big deal for anyone else to just rip up roots and go, so I got the raw deal of moving right at the end of last year. Senior year. No one is into making new friends in March of senior year, and I've never been a good friend-maker anyway. So, basically it was a big, lonely drag. I guess what I'm saying is even though it's a cool house they bought, I don't exactly share their big dream that *is* the Dream House."

True chucked the rest of her celery in the garbage and came over and laid down on her own bunk to stare at her side of the ceiling.

"Well, sorry that all happened. But home is where the family is, right?"

CHAPTER EIGHT

Julia knocked and knocked but there was no answer at Bianca's apartment. She located the key under the brick beside the doorstep and went in. Some of the lights were on, and several pairs of warm up pants were strewn across the bed along with two Reebok shoe boxes on the floor, one of them empty. Strange, she'd never known Bianca to take an interest in running, or in exercise of any sort. Julia sat down on the crusty vinyl beanbag chair and flipped through Bianca's cards, which she'd brought with her from Logan.

"Sunglasses are cool. But only if they are Raybans. Or if they are rose-colored or round. Like John Lennon's." Sunglasses. Julia had never owned a pair. She could see a lot better without them, no matter how sunny the day. Maybe the sunglasses she borrowed always had greasy fingerprints on them. But if they were necessary, she might be willing to risk her safety. Then again, she could seriously bump into something, negating the cool factor of the sunglasses. There were so many paradoxes. Wear tight jeans, but always walk gracefully. Be talented, but never admit to practicing.

Practicing. The practice rooms on campus simply didn't give her enough time on the keys. How was she going to get her pieces down well enough to make good grades? It scared her. She thought about just abandoning ship here and zooming up to Huntsville to get in a few hours with her favorite men—Bach, Strauss, and Schumann. But, dread of dreads, she had to go to Bianca's little get-together.

The new outfit selected by Bianca and Charmaine dangled off the side of the bed. Bianca canceled their shopping date, so Julia picked it up on her way over. Cream fisherman-knit sweater, sweet little denim skirt, cable knit tights, and boots. It was cute. Hot, but cute. Indian summer had kicked in—in a big way. Smells of fish and soy and burned cooking oil emanated forth from where they lay trapped in the brown shag carpet. Julia speculated that an Asian man had probably rented this room sometime in the last decade. She postponed donning the sweater until the last possible minute.

Of course, it might not be all that bad. It was, after all, her debut as the new Julia Cronquist with her new clothes, new information, new self. The time had finally come. But somehow she felt fake, as if everyone would be able to see through her little act. It was like in old movies where people with "old money" scorned people with "new money." She was scared she'd be transparent as the "newly cool." She shuddered.

Julia didn't really know anyone who was coming, either. They were all Bianca's friends and some co-workers from the mall. She didn't think much of the two she'd met: Troy and Pete. Why would her sister want to hang around with those brain donors? So they wore great sandals and had legs so tan the hair on them turned blonde. So what?

She turned over onto her back and closed her eyes. She imagined a black lacquer grand piano in front of her. She started ghost-playing the keys and could almost hear the rich resonance of Chopin as she pounded the imaginary bass ivories.

The front door rattled and she heard Bianca's voice outside say, "Thanks, Todd. You saved me," and then the door slammed shut.

"Bianca, hi."

"Oh! You scared me to death! Julia. You're here already." Bianca held her chest and sank down onto the brown couch then propped her Reeboked feet on the coffee table. She looked weary.

"What happened. What are you doing?"

"Oh, I got the cutest Juicy warmups. Like my shoes? So, I was out jogging, walking along the Ogden River Parkway with Kelli-Jill, and *bam!* I fainted. Luckily Todd, this cute bicycle cop, came along and found me. He brought me and her home in his squad car. He was even cuter than Bart, the parks landscaper I met when this happened before. I'm just so fragile." Boy, they broke the mold and *then* they made Bianca. Retelling the story seemed to bring a little of the color back to her cheeks. "But I'm glad you're here. We've got a party to plan!"

"What are you going to wear?" Julia knew Bianca's wardrobe was always a cheery topic.

"You've got to see this!" She pulled a Dillard's bag from behind the couch and lifted something black and fluttery from inside. "Should I try it on for you?" She didn't need to. Julia could already tell her own new outfit would be underdressing. Or overdressing. "I got it today. Payday, you know. It's just so the most." With its petal sleeves and wraparound, cross-my-heart style, Julia thought it fit more into the "just so the least" category.

"I got the cake. Mmm." She was rummaging through her closet for her black slingbacks.

"Bianca, do you think I'm ready to meet Scott yet?" She eyed herself doubtfully in the mirror.

"Yes. Absolutely. Be yourself, and he's going to fall flat on his face for you. But maybe—maybe I should give you a couple of extra last minute ideas on flirting. Some tactics."

"Like what?" Flirt tactics? Flirting sounded scary and impossible. Wearing clothes was one thing. Implementing actual behaviors was another. Bianca came over and sat on the foot of Julia's old bed.

"Okay. One is that you always turn your knees toward a person you're attracted to, or who you want to attract."

"Whom."

"Scott, of course." Bianca didn't get the grammar correction. That was probably best. Julia didn't want to start the evening as Snotty Grammar Correction Person. She might not be able to snap out of it.

"Okay."

"Also, touch his arm when you're talking to him. Just lightly rest your hand on it. It's a sign of possession. They like to be possessed."

"Really?" She had always heard men liked to be free. Good to know.

"Yes. And, this is key. Always listen carefully to everything he is saying. Be genuinely interested. If you get him to talk about himself, he'll think you're a great conversationalist. If you listen well to boot, he'll think you're a witty, brilliant queen of the world."

"Touching his arm the whole time?"

"You're getting it." Bianca hung up the flimsy dress and pulled out some jeans and a top.

"Anything else?"

"Let's see. Yeah. Okay, this is for riding in cars, but you might want to know it now anyway. Be sure and tilt your knees toward the gear shift so he can slide his hand off the stick and onto your knee. Zip, zip." Bianca demonstrated and giggled. "Which is why I always think that guys who drive cars with stick shifts instead of automatic transmissions are better targets. I mean, catches. Ha, ha." She paused to think for a moment as she tugged mightily at the zipper on her jeans. Once they were done up she stuck the side of her index finger in her mouth to heal it.

"You might want to know another car thing. It's a white lie. You tell them you don't know how to drive a stick shift. Ask them to teach you."

Was she kidding? That sounded dangerous. What about insurance issues? What about embarrassment issues?

"But I already know how to drive a stick."

"I know. I taught you over the summer, remember? That was the reason why. So, anyway, the *trick* is that you already know how. Then when they're 'teaching' you, you fake ineptness at first, and then make miraculous progress under their kind tutelage." Sneaky. "Remember. Never get involved unless you're already confident of your skill. And that goes for other things they might offer to teach you. Like tennis, or cards. Don't even bring it up if you're not sure."

Bianca's cell phone rang then, and she went giggling into the kitchen and left Julia to her thoughts. There was an underhanded pretense to the dating game that Julia had never considered. Was falsehood really as rampant as all that? All the unspoken signals, the playing dumb, the acrylic nails. It was a new world of façades and trickery. Could she master it?

If she could master Chopin's Water Music, she could do anything—including fooling this Scott person into liking her.

What was he like, her soon-to-be boyfriend?

Scott. Scott who? She didn't even know his last name—a name that she might someday take herself, if things worked out according to Bianca's predictions, assuming they didn't work out with Danny Boy Chitwood. Would Scott be courteous, kind, intelligent, hardworking? A young man of good character in addition to his good looks?

In quite a few of the evenings she spent at home and not on dates in her life, she'd used her hours constructively by defining just what kind of young man she would *like* to be on a date with, if she could. Once she listed them in a column in the back of her practice record. Qualities: kind, intelligent, hard-working. Supportive was one. Tuned-in to reality, another. Outgoing—although she herself wasn't. "One of us ought to be." She crossed out artistic and funny. Those would be nice but weren't necessary. Instead she penciled in faithful.

So, all those years in social exile at her piano, Julia had plenty of hours to concoct the perfect formula for her perfect match. He likely didn't exist. But why give up hope? Hopelessness was boring. After all, she did live in Utah now. Maybe, just maybe, he did exist. Could Bianca have some insight into both their souls? Could he be Scott?

No inch of her person had been spared Bianca's scrutiny. At 7:30, the proposed time of the party, Julia had looked as put-together as she had ever looked in her life. Her heart beat with anticipation. Even the sparkle stick perfume behind her ear was strategically placed.

The doorbell rang at twenty minutes past nine, and the first guests arrived. Kelli-Jill and Michelle ("Mi-shrill," as Bianca called her) came in bearing a two-liter bottle of pop.

"Hi, girls. Glad you could make it."

The two immediately sat down in the kitchen where Bianca was spreading the seven layers of the bean dip onto a tray, and they all began gossiping about people who worked at the mall. Julia sat back down on the couch to watch *Miami Vice* reruns and wait for the party to actually begin.

But, nearly forty minutes later, the clammy sweat on her hands had melted a bit of her makeup, and her well-ratted bangs were beginning to sag. Why she had let Bianca talk her into a fisherman-knit sweater for the middle of this heat wave she did not know. It was 88 degrees inside this apartment, for heaven's sake. So what if ecru was in her autumn color palette? It was blazing hot. The cable knit tights with the denim miniskirt were making her legs stick together like velcro. And for what? Scads of others sauntered in, but Mr. Love hadn't even shown his much-reputed pretty face.

She wandered through the crowds of other people saying weak hellos here and there. None of the conversations sounded remotely stimulating except one between a couple of guys who were debating whether zero percent financing was actually a good deal for a car. But then again, her own first car purchase was so far off that she stopped eavesdropping and sat down again to watch *Miami Vice*.

She gave in and pulled a carrot stick from the perfectly arranged vegetable tray on the table. It was her own birthday celebration, after all. She took five olives and began sticking them on all the fingers of her left hand when the doorbell rang again. Popping all five olives in her mouth, she answered the door.

"Hi. I'm Scott. Is this Bianca's place?" Scott? Scott! He was as tall and as dark and as meltingly beautiful as Bianca hinted. Julia tried to gulp down the olives and lamely pointed toward the kitchen. Scott stepped in.

"Scotty!" Bianca dropped her sour cream covered spatula and flew to his side, then she introduced him to Kelli-Jill and Mi-shrill, whose nasal voice squeaked a hello at the chic one. "And, over here, this is my sweet sister, Julia. Isn't she cute? Jules, isn't Scott great?"

There was an awkward pause, and Julia nodded again, weakly. "Jules, take Scotty in the living room and entertain him until I get this stuff ready." Scott followed Julia toward the brown, second-hand couch.

To be fair, he was chic. If that was the word for it. He was something, anyway. Something fashionably different. And hot. Although that might have been the weather.

His dark hair was parted in the middle and slicked back on the sides, and being a smidge too long in the back, flipped up in a fuzzy mange just under the ears and along his collar. Nothing a good haircut couldn't remedy. He was wearing a black vintage concert T-shirt with the words "Leftover Salmon" across the front and a long list of concert dates throughout Colorado down the back. Julia had never heard of such a group and wondered if it were a farce. But his olive drab pants with the big pockets on the thigh were nice and tucked neatly into his lace-up, high-top combat boots. At least Julia wasn't the only one with off-season footwear.

"So, you're Bianca's sister. What's she like to live with?"

Don't end the sentence with a preposition. "She's great fun. Very cool."

"Huh." He started flipping through the channels, just as the Vice were about to get the Jamaican drug lord. Ugh! Julia wanted to see that. But, no. She needed to focus. What exactly did Bianca say to do? The crash course info eluded her. Something about listening carefully. But to what?

"So, what's your deal?" What's your deal? Did she really just say that? It sounded so much like Bianca. Was it intelligible when it came from her own mouth?

"Mine? I'm into personal safety." At least Scott understood the question. But did she understand his answer? A NASCAR commercial came on for an upcoming race, and Scott turned up the sound. It gave Julia time to think. When it was over, she started the flirt tactics afresh.

"Personal safety, huh? Your own? You don't look all that danger-prone." Yessss. She couldn't believe the conversation was so zippy—

and coming from herself. With newfound confidence she turned her knees slightly toward Scott. His profile became more attractive as she studied it. He was still watching TV.

"I forgot. You're a girl. You probably don't know all the NRA lingo." What was the NRA? She'd heard that before somewhere. Not like OSHA, though that meant safety, too, she thought. "I guess I'm what you'd call a Second Amendment crusader." *We the people, in order to form a more perfect union . . . .* At that rate it would be twenty minutes before she could recall the Second Amendment. This was not going well.

"How so? And where's your chain mail and lance, if you're a crusader?" To her great surprise, Scott lifted up his T-shirt. "Is that a bullet-proof vest?"

"Exact-a-mundo. I just came from shooting practice."

"Were other people using you as a target? Why the vest?"

"Of course not. But you can never be too safe. Personal safety. Get it?"

"Cautious move. Well done." Then she remembered she was supposed to act extremely interested, even though guns held no appeal for her, and to listen attentively—dotingly. "So, are you packing heat right now?"

"No, I left my 'heat' in the truck. My concealed weapons permit is still in the works, but I ought to be getting it this fall, as soon as I work off those misdemeanor charges. You want to see my collection? Or, I should say, my *traveling* collection?"

"Sure," she replied buoyantly and wondered if she needed a concealed fright permit.

Together they walked out to his 1978 Chevy, and he pulled a large tool box from the truck bed. As he was fiddling with the combination, Julia took a look around the vehicle. There was something pointy in the back window, and she eventually deciphered its identity as a gun rack made from a mounted rack of deer horns. Creative. But whiplash would be a secondary concern in a collision. In the back window were several bumper stickers. *National Rifle Association Member.* (Oh, *that* was the NRA. Thank goodness—it was driving her nuts trying to remember what it stood for.) *Insured by Smith and Wesson. Guns don't kill people, people kill people.* Beside it, a similar saying, *Guns don't kill people, I kill people.* Yikes. *I didn't fight my way to the top of the food chain to be a vegetarian.* There were three or four others, but Scott had the lock open.

"This is my Winchester collection, in case I come across a charging elk, or a rabid racoon, or the like. You can never be too prepared." She knew rifles were the long ones. He started attaching numbers to the guns, like twenty-two and two-seventy, but it meant nothing to her. The bigger ones seemed to have higher numbers. Maybe it was how much they weighed. He put one in her hands, and it was certainly heavier than it looked. At least a five-fifty.

"But the beauty of them all is this Browning pump-action sweetie." He shut up the tool box and opened the truck door. From the antler rack he pulled a stainless steel-barreled shotgun and pumped a round into the chamber for effect. She acted impressed.

"Wow." But she didn't have any intelligent questions to ask, so she just kept listening. Apparently she'd hit a jackpot with this topic because he needed no encouragement. At all. Whatsoever.

"Don't fret. I know what I'm doing. Hey, I'm fixing to get me a job up by your guys's place in Huntsville someday. My dream job is up there at the Browning factory doing quality control. It's a dangerous job, but someone's got to brave it. And . . ." Wait. Browning was in Morgan, wasn't it? Wrong Ogden Canyon, dude. There were no gun factories or any other factories to be found in beautiful down-ghost-town Huntsville.

Fifteen minutes later, she'd viewed the entire traveling arsenal and heard more gibberish about guns than she'd ever understand in a lifetime. During their conversation she remembered Bianca's advice about resting her hand on his arm, but, under the circumstances, she thought it might not be wise. Darn. Maybe he wouldn't fall for her now. He locked up his truck, and they went back inside, but not before she noticed the mud flaps with pistol-packing Yosemite Sam underscored by the phrase "Back Off."

By then, yet another five guys, including Troy and Pete, had arrived. They came together in a herd and stuck together in a herd the rest of the night. A few fluffy mall girls circled them like satellites. Julia stuck to the kitchen table with Mi-shrill and the seven-layer dip, discussing what it was like to work at the housewares store House of Today. Mi-shrill already had her entire bathroom co-ordinated in yellow and powder blue. "I'm decorating my bedroom next. In silver and mauve. Won't that be soothing?" Julia could only imagine the room being soothing as long as Mi-shrill never spoke while there.

Scott left early. Bianca gave him a side-hug and discovered the body armor vest. "Bye, Scotty, you man of steel, you." Julia wished she'd thought of that line. As he left, Scott gave a shy wave Julia's way. Then he was gone, and she couldn't help but wonder, had she actually met her destiny?

CHAPTER NINE

Even though going home every weekend violated Bianca's triple-underlined rule, Julia's Saturdays teaching piano lessons at the Dream House had been surprisingly satisfying. Up until now, Julia had always surrounded herself with more accomplished artists, and it didn't occur to her there were kids just beginning to play who needed basic instruction. She fell into teaching mode quite naturally, and the students acted excited to learn. She knew that attitude might not last, but she decided to enjoy it while she could. At the time of Amanda's lesson, Jed dropped her off and came to pick her up, and Julia had a few minutes to visit with him.

"Do you want a Smartie?" He offered her a candy from the cellophane package.

"Sure, thanks." She took a white one, the best kind, and popped it into her mouth.

"Oh, a white one." He looked slightly surprised.

"Yeah. They're the best kind." She bit the crumbly edge off the powdery candy and then savored the solid center disk.

"You think so, too?" He riffled through the package for another white one and took it. Julia looked at Jed in wonder.

"I didn't know anyone else had bothered to taste the difference in the colors."

"Of course. Smarties are for the discerning palate." Jed offered her an orange and took a purple for himself. "Purple, orange, and white have the most distinct flavors. Actually, I can't tell the difference between the other ones."

"Oh, no. The yellow ones are gross. Banana."

"Huh. I think you're right." He flicked the yellow sugar drops into the gravel pile that was promising to become a circular driveway. "They'll disintegrate the first time it rains. It's not littering." Still, Julia decided not to mention this indiscretion to Cathy the Earth Girl.

They finished the rest of the package, and Jed wadded up the paper and put it in his pocket.

"One time I spent over an hour trying to taste the difference between M&M flavors. The only one with a clear flavor was blue. And not in a good way."

"Too chemical. I agree." Julia would have picked out and cast away the blue M&Ms if she wasn't always eating them while driving. Too hazardous a scruple for her.

"So, are you done for the day?"

"Amanda's my last lesson." Amanda was still inside at the piano playing, "Here we go, up a row, to a birthday party."

"I know." How did he know? Wait. Probably because he knew how many students she had—and had arranged all the times for her. What a good manager.

"And I want to tell you a great big thank you." She elbowed him. It wasn't the same as flirtingly touching his arm like Bianca said, but it was progress, at least, for Julia. "This has been great. I really like teaching."

"You sound surprised. Are you?"

"I guess so." She sat down on the rock wall that surrounded the flower bed of the Dream House, and Jed sat beside her. Amanda came out and shot baskets in the driveway. "The kids are funny and so excited, which I can't help but feel, too. I can't believe I never thought of trying it."

"Sometimes it only takes a friend to give you a nudge in the right direction."

She noticed her knees were turned toward him. Or, were his turned toward her? And he referred to himself as her friend. Nice. Well, obviously he was quite a good friend to her, doing all this stuff to help her get her teaching program going, including signing up his very own sister. My friend Jed. That sounded pretty good. It was odd to have someone be so nice to her just out of the blue. She was nothing to him—just Cathy's older sister.

CHAPTER TEN

Julia stopped by Bianca's place to pick her up one Friday afternoon. It was laundry time again.

"Thanks for stopping, but I gotta wait and go home a little later. That Dirksen guy's press conference is at five. Mayor George isn't going, but I totally think a press representative ought to be there. Do you want to go with me? He's announcing his fix-the-roads plan."

"Can't." Wouldn't dream of it was more like it. Was Bianca referring to herself as the press representative? Oh, dear.

"Okay. Do I look okay?"

"Yeah. You look . . . professional."

"I got this suit, can you believe it, for 75 percent off! It's so now. Do I look old enough?"

"For what?"

"Oh, never mind. If you're not going, I'll see you later. Take my laundry up to the Dream House, will you? I'll meet you there tonight. Can you put my delicates in the washer for me? Thanks."

The front doors of the Dream House slammed, and from her spot on the piano bench Julia heard the staccato of pumps clicking across the stone entryway. Bianca came into the piano room and sat down hard on the sofa, arms folded across her chest.

"Bad day?"

"Not my best. And I have to tell you, I am so done with politics. It's just cutthroat. And it's like there's no room for someone

56

with integrity. A person with real values just makes everyone else involved feel too guilty, I bet. And Josh and I are done. I'm not ashamed to say it—he dropped me. I'm sure it was only because his dad made him. See if I vote for him. Do you know where I can register, by the way? And I'm sick to death of journalism. Me, I'll stick to retail. I like it more, anyway." She was babbling, sounding quite nonsensical at this point.

"What happened? What were you doing, exactly?" Julia swivelled around to face her.

"Oh, nothing. I just went to that boring press conference."

"You didn't ask any questions, did you?"

"The public has a right to know these things, Julia. I couldn't sit back and let him slide into office. I have my integrity to protect."

It took some doing, but Julia finally got it out of Bianca, probably in a sanitized version, what went on at the Dirksen press conference. Bianca, in full business-suit attire, stood at the front of the press pack during the question-and-answer session so she could "look him in the eye," and shouted a few tough doozies regarding the alleged brother-in-law's alleged construction company and the fabled stolen car of decades ago. During a drinking fountain break, a legitimate political journalist, Chris VanNatter of Channel 4, cornered her in the hall, "And in a very mean way," Bianca asserted, "asked me pointed questions about who I was. When I told him I was a reporter, he *demanded* my credentials. Finally he forced me to tell him I was working on Josh's dad's campaign."

"You didn't. You didn't say that, did you?"

"Well, I am. I've walked more avenues to talk to voters than the mayor has himself." She brooded silently for a minute. Julia was too stunned to speak. "So, I'm sick of journalism. And Josh and I are totally through. Besides. I need to date someone more, like, more with a better last name. I am thinking if I could find someone with the last name Claiborne, that would be great because then if we got married my name would be Bianca Claiborne, and who wouldn't trust their makeup to a professional consultant named Bianca Claiborne?"

CHAPTER ELEVEN

— ⚜ —

Crisp fall days gave way to biting canyon winds and cold nights. Halloween was two weeks away, and midterms were right after that. The fisherman knit sweater was finally coming in handy.

Julia was settled into college life and had her daily schedule down to a science. Things were a lot less hectic since she dropped her Chemistry class just after Columbus Day. It wasn't serving any purpose but to ruin her GPA, make her a basket case and give her seven fewer practice hours per week. She realized she didn't need the science credit (she took A.P. Physics in high school which counted for that), and since no dates were possible from it (Bianca's requirement), it was easy to say good-bye. Now that she and True lived together, she wouldn't even miss out on the friend aspect of the lab.

Lately Julia spent as much time as possible in the practice rooms of the Fine Arts building at the piano, the keys of which were finally getting to feel better under the pressure of her fingers. Her three-credit lessons required nearly fifteen hours of practice each week, but she put in more whenever possible. Her professor made his expectations clear and pushed her to new limits. She couldn't deny that it was thrilling. Dr. Kitano had a reputation for being the most influential piano teacher in the West, and she was quickly coming to understand why.

In what was left of her time, she divided her hours into studying for her other classes and watching for a chance to bump into Dan. She'd figured out when his Institute class was and loitered in the lobby there twice a week, plus at the Nelson Gym. For some reason, he still hadn't mustered the nerve to say hello to her. She was sure he noticed her there. At least once they stood in the same line for the drinking fountain in the Student Center. Every morning she went over to the school an hour early to study trigonometry in the lobby of the Merrill Library in hopes of catching a glimpse of him as he swaggered past. It was hard to keep her mind from wandering to thoughts of what clever questions she might ask him if he finally decided to come and sit down by her as she studied.

"If only I could get a chance to say hello to him, I'm sure he'd take it from there." Julia trimmed her nails onto a Kleenex on her bunk while watching True piece together the last of her Halloween costume. "What do I know, though? This could just be some silly crush."

"You're just a freshman. You don't have to know everything."

"Thanks. So wise. I think I shall write that down and tape it to my wall." She wadded up the Kleenex and threw it in the garbage then pulled out her Trig book to look ahead a few pages.

"What do you think?" True lurched into a standing position in the white sheet which was spiraled around her and attached with brown packing tape. "Do I look skinny in it? I started my new 'Eat Right for Your Type' diet last week. It's based on your blood type." That sounded . . . effective.

"The costume's great. What's it supposed to be?"

"A weevil. Like in flour and stuff. The bug. Don't you think it looks like it?"

"Now that you mention it, yeah. But, you might need a sign or something."

"I have a move. Look." She squirmed like an earthworm.

"Oh. Now it's a dead giveaway." Julia hoped True wouldn't be too disappointed if she had to explain what her costume was a few times. She herself had yet to plan a costume. She wasn't sure what to do about Halloween. The school's Halloween Howl sounded like fun, but she also heard from a lot of people that it was packed—completely, to the point where it was nearly impossible to walk around. That part didn't sound so great. And Halloween was on a Friday night. She had to be in Huntsville fairly early the next morning for lessons, and late night driving on a party night was something her dad often warned her against. "You never know which drivers are impaired, sweetheart." And there were so many canyon roads between Logan and Huntsville. It was a dilemma.

"I wonder what Dan is going to go as. Probably James Bond or something suave and sophisticated like that." She fingered the edges of the cat calendar on her wall above her bed. She bought it and hung it the day after True posted her picture of a cat with a "no" symbol around it. True promptly vandalized the calendar by drawing little devil horns and protruding fangs on all the cats.

"You really should figure out a way to say hi to him. I bet he's waiting for you to make the first move."

"You think? But I get all flustered when I'm around him. I might say the wrong thing."

"You should write it down."

That wasn't a bad idea. A few phrases went through her head regularly. How you doing? What class do you have in here? Nice day, isn't it? Ever been skiing down Old Main hill? Do you need my number? Conversation openers.

"Hey, I drove past his house the other day." Julia made the trip to Providence regularly, if the truth be known. "I think he still lives at home." It was a two story brick colonial in Providence, a town five minutes south of Logan. It seemed kind of immature to still be under his mom and dad's wings at his age, but, then again, it might be the economically sound thing to do. He was a Business major. He probably thought about those things. She described the place to True, who concurred with her evaluation.

The phone rang in the dorm hall. It was for Julia. They didn't have a phone in their room, but they did have their own bathroom, with a tub, and Julia would opt for a private bath over a private telephone every time.

"Hi, Jules. It's me, Bianca. Long time no talky!" It had been a few weeks since she'd heard from Bianca.

"What's up? Anything new with you?"

"Yeah, actually. Totally exciting stuff! The Miss Weber County pageant is looking for contestants." She was almost breathless with excitement. "I'm totally thinking of trying out. They need girls. Do you think I should do it?"

"When is it?"

"It isn't until next June, so I have lots of time to get tan and stuff. It's a Miss America preliminary, you know. And I've always secretly dreamed of being Miss America. I mean, who hasn't?" Julia hadn't, but she didn't need to say so. "Winning the pageant would give me credibility as a journalist 'cause it would show I was good on my toes, and that I look good on the stage, and I'm not afraid to be in front of the public. So. What do you think? Should I do it?"

"Sure. Why not? What would you do for your talent?"

"Oh, that. Well. I haven't decided. I guess I could come up with an interpretive jazz dance—those seem good." All of Bianca's dance experience was from her years in cheer, but with her own choreography, who could tell, right? "And I've already found some gorgeous gowns online. Rhinestones, baby. Love it. Plus, and here's the best part (besides the crown): if I win, I would get my own float. How cool is that? To ride on in parades and stuff. So, should I go for it?"

"It sounds like fun."

"Oh, good. I think I will. I hoped you'd think it was great, too. Oh! Speaking of fun, I have the funnest idea." Most fun. The correct grammar is most fun. "We're planning Halloween stuff over here at your old haunt. Tons of people said they'd come, including Scott. It won't be the same without you."

Hey. A grand solution to Julia's Halloween problem! She could still celebrate the spooky holiday and not have to drive a long way in the night. Plus, she'd be at a smaller get-together with people she knew. Sort of. In all her machinations to get Dan's attention, she'd almost completely forgotten about Scott. It sounded great. Julia would be there for sure. Her only remaining problem was finding something to wear.

"I have a ponytail headache," True was saying as Julia came

back in the room. "And I'm going off beef. But don't tell my dad. He'll flip. Rancher at heart."

"You don't happen to have enough packing tape for one more of those do you?"

"So. Are you meeting any interesting people up at school?" Bianca was putting the final touches on a chip and salsa tray, while Julia mixed up another pitcher of Kool-Aid. "Guys, I mean." It was 7:30, and guests might arrive anytime after eight. Probably more like ten, though, knowing Bianca's group.

"Oh, one, I guess."

"Okay!" Bianca grabbed Julia by the hand and pulled her down beside her at the brass and glass table. "*Excellenté.* Tell me every little thing." She hunched forward on the wicker-backed brass chair and leaned her elbows on the glass tabletop.

"Well, I don't actually know him all that well yet."

"Doesn't matter. There's time for that. You're a freshman. Flirt-a-rama time. You don't have to even start thinking about getting serious until half-way through your sophomore year."

So soon? Yikes.

"His name is Dan. He's a Business major. He smells great."

"So, you're close enough to know that? This is good."

"Oh, it's not like that." She didn't realize it might come across like that. "At all."

"Sure. Anyway, go on."

"Well, I'm still just trying to get to know him and stuff. He's really cute. And quite athletic. Into rock climbing." Was she masking the situation well enough? Probably not. Bianca seemed slightly disappointed and got up to attend to her chip dip again.

"Julia. Can I tell you something frankly?" Julia nodded but hoped it wasn't too frank, like hurt-her-feelings frank. "You need something. *Seriously* need it." Bianca turned back around and looked Julia in the eye.

"What is it?"

"What you need is to be kissed. And often. And by someone who knows how." Julia had a vague feeling she'd heard that phraseology before but couldn't think where.

"I think Dan could fill that responsibility."

"Are you sure?" Was she? Not entirely, but he sure looked the part, so she nodded. "All right, then. Are you ready to make it happen?" Julia didn't say anything. It had been weeks since she'd looked at the cards. She might even have left them here in Bianca's apartment after the birthday bash. Shoot.

"Here's what you should do. Get yourself a subject to practice on. Then you'll be ready when the Dan opportunity affords itself." Bianca winked, as if the Dan opportunity were inevitable. Julia wished she could be so sure.

Nevertheless, it was a pretty good idea, once she gave it a little thought. Yeah. Armed with that scheme, as well as True's advice to plan her conversation ahead of time, she felt a new surge of confidence. Could Daniel Chitwood ever be her boyfriend? Sure. Why not! Julia and Daniel. Danny and Julie. Hmm. Dan and Jule. J and D. So many ways to say the right thing.

But who could she practice on? On whom could she practice? (That was better, although it did sound stilted and archaic.) There were no guys in her all-girl dorm. And, just as Bianca had warned, none in her major. Nobody from her math class caught her eye, perhaps because it was in the Ag building and made her think about farmers every day. She suddenly realized what a social desert she was living in. How depressing.

It was getting late, and the sisters changed into their costumes. The weevil sheet was truly weird, in an alluring way, Bianca said. "You have such a cute figure. A weevil costume shows it to advantage. Good choice." Julia wound the sheet mummy style around her whole body, wearing a white turtle neck leotard and white tights underneath. The brown packing tape had to be added a second time to keep the thing on her, but by the end, she was sure that at least no one would have a duplicate outfit. She examined herself in the full length mirror, satisfied with the result. Until, over her shoulder, she saw Bianca emerge from the bathroom in costume.

"How do I look? Is my crown on straight? This wig weighs a ton. And so do these bracelets." She crossed her arms martial arts style in front of her face, as if blocking punches. "Bullets and bracelets!" Bianca, in all her voluptuousness, made a stunning Wonder Woman, red undies and all. She even had the red vinyl knee boots and the gold eagle across her stomach and chest. She'd done her eyes and lips up to look just like Lynda Carter and made a show-stopping picture. Suddenly, being a form-fitting weevil didn't seem quite so la-di-da. "Have you seen my lasso of truth?"

The doorbell rang.

"Somebody's early." Bianca stalked off to answer it. Julia would have gone, but she just now realized she'd taped her legs together like a mermaid, and her evening would have to be spent hopping everywhere like a Veggie Tale veggie. Great. She'd better get a spot on the couch fast. From the other room she heard the conversation.

"Scotty! You look amazing!"

"So do you." Scott! Hearing his voice again made Julia's heart skip. She clutched her throat.

"Julia, guess who's here. Scott!" Bianca came into the bedroom alone and hiss-whispered to the alluring weevil. "I just had a brain flash. Your new practice subject is here in this very apartment."

Scott? Her practice subject? But he made her so nervous. Of course, if she could overcome that, it would be true practice for the Daniel problem. There were still some lingering fumes of the brief crash-and-burn crush she had on the gun man for a day last month, but compared with her feelings for Dan, they looked so immature. Still, she wasn't sure. Of course, tonight was a chance to test it out, give it a shot, in Scott-speak. Why not? He was here, anyway.

She leaned out of the bedroom and caught a glimpse of him. Something inside her sparked—a slight ignition of the old fumes. His face was quite attractive, more so than she remembered. He noticed her staring and flashed her a brief smile. Hmm. Once again, Bianca proved she knew her stuff. With a surge of weevil energy, she hopped into the living room and slinked as gracefully as possible onto the couch beside him. Let the games begin.

The following day, Julia lay on Cathy's bed at the Dream House reflecting on the events of the previous night, while Cathy sat at her desk making a poster for a school recycling drive.

"Do you ever say something, thinking you're funny, and then hear yourself and realize you're not funny?"

"You mean, like, when no one laughs?"

"Exactly."

"What did you say?"

"Oh, so many unfunny things, it's hard to recount them all. The lame comment about why you could eat a pound of licorice and gain more than a pound. Duh. And that may have been at a point when he was actually listening to what I was saying." Julia sighed and rubbed more white paint off the back of her hand. "It sank even beneath my usual level of lameness." But she did touch his arm while she said it. Bianca noticed it and winked at her in approval. Julia glanced at Scott to see if he observed the exchange and saw him wink back at Bianca. How embarrassing for him. He must have thought Bianca's wink was for him. An honest mistake. Julia could forgive it. Could happen to anyone.

"It sounds like you at least had more fun than I did." Cathy blew on the green poster paint to get it to dry. "Our school dance reeked. Even the deejay left early. That's the last time I leave it up to the sophomores to plan an important dance." Julia wondered what made it so bad.

"Didn't you dance with anyone?"

"Oh, yeah. But it wasn't that."

"What was it, then?" It was odd for Cathy to voice a negative opinion like this. Something was certainly up.

"Nothing. I mean—nothing. It's just someone I wanted to dance with came with someone else."

"I know how that goes." Julia did know. She'd spent many a stake dance sitting on the side chairs, watching her love interest enjoy himself on the dance floor with some other girl. She usually ended up despising the other girl and composing hate mail to her in her head. "Who was it?"

"Nobody you know." Cathy was being evasive. Also unlike her. But the answer was probably truthful. Julia had only met a handful of Cathy's friends. Jed was the only one she'd ever held a conversation with. With whom she'd ever held a conversation. He came to pick up Amanda after her lesson every Saturday and visited with Julia for a good hour.

The same thing happened earlier today. Jed mentioned he had a great time at the Halloween dance last night. He'd organized a group costume—he went as the Jolly Green Giant, a freshman was Little Sprout, and some girls were a box of peas. They all painted themselves green. He and Julia compared leftover paint on their hands and necks. He won because green paint still graced the crevice above his knee, a place Julia had opted to use tights instead of body paint. The thought of Jed made her giggle slightly under her breath. Cathy looked over at her questioningly.

"Nothing." She wasn't going to tell Cathy about that. Then again, Cathy already knew about the vegetable costume and could share the humor. "Jed just told me today about his Jolly Green Giant thing, and I thought it was so hilarious."

"Yeah, he made his date go as a pea." His date?

"How mean! What a dorky costume. I wouldn't have done it." But she *would* willingly dress as a *weevil* and be seen by a guy she was trying to entice into liking her. The irony hit her hard. But maybe Cathy was wrong on that. Jed didn't say anything about the box of peas being their dates. What would he be doing double dating with a freshman guy? Not likely.

Overall, Julia and Cathy agreed Halloween was mostly a bust.

CHAPTER TWELVE

Finals week. No one attended regular class schedules, which made it nearly impossible to run into Daniel. Even if she'd been able to get his finals schedule organized in her head, she wouldn't have had time to hang around waiting to see him. Things were just too hectic with her own studies. Her piano final was going to be a bear—a complete Beethoven piece, memorized, no mistakes. She practiced only it for seven whole hours one day.

By comparison, Trigonometry was a breeze. She came out of it so confident she almost felt like skipping. There was a freshly fallen snow, just a skiff, that powdered the sidewalk while she was confined in the Ag building. Seeing it and breathing the icy air gave her so much energy that she jumped down the last three steps on her way out.

Whiz—splat!

She landed on black ice, front leg sliding forward, and rear knee cracking down hard on the concrete, sending her sprawling into hurdler position. Ow! That killed! And there were her books and pencils, yard sale-ing it all over the sidewalk. She tried to pop back up and pretend it never happened, but her pack threw her off balance, and she sprawled out even further.

Help, I've fallen and I can't get up.

Had anyone seen? Was someone pointing and laughing? The walks were thronging with stressed-out finals takers with unkempt hair and granola bars in hand for energy. She squeezed her eyes shut in mortification. She hoped everyone was too engrossed in memorizing periodic tables of the elements to notice her crash.

But Providence smiled on her. As she opened her eyes, a gloved hand appeared, stretching toward her. She reached for it and looked up.

There he was! Daniel Chitwood! Coming to her rescue!

"Up you go." He lifted her, backpack and all, as though she were a feather. How wonderfully strong he was! She felt so pretty and helpless and, just like Bianca said, there he was to save her. She bent over to dust the snow from her jeans, and when she looked up, he was halfway down the sidewalk, striding off to the Business building. She hastily gathered up her books and things.

Up you go—the first words he'd ever spoken to her! She would remember them all her life. She didn't even get a chance to tell him thank you or give him her name or number—it all happened so fast. Her heart pulsed wildly under her black wool coat as she raced across campus to the library so she could tell True the news.

True was sitting on the fourth floor near the door to the computer lab. She had her Chemistry book open, and Julia breathed a sigh of relief that she put that class behind her. As she climbed up the final stairs, she noticed True's eyes were not on her textbook. Instead, they were staring instead into the open door of the lab. True gave a little nod and then turned, looking surprised to see Julia approaching.

"Hey. What are you doing here?"

Julia craned her neck to see what was so interesting in the adjacent room, but all she could see was some pasty moustache guy at the lab desk. Skinny. Shortish. Whatever held True's attention a moment ago must have disappeared.

"The most incredible thing just happened to me." Then Julia recounted the whole exciting incident to her rapt friend.

"Wow. So, that's twice you've fallen for him." True laughed at her own small joke. "Tell me the truth. Was this time accidental or strategic? Working your damsel in distress theory?"

"Purely accidental. I promise. I didn't even see him coming before I jumped."

True glanced furtively into the computer lab again. Lately she seemed to be spending more time than ever in the library. It was probably only due to finals. She seemed to be finding a new social circle among the library rats. The dorm girls held less fascination for her lately, apparently, although she was elected Activities Chairwoman for the upcoming winter quarter. Julia remained coolly aloof from both of those scenes. Dorm life and library rats both fit clearly into Bianca's off-limits zone, and she was determined to make a go of her older sister's advice to some extent. No sense having it if she didn't at least try to implement it. If only she could break into some upper crust social circle. Or figure out what one might be. She spent so much time in the practice room and at home on weekends, it was a little hard to find one.

"Hey, did I tell you? I lost two inches off my neck."

"You measured your neck?"

"Sure. Everyone takes measurements, don't they? So, I figured I'd measure some places I could always feel good about—my neck and my ankles. Everyone's perfect from the ankle down, right? That's why women love to shop for shoes." Julia glanced at her own ankle and thought about possible callouses on her heels. Sure, perfect from the ankle down so long as covered by socks and opaque footwear. "But then, surprise surprise! After I dieted a bit, boom. I'd lost two inches off my neck." Weird. Julia just smiled and nodded with feigned enthusiasm. "I like this gluten- and lactose-free diet." Julia felt her own neck and considered the skin around it a protective layer of fat for her vocal cords and esophagus and whatever else might be in there.

Later that afternoon, finals complete and dorm checkout passed, Julia loaded up the Century and headed south for home. With the most incredible luck, she passed her piano final with an A minus, and Dr. Kitano praised her hard work. She was on cloud nine. The day couldn't have been better if she'd invented it in her mind.

As she started up the first hill into Sardine Canyon, Julia began her weekly ritual of conjecture about Dan's personality and life. Today's incident added a new aspect to her ever-expanding picture of him. He was kind. Kind! Not only that, he was kind to her. In her lifelong daydream of what sort of man might be her own true love, she always included the requirement that he treat her well. Now Daniel placed a checkmark decisively in that column for himself. Well done, Mr. Chitwood. Well done.

His character was really starting to round out in her mind. Friendly: he was always surrounded by a group of friends. Athletic: obviously. Studious: he went to his classes nearly every day. Good sense of humor: didn't a smile tug at his mouth when he saw her fall into the hedge? Motivated: he was a Business major, right? Probably had an entrepreneurial spirit. Someday the two of them together would build their own Fortune 500 company from an idea only his brilliant mind could concoct. And now, add compassionate: Up you go. The words still echoed in her head.

All in all, her first quarter of college was pretty satisfactory. Good grades, good roommate, great job, a love interest. Not bad for someone who just turned eighteen.

She came to the hill overlooking Mantua, and the sun glinted on the snowfield, blinding her. Too bad she never picked up a pair of those Rayban sunglasses Bianca's card advised. Maybe Santa would remember her with those. Christmas was still a week away, and she was looking forward to a hiatus from the stresses of her life. She only had one more Saturday of lessons, and then her students had a break, too. It was a fun lesson—she'd assigned them all holiday music, which renewed some of their waning enthusiasm for practice. For springtime, she planned to rev them up with the threat of a recital in April. If she assigned them each a piece that was two steps above their current level, they'd rise to the challenge, she was sure. Her most effective piano teachers had done the same for her and gotten great results.

For the rest of the drive she amused herself by deciding which piece to assign which kid. In no time she found herself at the long gravel driveway of the Dream House. It was still early afternoon, and Cathy had school until three. Her mom must have been off shopping, so Julia had the house to herself. She unloaded the car and took her stuff into the bedroom she'd picked for herself. When her at-home weekends became the rule, she hesitated to entitle it her room, but it was undeniably becoming so.

The thought of practicing the piano just now made her a little sick. Overkill from finals. Instead she flopped down on her bed and began to study the course schedule for winter quarter. What should she take? So many to choose from. Music Theory, the next class in the series. More piano lessons, of course. Private vocal lessons? Probably not. She decided to get up the gumption to audition for women's ensemble this time. It was something she knew she ought to have done last time but didn't dare. Things were getting more comfortable-feeling, and she at least knew where all the bathrooms were in the Fine Arts building. What about a language? She didn't know. She couldn't decide right now. She needed to rest her eyes.

Some time later, the sound of voices awakened her.

"Gee, Cathy. I'm sorry about the dance."

"It's okay, Jed. You have to do what you have to do. I'll be all right. Seriously." Her tone connoted true reassurance, unusual for a phrase which often carries a meaning opposite its words.

Hearing the two talking, Julia chose that moment to appear. The sooner she came out, the less she'd be eavesdropping.

"Hi, gang. What's up?"

"Hi, Julia. I didn't know you would be here already." Cathy took a step backward, away from Jed. The foyer, though huge, was too full with three people. She made a motion for them to follow her into the living room. "Jed and I were just talking about the Christmas dance."

"When's that?"

"A week from Friday." Jed's voice was a little low, and he glanced at Cathy. "I already promised some people I'd go with them—before Cathy asked me to go with her group."

It seemed to Julia there might be a little more to the story, but she let it drop.

"Hey, I know." Jed brightened and made himself comfortable on the love seat. "To make it up to you, what if we go downtown and catch a screening of a Warren Miller ski movie? It's called *Steepest and Deepest*. You'll really like it."

"When is it?" Cathy hugged a large velvet pillow from her mother's prize sofa. Julia slid onto the piano bench.

"A week from tonight. You should come, too, Julia. Have you ever been to one?"

She'd never even heard of a Warren Miller, and wasn't much into skiing, and she didn't want to intrude on their good time, so she started to refuse.

"Aw, you have to come. It's this guy who loves to ski and make films, and he makes a new documentary every year with off-the-wall commentary and cool stunts like heli-skiing and stuff. I'll even pay your admission."

"Yeah, it'll be more fun with the three of us, Julia." Cathy sounded sincere. Julia had no big plans for next Wednesday, or for any other night during the holidays (except for New Year's Eve, a bash at Bianca's), so she relented.

"Good. It's all settled." Jed seemed especially happy. He was probably relieved that Cathy wasn't mad about the dance anymore, Julia surmised. "I'll drive my truck and we'll make a date of it." Home for the holidays two hours, and she already had a date. A threesome date, so maybe not exactly a date, but a fun plan, nevertheless. What a great day.

"So, are you going to that Christmas dance at your school tomorrow night?" Julia suddenly remembered to ask Cathy some details about her life. Her younger sister was super busy with school and student government, but school let out tomorrow—Friday, and then they would have more time to do things together.

Cathy was working on another poster at her desk, and Julia was studying the schedule for the umpteenth time, lying on Cathy's bed. She still hadn't done her hair or make-up for the day, and it was already 3:30. Vacation was glorious.

"Yeah." Cathy put down her paint marker and looked at Julia. "I finally got a date."

"Is it girl's choice?"

"Uh huh. My first person turned me down—but you heard all that." Jed was Cathy's first choice? It never occurred to Julia that Cathy might like Jed.

"Were you sad?"

"Oh, for a minute or two." She went back to her paint. "But I figured out he likes somebody else." He does? "And then, luckily, I figured out I like somebody else. So, you see, it all worked out great."

"Are you taking the person you like?"

"No. But I'm taking a person who would like to go. And that's what really matters." Was that what really mattered? Julia never considered that to be the point of a dance: making someone else have a good time. At the few dances she'd been to (stag), she was always too self-conscious and wondering why someone wasn't making *her* have a good time to think of that.

"Do you have a dress?"

"Yeah." Cathy left her markers again and pulled a shiny silk column dress from the closet. "Mom got me this pretty red one. For Christmas. Do you like the little Chinese collar?"

"That will look great on you with your dark hair. Are you going to put it up?"

"Yeah. With chopsticks. Funny, huh?" Cathy waved a pair of black lacquered chopsticks from her vanity and did a little oriental bow with them. "Nothing says 'Christmas' like chopsticks. So, Jules, what did you think about the movie last night?"

"Amazing. I had no idea that kind of stuff was out there. Movies like that, I mean. It made me want to quit school and move to a mountain."

"But you don't even ski."

"I know. Neither do you, but I bet you want to join me."

"You're right." Cathy finished her poster and fanned it a bit to dry it.

"How does this look?"

"Fine. You're getting pretty good at block letters."

"I practice a lot."

"Do you think Jed had fun?"

"Jed always has fun. He's fun incarnate."

"Is that why you liked him?"

"I never said I liked him. But that's why I like to be around him. Or part of it." She didn't blush or anything, so Cathy must be telling the truth about not ever like-liking him.

"What's the other part?"

"Oh, probably the fact that he's such a good person. Always thinking of what somebody else might need or want. That's attractive to me." This was a new definition of attractive. Where was the discussion of his winning smile, his deep brown eyes, his excellent, coarse hair? The way a person thinks can be the attraction?

"Will you get the door? I want to finish this." Julia didn't even hear the doorbell ring, her thoughts were so loud in her head. On her way down the hallway, she thought of Daniel for the first time in a few days. *He* was the type to think of others first, too. After all, he lifted her from her time of tragedy in the now-immortal "Up You Go" rescue. She decided that perhaps Dan's compassion might be his number one attraction as well. Or it could easily become so.

"Hello, Julia."

"Jed—how are you? Come in." He came in, bringing a gust of winter wind with him. She pushed the heavy wooden door shut behind him. A chunk of her red hair fell in her eyes, and she realized with horror how she must look.

"Thanks." He found his usual spot on the love seat but refrained from putting his snowy boots on the coffee table. He seemed a little less comfortable than usual. Julia sat near him on the adjacent couch. Her knees were unwittingly tilting his way.

"So, how'd you like the movie last night?"

"It was totally incredible. Cathy and I are quitting school and moving to a ski resort."

"Good. I knew you'd like it." He shifted in his seat.

"Do you want me to get Cathy? She's just in her room."

"Naw. She's probably getting some posters ready for tomorrow. I don't want to bother her." Then what was he doing here? She decided to put him at ease.

"Let me take your coat. You have to see this one Christmas card. My mom's Aunt Florene sent it. It seems to have been in her attic since 1975." She pulled it from the stack on the coffee table, and he moved over to the sofa, sitting beside her to better see the card. She was surprised to notice her hand resting on his arm. She hadn't even planned it!

"It even smells decades old." He lifted it to his nose and then to hers.

"Ew. You're right. Look at the fuzzy velvet poinsettia. If you brush it with your finger, it turns you red." She swiped it and held up her finger to show him. Then she rubbed it on his sleeve.

"Oh, thanks. Just what I needed. Old pollen."

"Merry Christmas."

Suddenly, she had a flash of brilliance. Practicing her flirt tactics on Jed just came so naturally, why not use him as her subject? She certainly saw him a lot more often than she saw Scott, and she needed quantity of practice as much as quality. And with Jed being a no-threat subject (i.e., younger than she was, liked someone else) he was a perfect target. Or guinea pig. Or whatever. Plus, it wouldn't hurt to practice on someone fun and cute and who returned the flirt every once in a while. Like last night when the three of them rode to the movie in his truck and she took the middle seat. Once or twice his hand fell off the gear shift onto her knee. Not that it remained there long, so it was probably accidental, but she couldn't deny the touch gave her a speck of a thrill. Maybe she was just imagining Dan's hand at that moment.

"So, what's the purpose of your visit?" She used her British customs official voice.

"Um, just here to see the sights. But I don't want to look like a tourist."

"Then you'll want to avoid gawking at St. Paul's from atop a double decker bus and wearing your camera on an embroidered strap about your neck as you're doing now."

"Thank you, ma'am. Words to live by. I mean, by which to live. I mean. So, actually, I came to see if you girls want to come to our New Year's Eve party. It's mostly going to be family—just a few friends—but it would be an honor to have the Cronquist girls in attendance."

When it rained it poured. Feast or famine. Never before in all her days had she received one invitation to a New Year's Eve party—let alone *two*. Would the wonders of this year never end? They'd have to. It was nearly the end of the year.

"I can't speak for Cathy, but it sounds like a great time to me."

Just then, Cathy piped up from the other room.

"I'll be there. Can I bring something?"

"Just yourself," he hollered down the hall. Then he turned back to Julia. "You can bring your impressive piano skills, though—if you would. My mom has been dying to hear you play." He told his mom about her piano playing? Wow. Oh. Wrong impression. He just meant as Amanda's piano teacher. Duh. It didn't matter anyway because his mom would have to wait to hear Julia play some other time. Bianca's party was already on the slate.

"Oh, shoot. I just remembered. I really wish I could be there. It's just that I already—"

"Oh, of course." He looked a little sheepish. She'd never seen Jed look sheepish. "Of course you have other plans."

"Yeah. Sorry." She felt sincerely sorry. "But if things wrap up there early, maybe I could hop over to your place. Would that be okay?"

"Sure." His face restored its normal cheer level. "We'd love to have you any time." It actually did sound more interesting than Bianca's bash, although she'd never tell anyone she thought a family party sounded better than a young single pals party. Too bad she'd already committed to bring the cheese ball. "And bring your music."

"If I can, I will."

"I'll be there," yelled Cathy. "With bells on."

"Great," Jed hollered back, then turned again to Julia. They walked into the kitchen and each got a piece of leftover apple pie and sat down at the bar to eat it. "So what have you been doing today?"

"Not much. Just trying to figure out my class schedule for next quarter." Julia wished her mom kept a squirt can of whipped cream on hand. Squirt whipped cream was something that definitely had a cool factor. "Any suggestions?"

"On what? For your classes?" She nodded as Jed put a huge bite of pie in his mouth and had to chew for a moment before he could answer. "Your major is Music, right?"

"For now, I guess." Despite pressure from her older sister, the department was a really good place for Julia—challenging and stimulating without the cutthroat competition she dissolved under, which would have been rampant at some of the other schools she'd wanted to apply to. But didn't. Because (though she'd never admit it aloud) for another reason besides missing the auditions, she was kind of scared to live far away from her parents. Who would fix her car if it broke down? And stuff. "It's not too bad so far. They're letting me keep my scholarship for another quarter."

"Well, I was just thinking." He took a swig of milk from the nearly empty jug. Huh. Making himself right at home. "If they offer a composition course, you should try it out."

"Composition?"

"Sure. You've fooled around with writing a little ditty here and there, haven't you?" He nudged her and raised his eyebrows up and down leadingly.

How would he know? As a matter of fact, she had never written anything down, but, sitting in front of the keys so many hours a day for so many years, there had certainly been times her own melodies rolled off her fingers—mostly variations of what she was working on at the time.

"Oh, not much more than a little chord progression. I doubt

I've got any creativity like that in me." The thought of creating something, whether it be a song or a little allegretto, scared her. What if she made it up and no one liked it? What if *she* didn't end up liking it? The fear of disappointing herself was too great.

"Sure you do. Everyone does. And it wouldn't matter if you never performed it at Carnegie Hall. Don't you think it would be fun to try it?"

"That might be an idea." Then again, it might not even merit idea status. She would mull it over and check the course offerings again to see if it were even in there. If not, argument solved.

Season Two: Winter

CHAPTER THIRTEEN

"Happy New Year!" Julia's mother called down the hall to awaken her sleeping daughters on Sunday morning. "The parade is starting!" It was a family tradition to hunker down in front of the TV on New Year's Day morning and watch the Rose Parade. Someday she and Cathy wanted to go to it and smell the rose petals in person. Julia rumbled out of bed and put on her slippers.

Cathy was already at the table, rubbing the sleep from her eyes.

"What time did you girls get in last night?" Family conversation ensued. More than anything, Julia wanted to put last evening's events out of her mind—forever.

It all started out fine, jingling all the way with her little bell earrings and her festive snowman sweater. The roads were slick, but she started for Bianca's early to help her get things ready for the grand fête.

"Oh, look at you. So fuzzy and cute! Love the sweater." Bianca made Julia do a twirl then gave her a warm hug. "This is going to be so fun tonight."

Julia admired Bianca's dark green crushed velvet mini dress. The satin spaghetti straps crossed in the back and matched the straps on her black satin shoes. A drapey crocheted shawl with the long fringe covered her shoulders—somewhat—from the cold. Her platinum coif was secured in a french twist. "Do you think it makes my neck look too long? I would wear my cubic-z choker, but I think the earrings are enough."

Julia helped arrange the shrimp and cocktail sauce on the lettuce leaves. She wondered how Bianca could keep splurging to feed her friends, who never seemed to contribute much to the parties other than a bottle of soda now and then.

"I think I've found another hobby I love," she bubbled. "Entertaining. It's challenging and satisfying. Planning stuff to keep the fun going for lots of different people with different interests and stuff—it's tricky. But I also get to try new recipes. And eat them. And make decorations. Now, where did I put that mistletoe?" Bianca rummaged through the drawer next to the telephone. "Here it is." It was a limp, crumpled specimen, obviously several years used. "A critical component of every New Year's Eve celebration. Would you hang it in the doorway there?" She pointed to the arch where the kitchen met the living room. "You'll have to pass under it a lot of times tonight." Bianca winked. "Take a deep breath, Julia. You're gonna be fine."

A blush rose to Julia's cheeks. It was imminent now: her first kiss. Of course, it couldn't happen the way she'd always dreamed of it, under the black wrought-iron lantern on the white-columned porch of the house where she grew up in Alexandria with the harvest moon shining and the smell of fallen leaves, private and romantic— but she felt the anticipation of it nonetheless. She wished they could turn the heat down to stop her nervous perspiration, but Bianca's dress was too scant for her to be comfortable with it any lower. Maybe Julia should trade in her 'fuzzy and cute' sweater for one of Bianca's shirts. But there were too many things to do, and by the time she had a chance to ask Bianca again, guests started to arrive—their signature ninety minutes late.

Mostly they consisted of people Julia didn't know. "There's a lot of turnover in retail, so you'll see some new faces tonight," Bianca warned, but, even then, Julia didn't expect it would be *all* new faces. Not even Mi-shrill remained. Then, just before eleven, Scott showed up. Scott. My, how he'd changed! His hair was all short, his clothes were untattered, his face shaven, loafers instead of combat boots. Almost looked like he belonged on Wall Street.

"Scott!" Bianca fluttered over to him as he brushed the snow from his shoulders. He smiled and looked around at the sea of faces eating and chatting in little groups. Julia felt herself blush and returned to the kitchen to hide and hyperventilate. Heart palpitations! Bianca's advice to be kissed, and often, and by someone who knew how—Scott would fit the bill, in style.

Bianca burst in and grabbed Julia by the arm, grinning like a Cheshire cat.

"Doesn't he look smashing?" she hissed in a loud, excited whisper. Julia just nodded dumbly. "Can you tell I've been doing duckling-to-swan practice on him? Pretty soon he'll be totally presentable—though I think he's pretty close now." This was like an alternate universe Cinderella story, and Julia couldn't wait for the stroke of midnight. So she could run away.

"Okay, Julia. It's time. Go start loitering under the mistletoe. I'll point him in the right direction."

Oh. Now? Not now! Not yet! She needed time to gear up for it. An hour, at least. Why hadn't she watched kissing scenes more closely on TV? What did they do? Just press lips together? Oh, no. She was *not* ready.

Julia fidgeted in the kitchen for fifteen minutes, pouring hot Wassail and rearranging pumpkin doughnuts on a platter. Sounds of laughter and flirtatious giggling wafted to her ears. The clock was about to strike midnight.

"Jules. Could you come out here?" Bianca called sweetly, and Julia knew there was no more avoiding fate. She took off her apron and went as far as the doorway. The matchmaker held up a hand for her to stop, then she shoved a thumb under Scott where he was sitting beside Bianca on the brown couch. Scott slowly got to his feet.

"Happy New Year," Bianca shouted, and all the guests repeated the salutation as they turned to watch the unfolding drama.

His steps toward her were unusually sluggish. Plodding

toward destiny. Julia didn't mind so much. The slower he went, the better—maybe the spit would return to her mouth before he reached her. The blood drained from her face, and her palms felt clammy. She grasped the door jamb to steady herself. Scott's face was nearly expressionless, but he turned back a moment to glance at Bianca, who smiled broadly and gave them a little prompting wave. He looked up at the mistletoe, back down at Julia's face, then took her chin in his hand. Everyone started cat calling. This was a nightmare. Julia closed her eyes and puckered. He leaned his lips down and touched hers. She suctioned in and . . . smack! Her first kiss set a record for the loudest kiss in all history, echoing like a hello called into the Grand Canyon.

The party-goers were silent for a moment and then burst into spontaneous laughter and applause. Mimicking smacking sounds were heard all through the room. Guffaws and slaps on Scott's back resounded. Julia, too mortified to soak any of it in, turned on her heel and fled to the kitchen for refuge. How could anything be more embarrassing? It was too bad to be true.

"Yeah, Cath, I wish I'd been there, too. It sounds like Jed's get-together was pretty fun."

"How many kids are in that family again?" Their mom tossed a chenille throw Cathy's way. The thin one was shivering again. "Twelve, or something?"

"No. Jed's the fifth of ten. Julia's piano student, Amanda, is the ninth. How old is she, Jule?"

"Ten or eleven, I think." Julia had all her students' stats written down in her file but didn't remember now. "She's one of my best little piano players. She practices."

"Their family seems pretty musical." Cathy took a sip of her hot chocolate. "You should have heard them singing together last night. All of them. Show tunes." She hummed a few bars from *The Sound of Music*'s "The Lonely Goatherd."

"The oldest brother accompanied them on the piano, and a sister played the guitar. We sang all the fun songs. I didn't talk to Jed much. More to his brother Matt, who's in my grade. Jed was busy talking to his grandpa really loudly. Going deaf. But now I know a lot more about raspberry farming in the 1940s than I did before yesterday." That really did sound like more fun than being humiliated in front of a bevy of Newgate Mall employees as she massacred her first kiss. Why, oh why didn't she try for leads in high school musicals while she had a chance? Then she could have *practiced* kissing prior to doing it in front of an audience!

Oh, well. It was all in the past. All last year, in fact. Now, thankfully, today was a whole new year with no humiliating mistakes in it. And school started tomorrow. New classes, new books, new friends, new life. And it was all more than a sixty-minute drive from that dreaded Newgate Mall. No one at Utah State knew about her first kiss, and no one would ever have to. As far as Julia was concerned, it didn't count. She'd never been kissed.

CHAPTER FOURTEEN

"It's a whole new quarter!" True was sporting a new sweater from Santa. It didn't hang on her quite right. Either that, or her bony shoulders looked like an actual wire hanger. "What classes do you have this time?"

"A bunch of music classes—piano lessons, Theory, a women's ensemble choir, and Composition, plus an English class. Poetry writing." Julia finished eating her toast from their shared toaster oven, the only appliance in their dorm room. She decided to save up for a microwave so she could eat instant oatmeal every once in a while.

"You're the queen of the humanities. I'll trade you."

"Why, what do you have?" She was watching True rat her hair into a perfect sphere, then spray it with Freeze and Shine for the third time. The world's most impenetrable bird's nest in for its daily tune-up.

"Lots of hard classes. Chemistry—the second one in the series. You're not missing out. Microbiology from Pedersen, who's the toughest prof on campus, I hear. A nursing orientation at the hospital. Human Anatomy. Oh, and ballroom dance."

"Don't you have to have a partner for that?"

"Not necessarily."

Old Main struck the quarter hour, and the two girls gathered their books for 8:30 classes. They crossed Seventh North together and then separated in their respective directions. Beginning the new quarter was so busy. Books to buy, professors to size up, homework levels to gauge. Yesterday was really hectic, but her ensemble tryout was fantastic. The director admitted her as one of only three second sopranos and told her he expected great things of her. It was shocking. She never supposed it would go so well and was glad she dared to try out. The ensemble practiced every afternoon at 3:30. Three-thirty? That reminded her. She had to get Dan's schedule, too. Three-thirty was his climbing hour last quarter. Darn. If he took that this quarter, too, she'd have to miss watching it again. Too bad. Anyway, she needed to check that out. Funny, she hadn't thought about it before now.

Composition was a two-credit class, Tuesdays and Thursdays at 8:30. She hurried to arrive on time at the Fine Arts building on the far side of campus. She wished she could move into the Golden Toaster, the funky double-barn-shaped church with a mustard-gold colored roof just across the street from Fine Arts, which was also home to all the Friday night Institute dances she was habitually missing. Living there would save so much time and energy. But the walk did her body good. Back and forth two or three times a day helped ease the guilt she felt about telling herself yes to Doritos and pizza so often. It kept her freshman fifteen in the wings.

"Welcome to Composition." The music professor Dr. Bailey had conservative hair and wore a white shirt and tie with his tweed pants. He held an ivory director's wand in one hand and a piece of chalk in the other. The chalk board had permanent music lines painted on it, with no clefs, just like her music classrooms at Duke Ellington. It was a comforting sight. "This class is scheduled for early in the morning, a time when we are at our freshest. You will be required to do your best creative thinking in here." He tapped his wand on the podium and stood up from his stool, walking randomly about the speaker's well.

"This class will not be easy. I guarantee it. In fact, many times it will be like opening a vein." Dr. Bailey proceeded to discuss the syllabus and class requirements. A challenge! The thought electrified her. Although the professor indicated it would be difficult, he also implied that success was likely—inevitable with hard work. She would prove him right.

"Finally, I will describe the quarter project." There were only a few moments left of class. He'd better be concise. "Each student will be required to compose a full-length song, for a choir of any size, on any theme appropriate to the given choir. This is a tall order. You will probably need to begin work on it right away."

"Does it need to have words?" a hand-raiser on the front row asked.

"Good question. Not necessarily. But if not, I will require designated 'ooos,' 'ahs,' and 'mms.'" Time was up, and students began packing up their notebooks and backpacks. "More details forthcoming," Dr. Bailey called as the students filed out. Julia was so excited she raced up the stairs to her practice room. Good thing she scheduled her piano time right after this class. She was ready to start plunking out melodies and rhythms immediately. Wow. What a great class Composition turned out to be. How lucky she signed up for it.

CHAPTER FIFTEEN

⚜

"You know I'm considering this as a career possibility, don't you? I can kind of see me as a professional floral arranger." Julia watched absently while Bianca frowned as she stabbed another silk daisy into her flower and fern assortment on the brass and glass table in her chilly brown kitchenette. It was a winter Friday afternoon. No fresh flowers were available from Rex Cronquist's prize-winning garden, even if it had been installed at the Dream House already, which it hadn't. Bianca had been pilfering blooms from his gardens all her life, sometimes to his chagrin. But even he admitted she was improving her eye for arrangement.

"Do you think I could parlay this into something I could get paid for?" For which I could get paid. "What this needs is irises. Too bad they were $2 more per bunch." Bianca's cash had run short with all her living expenses. Three roommates had moved in and out since Julia left for college, and right now no one was sharing the utilities. The heat was down. Bianca had even borrowed $7.50 from Julia for this little craft project.

Julia bent the wire back and forth in her hands, feeling it heat up in the friction. How much would it take to break it? She bent the wire back and forth quickly again and again. Even when the wire inside obviously broke the stem still didn't come apart. Plastic around the outside kept it together. Interesting.

"Too bad flower arranging can't be my talent for the pageant. I'm not getting a good vibe on my dance at this point. I know at first I was only doing Miss Weber County because of the journalism thing, but I realized I wanted to do it for *myself*. Not for some career path angle. I know I could do it really well, and I'd be a great spokesgirl for the county. Julia, I think all this politics and journalism stuff came into my life for a reason! Seriously, I think it was because I needed to find out about this pageant, and I never would have discovered it otherwise. Whew, I can't believe I almost missed it by telling Josh I wouldn't go out with him three times before I said yes. Weird. It's like fate was patient with me. Now. What should I do for my talent?"

The conversation drifted into Miss Weber County babble. Maybe it was the pageant preparation, but it seemed like ever since New Year's, Bianca had become more of a personality than a person—a personality with the volume permanently cranked to ten. She was acting like those people on TV Julia couldn't believe actually existed in real life without chemical enhancement. However, today Bianca seemed slightly off. Was something bothering her?

"Well, we'd better get going. Mom's waiting for us." They had messed around doing crafts long enough, and Julia wanted to get on the road to Huntsville before dark. Winter roads in the canyon were slick.

"The Ghia needs new tires. Let's take your car." They bundled up, and Bianca lugged her basket of laundry out to the Buick. Bianca hated the cold. Maybe the weather was what put her in this particularly caustic mood. All afternoon she'd been criticizing mall workers and people from her singles ward and old boyfriends. It seemed everyone was fair game in the bash-a-thon. Julia tried to turn the conversation several times, but even wardrobe topics proved useless.

"I know it's not nice of me to make fun of Becca's nose, but I've already got the mantra in my head, *Don't stare, don't stare, don't stare.* If you catch me staring, elbow me. And I have to stop calling her 'The Beak' in my mind. It's so wrong. It's going to slip out sometime." Bianca warmed her hands in front of the Buick's meager heater. Julia wished she'd remembered her other gloves from her backpack. It was a two-pair day. "But, dang it. You'd think, with that big engineer-essa salary, the first order of business would be a nose job. She might even have insurance to cover it. Maybe I could sneak it into the conversation. 'So, what all does your insurance plan cover? Any elective surgeries?' And then I'll know. Would that be a gentle enough hint?"

Julia glanced over at Bianca's profile. The makeup atop it was flawless, but the nose itself lacked distinction. And perfection. She felt her own nose. Brr. Too cold for that. But, yes, it was the Cronquist number through and through, just like Bianca's. Straight and narrow with a bit of a rounded tip. Nothing to sing about, that was for sure. Or to feel superior about. About which to feel superior.

"Oh, come on. Her nose is fine. Ted likes it, and he's all that really matters at this point."

"I guess you're right. It does have an undeniably conspicuous quality that *would* attract Tedious. But we all should make the most of what we've been given. And the least of what we haven't, I say. Enough with accentuating the negative." Amen, thought Julia. Let's change the topic here. Pronto.

"So, what do you think Ted is going to tell us tonight?"

"Duh. That he and Becca are engaged."

"That's what I'm guessing. When do you think they'll get married?"

"The sooner the better. Put us out of our misery."

"Misery? Why do you say that?"

"I love love, but mostly when it's people I'm interested in. And Ted is definitely not on that list. How can he be so smart and so boring at the same time? You'd think he'd be smart enough to know how to not bore others." All this negativity was boring Julia. Wow, was Bianca ever on one today. What was eating her? Maybe her sugar was crashing. Or maybe—maybe it was unresolved guilt for the embarrassing moment she'd inflicted on Julia via Scott's lips? Could that have been the source of the grumpiness and critical spew? An apology would be welcome—and readily accepted at any point here, she thought. But it had better be a good, thorough one.

Bianca sighed a big huff of steamy air. It froze white in front of her face and dissipated slowly. Sure, it was a dry cold, but it was still cold. Julia could never remember a winter in Virginia that stayed below freezing for nine weeks in a row. This was brutal. But the fog sure made for a sparkling, frosty winter wonderland. It left a residue of fluffy, furry crystals on every branch of every tree. The tree-filled campus of Utah State was spectacular after a foggy night. Julia thought to herself that there were as many branch-lets as there were sands of the sea. And now, driving through the gorgeous canyon, she predicted another beautiful frosty morning in Huntsville the next day.

"What do you think of Becca? Other than her nose."

"Oh, she's all right, I guess. I like her car." Becca drove a newish Jetta. "And once I heard her crack a joke. Ted didn't laugh, of course. He probably didn't get it. In a way I feel sorry for her."

"Why?"

"Because she'll be married to Ted, of course. And because she's stuck in that geeky life."

"Sometimes geeky lives can be pretty lucrative though." Julia tried appealing to Bianca's financial sensibilities.

"Oh, sometimes. But I will bet you twenty bucks they don't give awesome makeup bonus gifts at Christmas at the space technology plant. That's the shame of it, you see. Most corporate executives don't know anything about what would be a real reward for a working woman."

"Well, I like her, too. I wish I were as smart as she is at science. Did you know she has designed parts that have improved the space shuttle?"

"Nerd. Fest. And did you see her brows last time she was over? Time to pluck, Bert. Talk about mono-brow."

"Come on, Bianca. Don't you think that's even a little bit awesome? Think of the . . . astronauts."

"Okay. Okay, you're right. Astronauts are hot. So, yeah. You're right. Becca's pretty smart." Finally, something on which they agreed. "But most guys are intimidated by smart women. It's better to appear *less* smart to increase your potential dating pool."

To include '*less* smart' men? To include men who are intimidated by smart women? Julia didn't know if that was exactly what she was looking for in her true love, although she did admit Bianca had a point. There was a very good chance that Bianca got more dates than Becca ever did on that basis alone.

A good meal and a warm fire seemed to go a long way toward improving Bianca's mood, and after dinner that night, the family adjourned from the table to gather around the huge stone fireplace that graced the corner of the family room. Julia claimed her spot in the crook of the sectional couch and tossed the chenille throw to Cathy who nestled under it for warmth. Their dad set another log on the blaze and busied himself with nudging the embers with his poker. It made Julia want to roast a marshmallow like her dad used to let her and Cathy do when they were little.

"So, Ted. You asked us all to be here." Jan Cronquist extended the footrest on her favorite recliner. It was the only old piece of furniture (other than the antiques) in the Dream House. She refused to let it go. "Is there a reason you wanted us all to be here?" She looked over at Rex, who looked back at her and winked. A huge smile spread across Ted's face.

"As a matter of fact, Mom, Dad, everybody, I do have some important news. Becca and I are getting married! I asked her dad's permission this weekend, and I asked Becca last night. She said yes." Becca, who sat with her arms entwined around Ted's right arm, legs curled under her so she could lean against his side, blushed and dipped her eyelids. "We," Ted continued, "are planning to get married in the Ogden Temple at the end of May."

"Oh!" Their mom squealed with glee. Her footrest flashed downward, and she leapt over to the section of the sofa where Ted and his future bride sat, whereupon she smothered them with hugs of delight. "I'm so happy for you! This is wonderful news! Oh, Becca. We're so excited to have you become a part of our family."

It was the first time Julia had considered this: by marrying her brother, Becca would become Julia's sister. Another sister. An older sister. Another older sister. Weird. She looked at Bianca, expecting a continuation of today's cynical sneer, but to Julia's great surprise Bianca was smiling a genuine smile, even leaning toward Ted and patting him in congratulations. Was love—and its attendant joys—contagious? Julia certainly felt its tendrils pulling her in.

"That's great!" Bianca gushed. "So, what colors are you going to have for your wedding reception?"

"I don't know yet. I haven't given it much thought." Yeah, right. Bianca rolled her eyes at least at this, possibly thinking that every girl on the planet has been planning her own wedding reception since birth. Maybe since the pre-existence. "I like white. And I love flowers. It might be weird but I'm thinking of somehow doing all white and flowers. Do you think that would work?" This struck a chord with Bianca—and Julia detected a visible warming toward the new sister.

"That sounds fabulous. Can I help?"

"Sure. My folks are all in Oregon. I'm going to need lots of help. I'm glad it's not until May."

"Let's do a backyard reception!" Even their dad felt the excitement of it at discovering his own potential contribution. "I've been wanting to build a gazebo. I saw one in a do-it-yourself catalog." Rex Cronquist rubbed his hands together in delight and then shuffled over to give his dear son a hug of shared joy. Julia and Cathy exchanged looks of happy love, and Julia thought this was one of the best family moments she could ever recall.

"Congratulations," she said warmly, and a few notes of her Composition assignment spontaneously began forming in and twinkling through her mind.

CHAPTER SIXTEEN

—⚜—

"It seems like I haven't seen you forever. How are your classes?" True and Julia crossed the intersection of sidewalks between the library and the Geology building on their way to Valley View Towers. They agreed to have dinner together for the first time in two weeks. "I've gotten so busy with Dorm Activity Chair stuff for the Tower, I haven't been home much at all. How *are* you?"

"Things are going great. Mostly." Julia sidestepped a snowdrift in the late afternoon twilight. "What all are you doing with your chairwoman stuff?" True hardly had time to eat these days. She was looking so thin. Too thin.

"Tons. It's really fun. There are some cool people—you should come to one of our video parties sometime. We're doing anime this weekend."

Anime? Pokemon and such? Not really Julia's thing. Sure, there might be some interesting people there, but Julia wanted to get out of the freshman crowd—start getting to know some of USU's more, for lack of a better word, cool people. She didn't want to get sucked into the vortex of dorm sociality without giving the real campus life a try.

And she *was* giving it the old college try. She even went inside the Hub one time and tried to look like she belonged there, but no one talked to her. For David Letterman Week she forced herself to attend nearly every event. The Student Activities Board went the extra mile on that. Piano drop from the roof of the Business building was one day. (It was a yucky old piano, so Julia didn't cringe. Pianos don't improve with age.) Velcro suit jump was another day. People donned a suit covered in the scratchy part of velcro and vaulted from a mini trampoline onto a wall of the library that was covered in the fuzzy part. Only one guy, a lightweight, stuck. Everyone else peeled off.

The best day was Stupid Human Tricks, though. One girl copied Dave Barry's idea of catching hairspray-soaked underwear on fire by igniting them with the sparks from Rollerblade Barbie's skates. Apparently it was a tough trick to duplicate. They finally gonged her. Someone else wore a tutu and rode a unicycle while playing a song from the old punk group The Psychedelic Furs on the violin. Two of Dan's friends bobbed for carp in a big tin bucket—and one of them came up with a carp in his mouth—disgusting—especially when the carp's gill cut the guy's mouth and blood went everywhere.

Out of the corner of her eye, she saw Dan near the front, laughing his guts out. A girl was sitting next to him, but they didn't look like they were on a date. Or were they? Julia tried to get near him as he was leaving. She got to within five steps of him. She took a deep breath to introduce herself—but lost her nerve at the last minute. So much for her foray into the in-crowd.

"Video parties? Yeah. I might sometime. You know, you should have been there for Letterman Week. I needed somebody to sit by." By whom to sit.

"That's not my thing so much—lemminging along after the Beautiful People." True's definition of popular wannabes was broad. Besides, she obviously hadn't looked too closely at the main players on the Student Activities Board this year. Very few of them qualified as technically beautiful. Organizational whizzes, maybe. Creative social engineers, possibly. Beauty queens and kings, up for debate. "Dan came to one of our events, you know. A pizza party last night at the Junction. Does this coat make me look fat?"

"Puffy parkas make everyone look fat. But everyone wears them, so don't worry about it. Everyone wants a little blubber for warmth in this weather." Julia patted her thighs to demonstrate as they passed the snow-covered tennis courts just west of their dorm. "Dan was there? Why?"

"I think his fraternity got invited accidentally. They hogged the pizza, but other than that they were pretty well behaved. We invited them to participate in our line-up dance."

"Line up dance? What's that?" Flakes started fluttering down on their heads. Another blizzard was on its way.

"Just anyone who wants to sign up gets lined up for the dance. Then the guy gets the girl's address, goes and picks her up, and takes her to the dance. It's one giant blind date. Like a cult wedding." They arrived at their dormitory building and took the stairs instead of the elevator to the fourth floor. Heart health. "I want to lose three pounds before then. I think I'll try South Beach."

"Don't do that." They puffed their way to the final flight of stairs. "The dance sounds like fun. Can I go to that one?"

"Absolutely. And, I might be able to do more."

"What's that?" True inserted her key, and they stomped the snow off before going inside.

"If Dan signs up, I'm on the organization committee, and I might be able to pull a few strings so he gets your name." What? No way! Where did she sign? She was in.

This quarter was so busy, she didn't have time to loiter outside his classes like she wanted to. Their schedules didn't line up quite right. However, he crossed her path serendipitously twice a week or so. He always seemed to be around the Fine Arts building when her women's ensemble class let out. Once she even passed near enough to smell him again, but it wasn't quite the same. He didn't have rock climbing on his schedule this time, so no afternoon shower. Or maybe the cold just froze his smell. It froze Julia's nose often enough.

But this line-up dance was the breakthrough she'd been waiting for. For which she'd been waiting. Just the two of them, swaying on the dance floor. A Diana Krall or Harry Connick, Jr. (both great singing pianists) love song pulsing in the background. The brilliant conversations she imagined a million times floating off their lips. And then, the pièce de résistance: when he asked her for a second date! It was just two weeks away. True was the best roommate in the world.

CHAPTER SEVENTEEN

"So, you're finally going to officially meet him, huh?" Bianca sounded unimpressed with small progress. "Do you think you're ready?" Probably not. But Julia also didn't want to practice anything else on Scott. In fact, if she *never* saw him again it would be too soon.

They wrung out their rags into the old ice cream buckets and continued wiping Dream House baseboards. "I don't know how Mom shanghaied us into doing spring cleaning in the middle of winter." Picking up their buckets, they moved from the piano room to the entryway. "What a way to spend President's Day. I honestly doubt this is what the Foundling Fathers envisioned for us on their birthdays. Mops and buckets, happy birthday!" Bianca put her elbow into gear along the baseboards near the front door. "But I do like a shiny entryway. It makes it all worth it. Look at that shine." Inspired by Bianca's verve, Julia put her own elbow into gear, exuding grease she didn't know she had in there.

The three sisters scrubbed their little hearts out all morning. After lunch, their mom surprised them with an offer to take them shopping and for cheesecake at the Cheesecake Factory. She amply compensated for her taskmaster phase.

That evening, as Julia packed up for school again, Jed dropped by.

"This is a surprise. Thought you had enough of me after our three-hour chat on Saturday." Amanda and Cathy had played X Box for three hours while Jed and Julia sat at the piano, playing Name That Tune, and inventing new rhythms for Clementi and

Bartok. Jed wasn't a star pianist by any stretch, but he knew quite a few melodies. Some Julia hadn't even met yet.

"Not sick of you yet. Going for overdose here, I guess."

"Honestly, I never knew that Apaches point with their lips." He'd been full of trivia gems that day. Native American stuff, the exact length of an Earth year (365.24219 days), polar ice caps, and so on.

She showed him her new sweater and boots, describing the imperative need for arctic wear on the USU campus. "The wind just hurls out of Logan Canyon, frosting the tears in your eyeballs. If my hair would fit in a ski mask, I'd wear one."

"Maybe I'll knit you a big hair ski mask."

"You knit?"

"No, but I'd learn."

"Thanks." How sweet.

"That's what I came to talk to you about." Knitting? Couldn't be. "I have to drop off some application stuff up there next Thursday, and I wondered if you had time to show me around. I've only been to the campus a couple of times, so I'll probably get lost and never find the right building and miss the deadline—if someone doesn't show me around. Pretty please?"

Of course Julia would show him around. Not that she knew the campus all that well herself, but her four months there beat his none.

"Great. What time?"

"Two." That worked. Between classes. Before choir.

"Fine."

"Then it's a date." A date? A date. That was one day before the line-up dance date. Hey. A chance to practice date etiquette on her chosen guinea pig! It was unlikely any other practice opportunities were going to turn up before then for the flirt tactics. Her date with Jed was it. Perfect. She'd better look for the advice box as soon as she got in tonight.

⚜

"Never wear floral print to a dance—screams wallflower!" She reread the rule. Dang. Her new cornflower blue top had flower-shaped buttons. Did that count? It looked good on her.

"Never be seen without your makeup. You lose your mystery." No problem. She never went out without makeup, so one ever saw her without her makeup—except Jed that once when they were looking at Christmas cards. That was fun.

"Let him get your door. Helplessness is part of the feminine mystique." Got it. "Look at either his lips or his eyes whenever he talks. Then he knows you're interested—in more than just his words." Oh? She'd never thought of that before. No wonder things went so badly with Scott. She didn't do any of this on him. It was a good thing she located the box before her two dates.

Two dates in one week! The first two dates of her entire college life, and they fell within a two-day period. Okay, she admitted Jed only used the term "it's a date" as a cliché, and it was only Jed, and it was only a short, afternoon errand-run. She couldn't literally count it. But for the sake of scientific research she needed to treat it as such in her mind.

"Take his arm when you walk together. Rest your fingers lightly on his forearm." Oh, so let *him* be the man. Good. "He leads when you're dancing. Do what he does." She had no plans for dancing with Jed. But, with Dan . . . she needed to know that. Let him lead. Yippee! Slow dancing with Dan! Less than forty-eight hours away!

"What's that stuff?"

Julia didn't hear True come in. She stuffed the cards back in the box and hid it under her pillow.

"Nothing. Just flash cards for Theory. What are you doing home so soon?" Old Main struck eleven.

"Um, I have some bad news." True pulled her pajamas and a box of Saran Wrap from her drawer and started her nightly ritual of wrapping her thighs in plastic. She claimed the cellulose melted in the recirculating heat. It sounded like bunk to Julia, although she noticed True's legs did seem to be wasting away. Probably due more to her one-hundred-bite-per-day diet than to the body wrapping. "Things didn't quite work out like we planned."

"What do you mean?"

"I mean, there was a coup at the name drawing for the line-up dance, and Dan didn't get assigned your name. Before I could get there, some other chick on the board grabbed his paper and assigned him to herself."

"On purpose?"

"I don't know. If I hadn't gotten there ten minutes late, I might've stopped it. You probably want to kill me. I'm so sorry!" Her eyes pleaded for forgiveness. Julia knew it wasn't really True's fault their plot to cheat the system failed. It was fate. Every time Julia ever tried to cheat on anything it fell through. Luck kept her honest against her will.

"So, am I still in the mix? Or do I just drop out now?"

"No. You're still in." True didn't say anything else.

"Is it a big secret? Who am I going with?" With whom was she going?

"Now that the boys all know their dates' names, it's no secret. He should be calling you tonight or tomorrow." Who was it? Why didn't True just tell her?

"Tell me. Quick. Before I freak out."

"His name is . . . Elvin." Elvin? What in the world? Who named a kid *Elvin?* Oh, great. A foreign student. Expressly against Bianca's advice. But, then again, it was a somewhat European sounding name. Irish? Aren't elves in Ireland? Maybe he had a cool accent? No that was leprechauns. Elvin? Oh, dear.

"I've met him before," True was saying. "He's actually pretty fun. Not a rocket scientist. He's in the frat." A frat brother of Dan's. He might not be entirely useless. Maybe? Maybe she could use him as a frat "in" someday. Elvin? What a disaster.

Chapter Eighteen

"And this," she waved her arm in a massive *voilá*, "is the Fine Arts building, where I spend most of my waking hours. Would you like a tour of its halls prior to our parting?"

"Parting? Do you have to go somewhere?" They went inside, glad to be in the warmer air.

"Just a 3:30 class. Choir."

"Oh. Anything else this afternoon?" They walked through the big, hollow auditorium where orchestras played and keynote speakers preached to a thousand seats. "Or tonight?"

"Just class. I ought to get in some time on the piano, but Thursdays a practice room is hard to get for some reason." They walked down the long ramp to the Art wing. Hammers clinked against copper near the metal sculpting room. Someday that might be a fun class to take.

"Would it be okay if I hang around and wait until you're done with class? I'm not ready to face the slippery roads again yet. Plus, I'm starting to get hungry. We could grab a bite."

"Sure, I guess. If we go out here we can cut across the courtyard to that little museum. You can wait in there to keep yourself entertained. It has some arty artifacts and historical stuff. I sit in there to think sometimes." They crossed the snowy plaza. A whoosh of heated air blew past them as they opened the door and entered the warm building.

"But they charge admission," Jed pointed out as he opened the door for her to the Eccles Gallery inside, and she handed the lady four dollars. "What are you thinking about at two bucks a pop?"

She didn't want to tell him, but since he was the one who suggested she take the class in the first place, she relented.

"It helps me get my thoughts together for my composition class." There. That wasn't so painful. They found a bench, one she used frequently, and sat down in front of a painting of the Old Main building. It was an oil done by Ed Groutage, a local great. Collecting her scheme thoughts again, she wished she'd had the nerve to take Jed's arm while they were walking, but she didn't. She was failing at her own experiment. "And I have a poetry class, too. Brutal. This is the only place where I don't see any other students. I need solitude for creativity, I guess."

"How's your composition going?"

"I don't know yet. I can't quite get the feel for it." She spent an hour or more a day on it and had the basic melody, but knew it lacked inspiration.

"Maybe you could let me hear it sometime. It might help to let someone else listen."

"Maybe." She wasn't sure. Jed was a friend. Would he be an honest critic? She didn't need a yes man. "If you promise you won't just say, 'Oh, that's nice.' I need a true opinion."

"Of course." He turned and looked her in the eyes. "What are friends for, right?" Did he think they were just friends, too? Good. His arm slipped around her waist reassuringly. Hmm. "I was thinking—you might try working from lyrics. Already made-up lyrics."

That was an idea. She should try that.

They sat silently looking at the artifacts in the cases and on the walls around them.

"I like that painting." He indicated the oil of Old Main on the wall across from them. "I assume the letter A on the steeple stands for Aggies?"

"Probably. There's a little stone bench table thing on the lawn out front made of four letter A's and a slab of cement on top, too." It was not part of the Groutage picture, but Julia pointed out where its place was hidden under the fall foliage.

"What's it for? Picnics?"

"I'm not sure what its originally-intended purpose was, but the little legend is if two people kiss while standing atop the A during a full moon at midnight, they become 'True Aggies.' That is, if one of them is already a True Aggie." She thought about trying to rest her hand on his knee and look right into his face. Mouth, eyes, mouth. Bianca would be so proud of her for remembering. Too bad she didn't dare implement any of it. She was such a coward!

"Are you?"

"Am I what?" His question ripped her from her reverie.

"A True Aggie." He leaned a little closer to her as he pointed to the picture.

"Me?" She glanced up at his eye. But then his lip was more at her eye level. She tried to look back in his eye again. She was blowing it. "Not me. So, you'll have to find someone else to kiss you at midnight if you want to be one." She said it quietly. The museum was silent. The only sound was the chiming of Old Main's half-hour signal.

Three-thirty! She had to get to choir! The second sopranos were choosing soloists today.

"Hey, I'm late." She grabbed her backpack and hefted it onto her shoulder. "I'll be in choir. Do you still want to meet me after? We can take the cemetery tour. Maybe we can find the weeping lady." Please say yes.

"Sure. What's that?"

"I'm not totally sure, but I've heard it's a grave marker for a Danish lady who lost all her children crossing the plains. It's a statue of a woman. They say it cries in the moonlight. I'll tell you later."

"I'll be right here. I have some reading to do."

"See you in an hour—" Oh, she hoped he would stay. Please still be here in an hour. She dashed out of the gallery and up the stairs to her choir room. They were already warming up. Why did she want him to stay so much? She'd already proven herself incapable of applying Bianca's advice, hadn't she? Probably she just didn't want him to have to find somewhere to eat alone. Jed was a good friend, and she wanted to give him some company. Right?

"Soloists' names will be posted on the door of my office after lunchtime tomorrow. You all did well and should be congratulated."

Julia knew she had not done well. For some reason she was flustered during her audition. She couldn't concentrate on the runs. The blonde with the pouty lips probably got it. Oh, well. She had enough on her platter right now. Composition and poetry and piano practice and teaching lessons, as well as trying to overcome her social insignificance.

She gathered up her music and other things and filed out of the class with the other women. The audition was so stressful she almost forgot Jed sitting downstairs in the gallery and initially went the wrong way down the hall. When she turned the corner to correct her mistake, she nearly ran head-on into Daniel Chitwood. Her head filled with his ocean-fresh essence, and her knees buckled.

"Oh!" She caught herself on the railing of the stairwell. "Excuse me." At least she didn't fall a third time in front of him.

He said nothing but continued searching intently down the hall she just came from. From which she just came. Suddenly he seemed to awaken from his distraction, looked at Julia, and asked in a sincere tone, "Are you alright?" She nodded silently. He spoke to her! For the second time in her life! And she spoke (well, communicated) to him, too. The wheels were really turning now. It was only a matter of time before they would have a full-fledged conversation. "What are your hopes and dreams?" It was on the tip of her tongue, but he struck off down the hall before it could leave the tip.

In ecstasy, she wandered off toward the Eccles Gallery. Daniel Chitwood spoke to her! Ten thousand angels' voices couldn't be more lyrical. He cared about her safety—and proved it for a second time in a three-month span. Her feet clicked happily down the tiled halls. Daniel, Daniel, Daniel. What feelings you stir within me, her heart sang. And it sang more beautifully than any audition or performance of her life. If only their little run-in had happened an hour sooner, she'd be in business for that guaranteed "A" by now—the one granted to every soloist. Ah, the fates.

But, where was her little friend Jed? The museum was dark. She squinted to read the hours on the door. Noon to four, daily. Darn. Where was he? Four-thirty chimes cut the frozen air outside as she emerged into the courtyard in the dimming winter light. "Jed!" she called softly, not wanting to create an echo. No answer. Back inside she went, and this time she noticed a Post-it stuck inconspicuously to the door of the gallery.

J.C.— Sorry. Remembered I have to do something tonight. See you soon. J.S.

He was gone. So much for his big ideas of spending the rest of the day together. Oh, well. The tour as a whole was a success. Flirt tactics-wise, anyhow. But now Jed was gone, Dan was gone, and she should be gone. Hoisting her pack onto her shoulder once again, she tramped off toward home. Date number one down, one to go.

"I can't believe I let you talk me into this."

"Talk you into it? You begged to go. Remember?"

The girls were putting the finishing touches on their looks before the line-up dates were slated to arrive at 7:30. Julia caved and wore her new shirt, despite its flower buttons, and True sported an entire ensemble of floral prints. Hey, sometimes a girl has to take a risk—although she didn't consider floral for Elvin all that risky. The only real risk was being seen with him.

"Who are you lined up with, anyway?" With whom are you lined-up? "Did you end up choosing or just take luck of the draw yourself?" Julia touched a dab of vanilla scent to her neck and put her silver hoop earrings on, then did a final quick check for lipstick on teeth. Why was she bothering for someone called Elvin? Who knew.

"Me? Oh. The guy's name is Rory. Computer geek. You've probably seen me talking to him at the library fourth floor lab." Looking in the mirror, True cinched her belt another notch. She was proud of achieving her three pound goal and slimmed her pastel floral peasant blouse around her waist admiringly. "Does this make me look fat? It's so frilly."

"Not at all. You look as slim as can be." As slim as should be. "Rory, huh?" True never answered whether it were luck or whether it were fixed. Something told Julia no luck was involved. But why the pasty moustache guy? Did she like him for his brain? That must be it.

"Rory Avanti. Like the car." What car? There was a car called an Avanti? It sounded Italian.

"Sounds Italian."

"It is. And I forgot to tell you something about the dance which may save your chances with Dan."

"What's that?" She perked up.

"At the beginning of the night, every girl gets a dance card with five blank lines on it. You go around and get guys to sign a line on your card. Can I use some of your vanilla?"

"Sure." She handed over the perfume. "Like an autograph? What good is that? Handwriting analysis?" Some help.

"No. The deejay announces from time to time through the night that it's time for line three, or line one, or whatever is on the girl's dance card, and then you dance with that person. It's a good mixer, don't you think?" Not a bad idea. But how would that help? "So, you just get Daniel to sign your card, and he has to dance with you on that number of song. Get it?"

Hooray! True came through for her after all. Now, if she could get Danny Boy to sign her card on all the lines . . .

A knock came at the door. It was one of the other dorm girls, Amy.

"Hey, I saw your dates downstairs. They're waiting for you in the TV lounge. One of them is really cute." True blushed. Julia wondered if Amy had some sort of sight impairment.

"Let's take the elevator. No reason to add any unnecessary sweat." It also provided an opportunity for a grand entrance, as the elevator opened directly into the TV lounge.

When they came out of the elevator, the lounge was milling with people. Julia's eyes searched and searched, trying to determine which was her blind date, until True caught her and pulled her toward a couple of guys glued to ESPN, seated on a far couch.

"Hey, True-True-Truly Scrumptious!" Pasty stood up. Elfin magic followed suit. "Hi. You must be Julia. I'm Rory. This is Elvin." Elvin stretched forth a hand to greet her. "Elvin, Julia. True, Elvin." He shook True's hand, too. But Julia said nothing. Here before her was a darling, styling man, about age twenty-four, auburn hair, engaging smile, perfect teeth and skin, features that reminded her a bit of Errol Flynn's from the old movies. Very cute. He was dressed to kill, too. Not anything too fancy, but hip. Very hip. Bianca would term it chic. Right down to his copper bracelet and metal-beads-on-leather-strap-necklace. Very cute!

"Well, hello, Miss Julia." He stuck her hand into his, grasped tightly, and marched her out the door. "Rory and I thought we'd get a bite first. Cool guy. Met him tonight first time." The four of them slipped and slid out to the parking lot, Julia being glad she wore her new clodhoppers for safety, and piled into Rory's coupe.

"You two will have to get cozy back there." Rory started up his car and blasted the heat.

"Hey, Rory, old pal," Elvin called over the blowing air, "for a blind date, I sure scored. Julia's a babe." He flipped one of her red ringlets. "Gorgeous red locks." Then he whispered right in her ear, "I love reds."

"Yeah, but not quite as babe-ish as my date."

Flattery will get you everywhere, boys. She snuggled right up to Elvin, who snuggled right back. This line-up didn't turn out to be half the nightmare she expected.

"Hey, gals." The deejay muted the strains of the music to make his announcement. "The dance card numbers are coming right up, so don't forget to fill up your cards. Pick them up on the far wall." The volume came back up, and people resumed their bouncing. Elvin and Rory took the girls' coats.

"Let's go cut a rug, baby." Elvin pulled her toward the floor, where he began swirling her around swing style. The boy could dance! She was sorry she'd eaten so much Mexican at El Sol now. She had to break away and digest for a few minutes before she started dancing for real. True and Rory looked like ballroom dance swans together compared to all the chaotic geese flapping about to the music.

"I'm just going to run and pick up a dance card, my sweet." Elvin had been calling her pet names all night, and it was catching.

"Don't be long, sugar lips." What fun. Elvin was the best. The bestest. She plucked a piece of green card stock from the stack and a little mini golf pencil. With a wave and a "one minute, dear" signal to Elvin, she set out in search of her object. Daniel just had to be here.

For the duration of two entire songs, she scoured the mob for his face. Then, there he was! Near the punch bowl, talking to a bunch of his friends, including the carp bobber. She made a beeline for them.

"Now it's time for line number three. All you girls with dance cards out there, find the person who signed line number three on your card." The deejay played some vamping background music, like the Hokey Pokey, while everyone milled around looking for dance card signer number three. The shifting sands of the room unexpectedly swirled Dan and company away. Some tall people stood in front of her for a few minutes, crowding her and blocking her view until the music started. No sign of Dan. No sign of True and Pasty Moustache. But there was Elvin, right at the heart of the dancing crowd, going to town on the dance floor. The guy was breakin'. Elvin, buddy, where are your parachute pants? His number three dance partner was giggling and trying to copy him. They spun on their backs together, then got up and he switched gears. He was showing her the lumberjack, then the fisherman, the baseball player. She copied him for a few bars until he shifted to a new occupation dance. Soon, the whole floor was doing the Elvin. Hey, he was her date. And she was standing, wallflower style, on the sidelines.

Just then, her roving eye found Daniel Chitwood, doing the golfer along with the rest of the crowd, and she remembered her purpose. Predicting which way he would peel off when the song ended, she tried to position herself by the punch bowl where she could lie in wait. Unfortunately, when the song ended, Dan remained where he was on the floor and took his number three in his arms for the slow song. As they slowly rotated, Julia got a view of his partner's face. The pouty lips blonde from ensemble choir! Hair as stringy as ever! Now that she thought about it, she remembered seeing Stringy in the punch bowl crowd before the three dance. Were they together? No. Impossible. Impossibly unfair, considering Stringy *did* end up with the solo according to the list on Dr. Eberhard's door at noon today. What could Daniel be thinking? Stringy hung on him like a bad shirt.

But the song was ending, and couples made their way to the sides of the hall again. He was coming her way! She clutched her sweaty dance card in her hand.

"Hi, would you sign my card?" The words came breathlessly. Softly. He seemed as though he didn't hear them. He *hadn't* heard them! His gait didn't slow. He was getting away! She could not allow this chance to slip past her! "Excuse me!" She shouted it this time, just as the music ceased. The whole room seemed to turn toward her. Dan, obviously startled, looked her way. Politely he dropped Stringy's hand and listened to Julia's words. "Would you please sign my dance card?"

He fumbled for a pen, a pencil. Where was her mini golf pencil? Gone! Horrors! She desperately grabbed for a spare from her own pocket. Nothing. There! A guy had one in the front pocket of his Oxford. She snatched it without asking and handed it to Dan, who looked a little distracted, but he signed. He signed!

"Next, ladies, we will be dancing with line number five, so get ready. Number one will be after that, so get your cards filled while you can." The deejay played the Hokey Pokey music again while people milled around. Julia clasped the wrinkled card to her heart. When would it be? How long? Number five, one, or later on two or four? So many chances. So many dances.

She looked down at the card. There was his name. His autograph, quite legible. Impressive. Ah, he wrote it so lovingly. Right next to the number three. Three! Three? But three was already finished! The deejay wasn't going to be calling line number three again. *Wait! There's been a mistake!* She wanted to chase after him, but the tall people surrounded her again, and his form disappeared in the mix. Strains of "The Wind Beneath My Wings" began to fill the air, and Julia stood cold there in his shadow.

He didn't even know that he was her hero.

Eventually she caught up with Elvin and Pasty Moustache and True.

"We've been looking for you. You ready to roll? This place is getting stale."

Julia hadn't danced one complete dance. "Okay." Not even one with her date. The curse of the floral-accent shirt struck again.

"The only regret I have about the dance is that I even bothered to get ready." Julia lay on her bed looking up at the ceiling, poetry book lying open and face down across her stomach. She was too depressed to read, even though the mid-term was Monday morning.

True, on the other hand, was light as a feather, wafting in and out of the bathroom, taking off her makeup with Sea Breeze and cotton balls. "What's the matter? I thought Elvin was cute. Didn't you?"

Elvin. He would probably never call her either. "Yeah. Really cute." Not her type but very cute. "Rory sure seems to think you're a fair and desirable maiden."

"Really? You think so?" Suddenly True got interested in the conversation. "How can you tell?" They spent the rest of the night talking about ways Pasty Moustache looked at True or laughed at her quips, until Julia realized how drained she felt and turned in. Two very weird days of unprecedented events now lay behind her. Her first two dates lay behind her. Three, if she counted the one to the play in high school with the vocal coach's son. She counted it. And the one with Jed on tour yesterday. Should she count that? She should. And the dance with Elvin. All over, finished. Three dates made her a dating veteran. In the future she could date with confidence, certain that the worst was behind her, the best ahead. Either that, or three down, none to go.

She drifted off to sleep with visions of occupational dancers dancing in her head.

CHAPTER NINETEEN

"How's the composition going?" Jed tossed a crusty snowball her way. Julia caught it with an ungloved hand. It stung, and she crushed it to reveal little pieces of gravel from the driveway. The winter air had given way to early spring air, and this particular Saturday afternoon felt almost vernal. Despite the fact that the temperature barely broke forty degrees, it felt so much warmer than it had for months that the two wore short sleeves and no jackets while they basked in the drift-melting sun.

"Better. Not *much* better, but I took your suggestion about writing to lyrics, and it gave me a breakthrough." She wiped her dripping hands on the thighs of her blue jeans. Gingerly she cleared a pile of snow from her mother's flower box on the outside chance that the crocuses might bloom a day sooner. "But I think my lingering problem is I tried to use my own inferior poetry—the stuff I wrote for the class I'm taking now. It stinks, and it's hard to be lyrical over something that lacks both rhythm *and* beauty." The staccato of Amanda and Cathy's bouncing basketball broke the air. Everyone knew it was good to be outside again.

"I see." Jed left off snowball catch playing and came to sit beside Julia on the rock wall, their usual place from the last warm season. "Even though I doubt it's as bad as you say, I think I know what you mean. Who wants to sing about something you don't want to sing about?"

"Exactly. There's a melody in my head. It needs to find its words." She hummed it faintly.

"What was that?" He urged her to sing it louder. "Let me hear it again." Against her will she relented, and he listened carefully. "I like it. I really do think it's a start." She was pleased at his praise but didn't want to make too much of it. "Hey, Jules, let me look through some of my parents' books and see if I can find something for you, words-wise. Would you mind? You wouldn't *have* to use them, of course. But it might be a jumpstart. Can I?"

"Sure. Why not? I mean, I'm not coming up with any hot ideas on my own. And, yeah, I'd really appreciate it." That *was* a good idea, taking something already written and putting it to music—she should have thought of that—rather than mucking through her own crippled poetic attempts. If this quarter taught her one thing, it was she should stick to the notes and not the words. If she didn't fail her poetry class it would be due to the mercy of the English professor and nothing else.

"Hey, Cathy." Finished with that subject, Jed called to the basketball players. "You ready for the canned food drive next week?" Cathy stopped dribbling and held the ball under her arm long enough to give him a thumbs-up. He turned back to Julia. "Your sister is pretty amazing." Cathy resumed play, passing the ball to Amanda. "She has really mobilized the school—recycling, sub for Santa, canned food drive, Big Brother and Sister program." Wow. Cathy did all that? Julia had no idea. "We're sure lucky you Cronquists moved here." He got up and ran toward the court calling, "I'm open."

Julia wished for the hundredth time she had an athletic bone in her body somewhere. What all did Jed mean by that? Was that a look of more than admiration in his eye when he spoke about her little sister? If it was, she couldn't blame him. Cathy was a pretty neat chick. She never bragged about all the good she was doing—not even to Julia, who was clueless about all those service projects except the recycling drive, which she saw the poster for. For which she saw the poster.

Good for Jed, seeing Cathy's great qualities. Good for Cathy, being so great. Lucky girl, getting a guy like Jed.

Yeah. Lucky Cathy.

CHAPTER TWENTY

❧

"Mail for you." True tossed the envelope onto Julia's bed. Julia put down her poetry notebook, glad for the distraction from her most dreaded homework.

"Where have you been so late?" Julia asked, tearing open the letter. It was from Jed. Suddenly she didn't want to make small talk with True about her whereabouts—she wanted to retreat into silent solitude to enjoy this surprise communication. Fortunately, True's answer was short, library and chem lab, so Julia got her wish.

Dear Julia,

So, there I was, thinking about your composition assignment, and I decided I should write to you and tell you what I found in my very own living room. Sorry so soon. I know it's only been a day since you saw me and put up with my glomming onto you, but I want you to know I fulfilled my little promise to try to find you some poetry for your lyrics. My parents have a zillion books, so I know I didn't cover all possible territory, but I copied a few for you. Hope it gives you some ideas. I like Robert Herrick the best. Not very modern, but the guy can turn a phrase. While I was looking through stuff I thought his poems seemed to fit your melody better than Dickinson's or Frost's, although I liked Frost a lot—easy to understand.

Have I ever mentioned how glad I am your family moved to Huntsville? I should buy your dad a cigar or something, if either of us smoked. Offer to mow his lawn for free.

Hey, thanks again for the little tour. You'll have to show me that 'weeping lady' sometime. Sounds pretty creepy. If I have more paperwork to hand in, I'll call you. Study hard. Don't dent the museum benches sitting there too long.

Jed

Enclosed were four photocopied pages from poetry books. Emily Dickinson's "That love is all there is, is all we know of love." Four lines. Nice. But a mite short for what she needed. Another Dickinson about a bee and clover. Okay. Not her style as much. She wasn't so into nature as to sing about it. Especially bees, which she was allergic to. To which she was allergic.

Next were four or five of Robert Frost's poems. Two she'd seen as examples in her poetry class, "Fire and Ice" and "Nothing Gold Can Stay." Then there was one that struck her as funny, called "On Being Idolized." The man in the poem is standing in the surf, seaweed around his ankles, shifting sand under his feet. He has to take a step so he won't tip over on the moving sand, "like the ideal of some mistaken lover."

Ha, ha. That had possibilities. At least it was something she might relate to. To which she might relate. She needed to stop correcting her own thought-grammar. It was starting to make her crazy.

There were a couple of pages of poets she'd never heard of, Anne Bradstreet, William Carlos Williams, Ben Jonson, although she recognized some of Jonson's words from an art song assigned by her vocal coach, "Drink to Me Only With Thine Eyes." Been done, and she knew she couldn't compete or compare, so she skipped him and came to Robert Herrick.

On the Herrick page were several poems, and Jed had taken a yellow highlighter to one, apparently the most promising in his opinion: "To Electra." The title sounded a little risqué to Julia's mind. Then she read the words:

I dare not ask a kiss,
I dare not beg a smile,

Lest having that or this,
 I might grow proud the while.

No, no, the utmost share
 Of my desire shall be
Only to kiss that air
 That lately kissed thee.

Wow. Wow, that was good. And the rhythm was very good. She
hummed her head's melody once through, then tried adding the
words to the poem. Hey, it just might work! Jed was a genius! She
ran it through her head a few more times. Better and better! The
dynamics started coming to her—they worked so naturally with
the music and the words. Oh, she couldn't wait to see him and tell
him how great it was! She wanted to call him this very second in
all her ecstatic ravings. But she knew it was too late, particularly
on a school night, and he was still a high schooler, living at home.
Hmm. That Jed. He seemed so together for a high school guy. And
what high school boy knows anything about music or poetry (non-
offensive poetry), let alone cares about it? Jed was just too amazing
for words.

She glanced back down at the Robert Herrick page to reread
"To Electra" and commit it to memory. Off to the side of Electra
were several unhighlighted poems, apparently from the same page
of the poetry book he photocopied. "The Fairies." She glanced
through it. Cute. "The Amber Bead," about a fly stuck in amber.
Interesting. She could see why they weren't highlighted, though.
Then the last two caught her eye: "The Night Piece, To Julia" and
"Upon Julia's Clothes." Hey, neato. Two poems with her own name
in them. Her poems. Ha. A poem about *her* clothes? Very funny.
Mr. Herrick had obviously not taken a look in her closet.

Whenas in silks my Julia goes,
Then, then, methinks how sweetly flows
That liquefaction of her clothes.

*Next, when I cast mine eyes and see
That brave vibration each way free,
Oh, how that glittering taketh me!*

Well, well. Very nice, Mr. Herrick. Maybe she ought to look into buying something silk. Her eye scanned the final poem, and its last verse arrested her.

*Then, Julia, let me woo thee,
Thus, thus to come unto me;
 And when I shall meet
 Thy silv'ry feet,
My soul I'll pour into thee.*

Mmm. Soul pouring. She mused a moment on what that might entail. Sometimes she felt so empty—needing another soul for company—and thought she had a great deal of room for another, large soul. No doubt of all the souls she knew, Jed's had the most substance. And he was such easy company, no doubt he'd make himself right at home, just like on her mother's prize sofa. Hmm. Just how might he woo her? Too bad he was so young. Born . . . too late . . . for you to love me.

Oh, and not to mention the fact that he had a thing for her sister Cathy. We could have written beautiful music together, my friend. Too bad.

She tried picking up Dan's picture from his high school yearbook that she procured from his high school's library to push Jed from her mind. Dan was so cute. So, handsome. And mature. Compared to Jed, at least. If only she could get Dan to notice her—not just by signing line three on her dance card—she'd have it made. Her social status at USU was guaranteed: to be dating the best-looking guy on campus would give her a deadlock on it.

But, how? How could she legitimately meet him? Aha. The Hub. He studied in there. She just needed to present herself casually to him, make the witty comments she'd been rehearsing for months, and he was hers. She was his. With the composition stress somewhat allayed, she gave herself permission to spend some time in social pursuits. She resolved to approach him there the very next day.

Scents of burgers, chili and fried food filled the air. Venturing past her usual barrier of the front threshold, Julia hoisted her slipping pack back into place on her right shoulder, and made her way to the deep recesses of the buffet line. She selected an orange fiberglass tray from the top of the stack and started nosing around the dim cafeteria. Dan, whom she saw as she entered the Hub, sat alone at a booth near a window. *Wait for me, my love. I'll be there with my submarine sandwich soon.* Hurriedly she found some food, fumbled for change in her pocket at the cash register, then tried to walk nonchalantly toward the cafeteria's eating area. True's words echoed in her head, *It's just a bunch of wannabe Beautiful People, sitting there to be seen. I wouldn't go in there if my life depended on it. If it were the last food on earth.* But Julia wasn't going to let that accusation stop her today, although she suspected it could be at least partly true for herself.

Cautiously she approached his table. He was reading the school paper, the funnies page. She made just enough sound in coming up behind him so as not to startle him. The moment of her test had arrived! Would she have the courage, the self-confidence to follow through? She must! It was now or never! She must speak to him!

"Excuse me, is this seat taken?" Her backpack slipped from her shoulder, jostling her orange tray in its heaviness, nearly spilling the contents of her sandwich onto the table. He looked up at her in surprise but said nothing. "May I sit here?" She should have said *May I join you?* But it was too late. Did it matter? Did lacking the perfect phrase make any difference? Only he could answer that question.

Quickly folding his newspaper, he stood slightly. "Oh, sure.

It's all yours." To her great surprise, he chivalrously took her tray and deftly pulled her chair out for her to sit down. What stunning politeness! She sat throwing a smile up at him and expecting one back—a witty phrase and conversation starter poised on the tip of her tongue.

But to no avail. Rather than sitting back down to join her, Daniel simply picked up his book and jacket and distractedly wandered out of the Hub, leaving the *Utah Statesman* in a neatly folded pile for her enjoyment. It was no use. No bubbling witty banter. No getting-to-know-you jokes. Not even a chance to tell him thank you for the service he rendered. Gone. She took a bite out of her submarine sandwich, emphasis on *sand*, and wished she'd had enough change for a carton of milk. But it was the most polite disaster ever. He deserved one more chance.

CHAPTER TWENTY-ONE

Dr. Bailey shuffled papers atop his podium. The atmosphere in the room was thick with anticipation. He returned the composition finals today. Julia's heart outpounded every other heart in the room. She could actually hear it pulsing in her ear drums. Finally! Her last final of the ten-week quarter.

"I have good news." The professor began distributing the sheets of hand-written music. "There is a piece of information I withheld from you students throughout the quarter, on the chance that no composition meriting this reward would surface in this class." What was he talking about? He claimed about two-thirds of the students' attention, the other third being engrossed in looking over the results of their work. Dr. Bailey continued passing out papers and methodically revealing his secret.

"Each quarter my colleagues and I review the results of this course's student efforts. On occasion we are pleased to find a composition worthy of public performance. This quarter we happily found several numbers which were quite impressive, especially as student output. However, one outshone the others." Whose could it be? He continued slowly distributing the papers. Julia looked around expectantly to see if one student wore an irrepressible grin revealing his success.

"That you all may know, the piece was written in three part harmony for female voices, arranged perceptively to allow for the well-chosen lyrics to be understood and emphasized in proper places. In short, it is the best student composition I have seen come from this entry-level class." Still no revealing looks from among the writers.

"With the author's permission, my colleagues and I would like to see this excellent composition performed by the women's ensemble choir at their recital at the end of next quarter. I encourage you all to be there to hear and enjoy it. So that you can distinguish it from the other composers' work, and this may be the only way you can, for you won't see a dip in quality, the title is 'To Electra,' and I congratulate Miss Julia Cronquist on her fine work." Dr. Bailey handed Julia her sheet of paper with its familiar eraser smudges and pencil lead smears. Across the top in the professor's handwriting were the words, "Superb. See me."

Her work? Of course, she knew it flowed well; the rhythms and harmonies rang true in her ears. The lyrics were as perfect as could be—through no merit of her own—and listening to it filled her with joy at her own creation. But she never dreamed it would touch someone else in the same way, especially a loveless old conservative like Dr. Bailey. Oh! And her own choir would get to perform it! Of course, she wrote it with their very voices in mind, as they were the only women's choir she knew well enough to prepare something like this for. She never, ever dreamed they or anyone would actually sing it. She had to tell someone! But who? Who could appreciate this grand surprise? Jed! Only Jed.

She literally ran, windbreaker over her arm, backpack bouncing jauntily on her sore rib cage all the way to her dorm where her loaded car sat ready to take her back to Huntsville for spring break. Without even going upstairs to say goodbye to True, she climbed in the Century and sped off for home.

"What do you mean he's not around?"

"It's spring break for us, too. Lake Powell. Everyone's there. I'd be there, too, if I didn't have to get this Earth Day thing organized." He was gone. No one could share her joy. She didn't want to diminish the excitement of it by telling someone else first. "What's the deal? Are you suddenly taking an interest in Jed?"

"No. It's just—" Julia was definitely not trying to barge in on her younger sister's boy territory. Did she detect the slightest hint of jealousy in Cathy's voice? "Never mind. I just had some school stuff to tell him. It can wait." Lie. But she couldn't see herself driving however many hours south to Lake Powell and then scouring the zillion miles of beaches to find him. It could wait. Sort of.

"Well, he's coming back on Saturday night. His parents have a thing about Sunday dinner together. And church, naturally." Well. Saturday. That was only three days away.

Three *vacation* days. Spring break her freshman year of college! Time to kick back. Too bad she didn't have any big plans. It seemed like everyone at school was talking about their fun trips for the break. Florida. Mexico. California. Anywhere warmer than Logan, Utah.

California? Wasn't Bianca tripping off to the sunny climes and TV game shows along with all the baseball players from Weber State? Julia should call her and find out. She picked up and dialed B's cell.

"So, who all is going?" Julia tried to act mildly uninterested, as though she had several offers and was trying to choose between them.

"Scott and me for sure. We think. It's all about work schedules, you know. And, dang it, the baseball team had to ditch out on us. Spring training or some other cheap excuse. I'm waiting to hear from Shanna and Kiki and their roommates. We were going to caravan, but nothing's set. So, basically the answer is we're not sure yet. We'll keep you posted." Good enough.

Hooray! Fun road trip with cool people, or at least coolish older-sister-person and mildly annoying sidekick. Scott never had any range of conversation, it seemed. But anything was better than Huntsville, boringville, for ten long days.

"By the way, I got my talent number all ready. You should come down Saturday afternoon and see it. We'll hang out."

⚜

"So, that was my talent. What did you think? I totally like this 'Walkin' In Memphis' number, but I'm not sure. Do you think it has enough range of emotion? Callie told me that was vital, and she's been in pageants for years. It's something they dock points for, and everything." Bianca hoisted her dance bag onto the crook of her arm, and she and Julia headed out to the Buick.

"Bye, Sharon. See you Tuesday," she called over her shoulder to the dance studio manager. "Sharon is such a great dancer. You should see her in toe shoes sometime. Eventually I'd love to be en pointe myself. Am I getting too late of a start, do you think?" Julia thought so, as most ballerinas start much younger than twenty, but no sense squelching someone's dream.

"I don't know very much about dance, but you might as well try. And, as for the number, it's good. I like it. Did you have other options?"

"Not really, unless I sing that Trisha Yearwood song. Either way, I still have time to work something up if this isn't the perfect thing. I love the creativity of it all. Now, what do you say to stopping for fries and frozen custard? I'm telling myself and you yes to this!"

Over a triple chocolate fudge sundae and a humongous pile of french fries, Bianca rattled on about the pageant, and who was dating whom at the mall, and other aspects of her life. Julia didn't have a lot of interest in the mall gossip, so she changed the subject again.

"What are you going to wear for your talent number? Have you found anything yet?"

Bianca gulped another bite of ice cream and answered, "Nothing for sure yet, but I'm thinking white. Winners wear white is what all the pageant people say. And most are, even though I know it's cliché, blonde. So, with those two factors, I think I'm increasing my shot at it appearance-wise." She took another big bite and looked thoughtfully at Julia. "You should think about going blonde yourself, Jules. Just some highlights or streaks here and there. Loréal has a great streak kit in Bold as Brass. I've been envisioning that for you for months. Sometimes I think that other

cliché, that blondes have more fun, might actually be true. Do
you?" Bianca heaved a heavy sigh and took her last bite of fudge.
"So. On to other exciting things! Are we going to California next
week, or what?"

By the time they got back to Bianca's apartment, Julia was
anxious to head back to Huntsville. She had some pieces she needed
to do some practicing on, and—more importantly—Jed should be
getting home soon.

"We got some new Jordan Carlisle perfumes in," Bianca called
from the bedroom where she was changing back into jeans from
her dance clothing. "I brought home a couple of testers. You want
to try them? They're in the video cupboard."

Next to the perfume testers, which smelled too musky for Julia's
nose, was a stack of photos. Idly she picked them up and thumbed
through them. Some from the Halloween party. Who was that
sexy weevil? Oh, that was Julia. Ha, ha. Somehow the photo made
Bianca's Wonder Woman costume look gaudy and ridiculous—not
at all like Julia remembered the real thing. Here was one from last
summer—the outing to Willard Bay. Boy, her hair was a bristle
brush! A red one. Yikes. Get a comb, girl. Another from the New
Year's Eve disaster. It was a candid of Bianca draped across Scott's
lap.

Then a little strip of photo booth black and whites slid out.
They were silly face pictures of Scott and Bianca. In the last one they
were . . . kissing. She flipped it over to see if a date were printed on
the back. January. Hey. That was *right* after Bianca made him kiss
Julia on New Year's Eve in front of all the retail rats. What? Why? If
Bianca wanted to kiss Scott, why would she want him to kiss Julia?
Why would she do that to Scott? And, more than that, why would
she do that to Julia—her own sister?

A reflexive swell of anger and embarrassment rose in her chest
and manifested itself on her burning cheeks. She replaced the

pictures on the end table and sat quietly, breathing deeply to keep her temper in check. She would leave as soon as she could walk out without slamming the door. Bianca jabbered on from the other room as though she'd never betrayed her sister, while Julia ground her teeth.

It wasn't fair! Julia couldn't even snag a guy she *didn't* want. What was wrong with her? *What* already! No matter how hard she tried she couldn't get anything right. No boy would ever be attracted to her. No male person would ever notice she was alive. At this she cocked her head in a huff, and a lock of hair fell across her eyes. She pushed it back angrily.

Then, it came to her.

It *was* this red hair, after all. Hair color defines people, she reasoned. Redheads were known for their fiery tempers. Mousy brown haired women were destined for careers as librarians or school lunch cafeteria workers. Brunettes? No one ever generalized much about brunettes. But like Bianca said, blondes had more fun. From the look of the photo pile, blonde Bianca was definitely having more fun. At least she was having some fun behind Julia's back. It totally frosted her and pierced her heart at the same time. But what could she do about it?

"Oh, look there's a message." Bianca tripped lightly back into the living room where the answering machine flashed. She pressed the button on the old silver tape-to-tape machine.

"You girls. I expect all three of my daughters home on Wednesday night for family dinner." Jan Cronquist seldom laid out requirements for her grown daughters these days, but when she did, she expected them to be obeyed. "Your brother is coming and bringing Becca as his guest. Six-thirty on the dot."

"Oh, great. Ted-ious. That engaged killjoy just submarined our trip to L.A." She came back in the room bearing a tin of bean dip and some Doritos. Julia refused to tell herself yes. Bianca took a huge scoop of beans and filled her mouth.

A surge of thankfulness rushed through Julia, as the dinner let her off the hook for *The Price is Right.* Since seeing the photo booth photo, Julia was getting a rotten feeling about it, and she was aching for an easy out. Thank you, Ted.

At that, her anger subsided a bit. She shuddered to shake off the hot emotions. She'd have to deal with those later. Nevertheless, her other problem—the hair problem—remained. It obviously wouldn't be by Scott (thank heavens), but if she was ever going to be kissed and often, drastic measures needed to be taken in regards to the Raggedy Ann hair transplant atop her head. Too much time of her life had been frittered away already. Action was required, and Julia felt like taking it immediately. From somewhere far away, a lilting song called to her, so Julia said good-bye to Bianca, whose indiscretions she'd deal with later, and then followed the call all the way to the Loréal Bold as Brass highlighting kit on the Smith's supermarket shelf and then home to Huntsville.

Jed was coming home in just a few hours! And she planned to be ready.

"Didn't you *ever* read *Anne of Green Gables*?" Cathy hissed, leaning over her sobbing older sister with the kitchen faucet's sprayer in hand. Julia was bent headfirst over the sink.

"No," Julia blubbered. She wiped the drips from her eyes, wondering which were tears and which were water and which were the hair dye solution.

"Duh. Her hair is only half as red as yours, and it turns *green* when she dyes it." Some of the color was washing down the sink in big yellow glops. "What were you thinking?"

"That blondes have more fun." The tears came freely now, along with sobs. What *was* she thinking? What a mess she created for herself. And her hair.

"I can't believe you." For the first time possibly ever, Cathy showed no mercy. "You have the longest, most gorgeous auburn hair, curled to perfection, the envy of the hemisphere. And what do you do? You put *cheap bleach* on it."

Cheap bleach! That was exactly what Julia had done.

"Don't you know? Hair dye is for people who look *bad* with their natural hair color. Your beautiful, long, million-dollar auburn hair! Rich women in huge cities pay thousands of dollars to professionals to merely approach your perfect natural color. What were you thinking?"

Oh, no. What had she done? It was too awful to accept as reality.

"Worse, what is Jed going to say when he sees it? He's going to be here at nine, you know."

Why would Jed give a hoot? He was just his younger sister's admirer. True, he was also practically her best friend and biggest supporter, but about her hair—why would he care? Wait. Nine o'clock?

"What time is it?" Julia asked frantically.

"Eight-thirty. You need to stay under this sink at least another few minutes, although I'm pretty sure the damage is done." Cathy loyally held the sprayer over her sister's ruined locks for the remaining time necessary, and then the two of them retired to the bathroom to dry it and survey the damage. It was true. Bold as Brass certainly was not the outcome of her first home coloring experiment. More like Bold as Marmalade. Or Bold as Canned Mandarin Oranges. Luckily, she only applied it in streaks. Or, *was* that lucky? There was an undeniable skunkiness about it. A bright orange skunk. Unknown to nature.

She attempted to separate the two colors, orange in one clip on top, auburn pieces left hanging down on her shoulders. You never know what you have until you've lost it. Suddenly, for the first time in her life she realized what a great color her natural hair was. Mahogany red, like expensive furniture. Big, loose natural curls. Long and healthy. Now, as it dried without the benefit of Tigi Bed Head or Shiners, its natural beauty lain bare before her eyes, the full force of the tragically frizzy, burnt strips hit her like a gut punch.

"It might be possible to weave these orange pieces underneath. Er, to hide them somewhat." Cathy sounded hopeful. For five whole minutes the two of them made the attempt. Parts were concealable but not the roots. "You could become one of those bandana women. I hear it's coming back in style."

"I think that's used as a belt." Either that or it was necktie belts. "What about a hat?"

"Maybe. Bianca's probably got a hundred. I bet she left one in a closet here somewhere."

The doorbell rang.

"You get it. I'm . . . indisposed." Cathy left, and Julia continued wrestling with her hair. The best bet was a french braid, or a twist braid. Both worked pretty well. Not completely, but either was much better than down. She heard Jed and Cathy's voices in the front room and decided to give up and join them. Jed had already seen her at her least attractive many times. What was once more?

The two high schoolers were whispering as Julia came down the hall.

"Jed. Hello. How was Lake Powell?" She tried to sound buoyant—not as if she'd just had the wind knocked out of her by simply looking in the mirror. Wow. She'd been biding her time all through the first half of spring break awaiting his return so she could talk to him, and, now, here he was at last.

"Great." He got up and walked over to Julia, steering her with his hand on her back into the piano room. They sat down together. "Look. I brought you a souvenir." From the table he pulled a khaki ball cap that read Lake Powell embroidered across the front. He placed it atop her head and made sure it fit snugly around her hair. How coincidental. And how nice, as now she could talk to him without feeling self-conscious about her home-salon disaster. Almost as good as a knitted big-hair ski mask.

"Like my tan?" He showed off his new tan line, and the girls listened to his cliff diving adventures and waterskiing wipe out stories. The girls kicked back on the couch while Jed fingered through the Cronquists' CD collection, pulling interesting titles here and there, and reading off the credits to the girls, making them guess the technical people's names by giving them silly hints. It was just like the fun they had together over Christmas break.

Eventually they fell into their trivia banter challenge routine. Julia and Jed sat by each other on the squishy sofa, and Cathy perched atop the coffee table with the chip bag on her lap. They all tried to impress each other with tidbits they'd picked up since their last technicality-slam. It only intensified when Julia broke out in hiccups, which happened to be the topic of Cathy's recently completed school research paper.

"Hey, did you know they think it might be a residual function? They think fetuses hiccup to strengthen the breathing muscles. So, hiccups are leftover from before we were born and serve no purpose now." Cathy took another sour cream and onion potato chip from the sack. "Babies hiccup way more than adults." The three lounged on the sofas that surrounded the piano in the front room. Jed was flipping through the Cronquists' classic movie collection now.

"What about when you eat a bunch of dry bread? What makes you hiccup then?" He selected a compilation and opened the case for further inspection.

"They don't think that's related to being in the womb. No bread there."

"Here's my stumper for you: why don't quick and Buick rhyme? They're spelled the same but for one letter."

"Mysterious. *Hic.* Excuse me. And why would you want to name a car anything that rhymes with 'ick.' I don't get it. *Hic.* Now here's mine: why is yawning contagious? That's what I want to know," Julia asked and then helplessly yawned a yawn cut short by another hiccup.

"Questions for the ages, guys. Speaking of yawns, I'm turning in. It's late." It was only 10:30, but Cathy always crashed early. "Good night, kids." Cathy yawned loudly and waved good-bye as she headed down the hall. "Don't say anything interesting without me."

"Don't worry, sis." Then Jed, too, bid Cathy good night and, finally, Julia had her chance to talk to him alone. As soon as she heard the water running in Cathy's shower, she blurted out the good news about her composition.

"That's tremendous!" Jed clapped his hands together loudly enough to wake the whole family. It was as much enthusiasm as Julia hoped he would show. "I knew you could do it all along."

"Well, I owe it all to you."

"Let me hear how it turned out. Can you sing it for me?" Sing it? Hmm. She could play it on the piano. But sitting here so close to him felt so relaxing, comforting, she didn't want to get up. And he did request that she sing.

"Really? Okay. Here goes." She began to sing the soprano part, which carried the melody. "I dare not ask a kiss, I dare not beg a smile . . ." Her voice was soft, so as not to disturb the other members of the household or draw their attention. This song was only for Jed right now. "No, no, the utmost share, Of my desire shall be, Only to kiss that air, That lately kissèd thee." She brought it to its ethereal, high F-sharp culmination. Although she stopped singing, the note still hung in the air. Jed looked intently into her eyes, and then leaned toward her lips. He pulled her close and kissed her.

It lasted an hour—a year—a lifetime—though barely five seconds of actual time passed. He might be young, but this strapping youth knew how to kiss. It was firm, sincere, filled with tenderness and wishing all at once. Jed was someone who knew how. She felt that connection from everywhere to everywhere. He pulled back and looked in her eyes. She didn't say a thing. She couldn't. What a surprise he turned out to be.

Then, rising to his feet, he leaned in, gave her a light kiss on the head, just atop the brim of her upturned hat and strode toward the door. As he began to let himself out, he turned and smiled.

"Julia. I'm really happy for you. I have to go. Will you save Tuesday afternoon for me?" She nodded and he was gone.

It was too late to talk to anyone that night, though she was fairly bursting with bliss. Her first kiss! Well, the first one she counted. Not playground kissing tag or a forced public display of mock affection, but a bona fide, sincere kiss. She couldn't wait to tell someone. But, not Bianca. She was with Scott tonight, dancing at the country swing club. Plus, Julia could almost hear the reprimand now: "A high school boy? Are you kidding me?" No. Bianca couldn't know.

Cathy. Oh, no. Cathy! What had she done? Did she just kiss her darling, true blue little sister's sweetheart? Oh, dear. What was she thinking? How could she be so cruel and unfeeling—especially after all Cathy did for her tonight, faucet sprayer and all! Cathy must never know.

But, despite that horrible consequence, Julia still felt the exhilaration of the kiss! If only she could call True, who was off in Wyoming for the break. Or, was she? They spoke so little before parting for vacation, only so Julia could reassure her she looked thin in her new size three jeans. But she thought she remembered True saying something about maybe running into her in Huntsville. Now, why would she do that?

The only other close friend she had was Jed. And he already knew. And he probably shouldn't know exactly how much of a thrill it gave her. Instead, she ran through the possible conversation in her head. Hi. Is Jed there? Hey, Jed. The most incredible thing just happened. I had to call and tell you, since you're such a great friend and all. Yeah, I was just sitting there on my mother's couch with this very cool guy, and he asked me to sing to him, so I did. I was just singing along, and then, when I finished, he leaned over to me, and then this most awesome person gave me the best, most staggeringly good kiss history has ever known. So good I couldn't speak. So good I almost melted like spring snow. So good I almost fell in love.

In love? Where did that come from? No. This was all a practice. Wasn't it? For science's sake. Preparing her for some future event. Not the real thing. Not with Jed. Was it?

She lay on her back in bed, staring at the ceiling and trying to recreate the moment in her mind over and over. Each time she relived it, she recaptured the soaring feeling. Oh, Jed. What an amazing person you are. Tuesday was only three days away. Less than that because he requested the afternoon. How could she stand the wait?

CHAPTER TWENTY-TWO

"Julia, would you come in here, please?" Her dad called to her from his study, a nook just off the family room where Julia was looking through the *New Era* on Sunday morning. "I need some brainstorming help with my Sunday School lesson." Now that Julia was in Gospel Doctrine, her dad picked her brain pretty often, although a lot of times it seemed that what he really wanted was someone to bounce his ideas off. Off whom to bounce his ideas. A sounding board. Or someone else to listen while he thought out loud to formulate his thoughts. That was fine with her. She was happy to oblige. It kind of made Sunday School more interesting because she saw the behind-the-scenes of how he came to his conclusions.

"Sure, Dad. What are we studying this week?"

"The part in Mosiah chapter eighteen that talks about the baptismal covenant."

"Oh, sure the 'mourn with those that mourn' part."

"Exactly. You've been reading." He looked at her in surprise, which surprised her. Of course she'd been reading her scriptures. Wasn't everyone supposed to read them every day? He taught her that himself when he was her early-morning Seminary teacher for two years. What was the big deal? "That's great. So, the part I'm working on is the 'bear one another's burdens' part."

"Okay." Oh, great. She'd always been a little wary of that part. She kind of wanted to say, *Sure I'd be glad to bear one, maybe two, depending on how heavy, but can I pick and choose? To be honest, I'd really rather wait and decide after I have more information.* Naturally her dad would select that part for her to comment on. It was like he knew her weakness and read her mind.

"I'm trying to put together a little list of what some burdens are. I've got a few, like losing a loved one, poor health, poverty, illiteracy, being born into a family that doesn't have the gospel. And it's fairly easy to see how to help bear those burdens, but I wanted a few others. More creative ones. Any thoughts?"

Julia bit her lip in deliberation. She'd always figured tone deafness would be a serious burden—a real detriment to someone's enjoyment of life, but that probably wasn't what her dad was looking for. A burden? A burden. What might be a burden?

"What about, um, a personality defect, like getting angry easily?"

"Good. Very good. And how can we help bear that? Maybe by being patient, or maybe by teaching them that the Lord will help us work on our weaknesses. Good. You're thinking. What about more for my list?" Oh, dear. She'd already drained the well, and now he wanted more. She tried one of the random go-to-church-read-the-scriptures-keep-the-commandments standard Sunday School answers.

"Okay. Um, what about sin?" She was glad she had come up with something, although her dad probably wasn't looking for that one, either.

"Sin. Oh." He was quiet and thinking, most likely trying to come up with a tactful way to tell her to keep firing away at this target because she hadn't hit the bull's-eye yet. But he got a different thinking look on his face next, a mulling-it-over look. "Right. Very good. Sin is definitely one of the heaviest burdens we will ever carry. Right." He was mulling again. Julia was surprised that her answer wasn't so bad after all. "But," he continued, this time doing his thinking aloud routine, "how could we bear the burden of another person's sin? We can't repent for someone else. No. We can't take the burden that way. . . . I'll have to think on that one. Thanks, Julia."

Julia looked at her dad's furrowed brow as he contemplated

so thoroughly his upcoming lesson. She thought he was a great teacher. Why did he end up picking the career he chose—mortician? Well, he *had* been a mortician and then recently moved up in the company, and their family moved to Utah. But, anyway, it just seemed like the wrong fit. He was somehow squandering his talents. She'd been planning to ask him about it for a long time. Now seemed as good a time as any.

"Dad, can I ask you something?" He spun in his swivel chair to face her again.

"Sure. Anytime. Shoot."

"How come you decided to become a mortician?" She hoped the question didn't bug him. Sometimes he got kind of sensitive about his occupation, like when people cracked jokes about dead bodies. He didn't think there was any humor in that—he always treated the dead with a kind of reverence, and she'd heard enough of his experiences through the years to know it was a spiritual kind of job, at least to him, and he didn't appreciate wisecracks.

"Oh, have I never told you about that?" She shook her head, and he set down his scriptures and his yellow legal pad where he'd been taking notes. "Well, I got home from my mission and decided I wanted to be a Seminary teacher. There was something in my patriarchal blessing about that, so I figured, you know, I should go that direction. But things kept coming up and getting in my way. Weird obstacles. At the time I had a job at the funeral home in Star Valley, and it didn't take me long to notice that the funeral director there was doing something pretty similar to what I'd been doing for the past two years: teaching about the plan of salvation every day. I filled in one time for him when he was ill, and bingo! I knew exactly what I wanted to do." He smiled a satisfied smile.

"And you still got to do the Seminary thing, too."

"Right. Just not full time. And that was for the best, too. I liked it for one hour a day, but I don't know if I could have done five or six. You little teenage twerps did your best to—"

"I know, Dad. Sorry. We *were* twerps. But you were a good teacher."

"Thanks."

Julia patted her dad's shoulder and left him to his lesson. She went off to run through the hymns she'd be playing for sacrament meeting later today, glad to have a music calling and not a teaching one.

CHAPTER TWENTY-THREE

Tuesday came sooner than it might have if Julia had been idle. Their mother prevented that, mercifully. She set both Julia and Cathy to work spring cleaning—once again. Mops, buckets, rags. The works. "I want this house to shine by Wednesday." As if the brand-newness of the Dream House didn't make it sparkle enough, with its turret and curving bannisters and leaded glass windows. Julia started to notice a little shift in her attitude toward the house as she cleaned, however. Perhaps investing time and effort in it gave her a tiny sense of pride of ownership and she began to despise it less. Besides, the Dream Home was the site of her first, life-changing kiss. Her feet were still light as air while she fluffed the feather duster around on Tuesday morning. Just four more hours to Jed. Just three and a half more hours to Jed. Cathy asked her one time what was on her mind, seeing she acted so strangely.

"Who, me? Nothing." But she had to say something. "Didn't I tell you about my composition? It's going to get a live airing—my choir is singing it at the spring quarter recital in May." A good cover.

"Really? That's so great! Wow! No wonder you're so happy! I know you worked hard on that. Jed told me how much it stressed you out." He did? He talked about her with Cathy? Of course he did. They were close. Very close, maybe. It deflated her slightly to recall how untrue she'd been to her dear little sister. Did this make her as bad as Bianca kissing Scott? But Cathy continued buoyantly, "Hey! Mom! Did you hear? Julia's going to be famous!" And Cathy made Julia tell their mom the whole tale.

"I'd love to hear it. Would you like to sing it to us tomorrow night when Ted and Becca are here?"

"Oh, Mom. I don't think it's really a solo piece. Can you just wait and hear the full choir sing it in a few weeks?"

Her mom was understanding. "Sure, sweetheart. We'll take the video camera and record it that night—for posterity." Jan Cronquist liked going the extra mile technologically.

"Mom, I have some plans this afternoon. What time do you think we'll be finishing up here?"

"Oh, Julia, honey. Didn't you remember? This was the day we all agreed to put the yard in. Dad is coming home from work early, and everything." She sighed at her middle daughter's forgetfulness. "Are these 'plans' anything that could be rescheduled?"

Yard work! Yard work instead of a date with Jed? If it was a date. Maybe he had no actual plans. Perhaps he would forget anyway. Not that he ever forgot before when he promised to do something. But of all days, today would probably be it. No use putting up a stink.

"I guess so, Mom. What all are we doing out there?"

"Just the whole back yard. We need as many bodies as possible for hauling rocks and leveling the ground. Your dad wants to put in the lawn and clear ground for his gazebo." Bummer. She looked at her newly painted fingernails, imagining the grime they would soon meet. But when the time came, she dug in and made herself so useful she didn't even hear the car pull up in the driveway, or the chimes of the grand doorbell of the Dream House, or the persistent knocking on the front door. And she didn't see a dejected young man slink away, worried sick that he'd offended the most beautiful, talented girl he'd ever meet by presuming to kiss her uninvited.

Season Three: Spring

CHAPTER TWENTY-FOUR

Spring was well underway. Tulips and daffodils lined the walks between every building on campus. Classes were easier—even professors proved distractedly feverish at the warming change of seasons. Little homework was assigned, particularly on weekends, and hardly a soul could be found indoors in the afternoons.

One evening, in need of some non-recirculated air, Julia bundled up her books in her backpack and ventured forth from the Fine Arts building. Soon she found herself taking a little walk along Fourth North, heading toward Logan Canyon. Generally traffic moves swiftly along the four-lane highway there, but the paved walking trail adjacent to the road winds through part of the Country Club's golf course and past a covered picnic area, making it a nice place for a stroll.

As she rounded a little bend to begin her descent into the mouth of the canyon, to her surprise Julia saw a pond and park—green, grassy, inviting. How could she have lived in Logan for nearly a year and never seen this great little place? Once or twice during the winter she traveled this road on her way up the canyon but always looked at the evenly engineered waterfall on the hydroelectric plant across the road from the park, so she missed it. What a delightful place! She tripped on down the hill and soon seated herself on a wooden bench to watch children feed the ducks and geese that flocked in the pond.

A mother, frazzled-looking but kind-faced, stood nearby. Julia had to ask.

"What is this neat little place?"

"Logan? Oh, you mean First Dam Park." From a wrinkly Wonder Bread bag she handed another piece of dry bread to her toddler, who chucked the whole thing into the water then giggled as the geese fought it out. "It's a great park, especially this time of year. Sometimes you see the most exotic birds. My kids love it." Just as she said the words, Julia noticed a long-legged bird, a heron or a crane, descend on a quiet, far side of the pond. It was so peaceful. Idyllic. Soothing. If only she had someone to share it with. With whom to share it.

She'd taken to correcting her own grammar again—about the same time her social life went south. In the four weeks since classes began, Jed had come no times to pick up Amanda after her lesson. The kiss was the last time she saw him. She knew she couldn't kiss well, she but didn't think she was that bad. Oh, it hurt too much to think about it—even though Jed was just a high school boy and ought to elicit no feeling from her. She refused to think badly of him, however. It must have been something she did that made him stand her up for that Tuesday on spring break. He was probably feeling guilty for being untrue to Cathy.

Julia never should have kissed him.

In addition to the dismal Jed story, Dan was completely invisible this quarter. Granted, she still needed to get over to the Student Center to look up his schedule, but in fall and winter he was everywhere, it seemed. Just once she thought she caught a glimpse of him outside women's ensemble, but she had to stay and talk to the director after class so she didn't have a chance to say hi. Was his head shaved? Maybe it was just bad lighting. Somehow with a shaved head he wasn't as cute as he was in her mind. But if he were under her direction, she could encourage him to keep it just a bit longer.

Speaking of hair, her own was still fairly disastrous. Happily, the hat from Jed made it a little less noticeable. True suggested getting it thinned, mostly on the orange parts, and then hoping for the best. Braids every day were getting old.

Still speaking of hair, True's seemed to be everywhere these days.

And not just in the spherical nest. It was falling out in big chunks every time she brushed it. Julia suggested she change shampoos, but True claimed to have changed twice to no avail.

"I saw an ad for hair vitamins in a magazine," True had complained. "The woman in the picture looked like a cross between a water nymph and Medusa. But no snakes. Pretty, snaky curls instead. I decided against ordering." It was all a little gross, and Julia didn't dare eat anything sticky in their dorm. True never seemed to eat anything at all, so that wasn't a concern for her.

Every time she went home for the weekend, the Dream Home flurried with activity. Spring plantings took everyone's energy, and their dad's gazebo was well underway. Mom wanted everything to be just perfect for Ted and Becca's reception at the end of May.

Julia secretly looked forward to getting a heavy satin bridesmaid dress and putting her hair up with baby's breath and gardenias. A backyard wedding reception in Huntsville in May sounded heavenly to her. The preparations for the quickly approaching ceremony filled every weekend she spent at home.

Ah, springtime. It felt so good just sitting there in the park beside the waters, pondering life, and breathing the new air. But the daylight began to wane, and she had quite a distance uphill to walk home before dark. She bid goodbye to the busy mother, who was also gathering things and children to go home. With a lurch she hoisted that heavy backpack and turned to go.

Suddenly, the next thing she knew she was on the ground, writhing in pain. Not really writhing—she was too paralyzed to writhe. She must have cried out because several concern-filled faces hovered over her.

"Do you need help?"

"What happened?"

"Are you okay?"

She didn't know what happened. She didn't know if she was okay. She did need help. Someone extracted her from her position as an upside down tortoise on its shell and lifted her to the bench.

Another kind stranger gathered her books, which spewed forth from her ripped pack.

"This thing weighs a ton. She shouldn't be carrying this much weight around."

"I bet that's what caused it."

For several minutes, strangers talked nervously about her condition as she lay with her eyes closed, letting the tears seep out the edges and run down her temples into her hair. No one knew quite what to do. It was getting much darker now, and the kind helpers began to disperse. The frazzled mom offered to take Julia home in her minivan. Julia accepted, trying to force back the tears and sobs that seemed determined to escape her eyes and mouth. She also accepted a large grandfatherly man's offer to carry her to the van. Sharp, shooting pains in her back made voluntary movement close to impossible. She muttered a weak thanks as he jostled her into the passenger seat, which the generous mom mercifully reclined.

"I live at Valley View Towers. Can you take me there?"

"Sure. Don't you want to go to the hospital? The emergency room is a familiar sight for me with my three boys." No, the hospital couldn't do anything for her. She just needed her bed and an ice pack. Thank goodness she and True had a full length tub in their dorm room. With great effort and extreme pain, she limped rigidly to the dorm and the elevator. The kind mom, whose name was Deborah, enlisted a passerby's help to get Julia's backpack upstairs for her. Julia spent the remainder of the night popping Advil and alternating heat and cold packs. Eventually the pain subsided under the influence of eight hundred milligrams of ibuprofen, and the crippled girl dropped off to sleep.

The next morning, she awoke to a sharp pain in her neck and upper back as she tried to roll over in bed. She could hardly turn her head. Fumbling on her night stand for the pill bottle and her alarm clock, she ascertained the time to be 7:45. Good. The student health center would be open in fifteen minutes. She could dash right over there and be first in line. Ow. If she could walk.

Ultimately, it took her nearly ninety minutes to make her way over to the Student Center's ground level health clinic. Wisely, she took ten minutes of concentrated stretching time before setting out, which likely sped her journey by at least ten minutes, although it didn't do much to ease the pain.

"Julia Cronquist," she told the receptionist and gave her student ID number.

"Wait over there. The doctor sees patients in the order they arrive. Standard student insurance?" She attempted to nod yes, but a popping sting from her spine stopped her, and she answered aloud instead. She hobbled over to an orange vinyl and steel chair and sat down.

Her arms still worked, so she picked up a *People* magazine for brain candy. The office smelled like a mixture of blood, sweat and tears, with a heavy emphasis on the sweat. Ah, the good old days. Where was the excellently sweaty Dan now?

Incredibly, just then the heavy wooden door to the health center opened, and her question was answered, nearly instantaneously upon her thinking it. Dan Chitwood! Her heart skipped a beat. The old magic returned, despite the now-fuzzing butch haircut. Oh Dan oh Dan. You have come to me at last. Her heart sang as it danced the rumba, the dance of love.

He approached the receptionist, and she overheard his distinctive, friendly voice. "I'm here to give blood." Best looking guy on planet Earth and a good Samaritan to boot! If only she needed blood. That was one way he might pour his soul into her, as her cherished poem suggested. If she slashed her wrists right here . . . But someone was calling her name.

"Julia Cronquist. Julia Cronquist?"

She lifted a finger to indicate her presence and turned her neck slowly toward the nurse in white scrubs, who was leaning out of the examining room door and holding a clip board.

"Yes." Julia attempted to rise with grace in the sight of her beloved. It was tough.

"Miss Cronquist. The results of your spleen screening are negative." Spleen screening? What spleen screening? There was no

spleen screening! Yuck! Not in front of the whole waiting room—
Dan! She creaked her head toward him, a glutton for punishment,
to observe his reaction to this mortifying announcement. To her
great relief, his eyes didn't divert an iota from the *Sports Illustrated* in
his hands. Slowly, calmly, she limped toward the nurse, attempting
to whisper discreetly there had been a mistake.

"Oh, I apologize. There has been a mistake. The doctor will see
you now, Miss Cronquist. Miss Tennyson. Miss Stella Tennyson?
The results of *your* spleen screening are negative." The examining
room door closed behind her, and Julia heard no more spleen test
results that day.

"It appears," the doctor smiled plastically, "you are suffering
from a malady quite common to this campus in the last decade."
He was scribbling something on a small white notepad. For the past
twenty minutes Dr. Generic had prodded her back and examined
her spine and its surrounding muscles.

"Yes, sir? Is that so?"

"Yes. It begins with a mild, very mild case of preexisting scoliosis,
or curvature of the spine, and escalates under intense daily pressure
from heavy burdens placed on the back. Can I assume correctly
that you intentionally carry your backpack over just one shoulder
at all times?"

Julia nodded guiltily.

"Right. Under that intense strain, even the strongest Lumbar
muscle groups will wear. I'm afraid you've pulled one of these
muscles, and at worst, compressed a disc. There is no way to tell
externally, and I doubt an X-ray would give us much more useful
information." This was terrible. She would be in traction for
months. "The best advice I can give you is to continue the hot and
cold packs. I will prescribe a muscle relaxant for use in the next
few days, just to get things going again, and then for extreme cases
in the future only, along with some industrial strength Tylenol.
And, finally, keep a lightweight backpack balanced evenly on both
shoulders." But that was explicitly against the doctrine of the box!
That was relegating herself to hopeless geek-dom!

She slowly exited the office, wishing he'd prescribed a wheelchair and a masseur.

Two strap pack? Ugh! But, then again, what was one more broken rule of the advice box? She already lived in the dorms, went home every weekend, enrolled in a practically all-girl major, and wore a floral shirt to a dance. Her every effort to break into the Beautiful People scene on campus had been rebuffed, and Daniel Chitwood just heard her name associated with the word spleen. Really, could wearing a back pack on both shoulders make it much worse? Obviously, the worst nerdish thing would be lying on her compressed disc back like a fool tortoise, writhing in pain. She clutched the prescription and gimped her way to the student pharmacy in the convenience shop near the bookstore.

CHAPTER TWENTY-FIVE

"So, what do *you* think it is, Cathy, that makes me so undatable?" The two sisters' hands were crusted in soil as they inserted peat pots of marigolds and petunias into their mother's mounded flower bed. The back yard of the Dream Home was quickly becoming *Better Homes and Gardens* material. "I mean, I've been on fewer dates than I can count on one hand. That's counting my whole life."

Cathy rubbed her nose with the back of her hand, leaving a smudge of dirt there beside the others that adorned her now bronze face.

"It's not something wrong with you. Trust me. It's like too much right instead."

"What are you talking about?" Julia took another six pack of pansies from the red wagon and started on the next section.

"You know, too pretty. Too smart. Too talented. Too humble." Who was Cathy talking about? "Guys get intimidated by that."

"You're up in the night. No guy in his right mind would be intimidated by dumb old me."

"Julia, you underestimate yourself." They hauled the wagon over to the garage for another load. The wedding reception was a month away, and things needed time to fill in and look natural, not forced, before then. Jan Cronquist had her girls gardening five hours every Saturday and some Fridays, too. She kept them working diligently with promises of a trip to wherever they wanted to go this summer—Bear Lake, Yellowstone, Ft. Collins, anywhere.

"Maybe I want to change my answer to that question," Cathy called to her sister from the other side of the mound a few minutes later. Of course. She'd come to her senses and was going to answer Julia honestly about what was wrong with her to make her so undatable. Hey, those words fit perfectly with the Nat King Cole song, "Unforgettable." She sang them in her mind. *So undatable. That's what you are. So undatable both near and far.* What would her answer be? Her lame attempts at humor? Her classical music obsession? Her affinity for bad fashion? But Cathy interrupted these toxic thoughts.

"Instead, I think your problem is you think you want to date the wrong kind of guys."

Julia reached for a trowel and patted down the earth around the plant start. "What kind of guys are wrong?" As far as she was concerned, any guy was right if he paid attention to her. Sort of. There were a few off her list. Scott. Some others.

"What I mean is you call yourself undatable to the type of guys you think you want to date. But in reality they're undatable for you. They're so far beneath you, even their lame brains know you're out of their league."

"But Bianca seems to get asked out all the time."

"By that type of guy."

"Yeah, so?"

"Exactly my point."

"But, Cathy, you're sixteen. Already you've been on twice as many dates as I have. At least twice as many."

"I doubt that."

"Okay, how many have you been on?"

"Six or seven." Cathy wasn't sure. She wasn't keeping count. Not keeping count? How could that be?

"See. I'm right."

"But what about those dates with Jed?"

"What dates with Jed?" The only date-ish thing Julia recalled was the campus tour, and that hardly mattered. Plus, he went undercover stealth man after kissing her, and that was as bad as if he hated her guts from the beginning. She was starting to feel like a social leper.

"All the dates. The Warren Miller ski movie."

"You were with us. A threesome date."

"Whatever. Ice skating." She'd forgotten about that. More Christmas break fun. Back when Jed acted like she was alive. "And your weekly date for the Saturday flirt-and-chat after Amanda's piano lesson."

"Those aren't dates. I couldn't possibly count them as dates."

"Jed does."

No way. Jed did not count them as dates.

"Yes. He plans to be there and plans that you'll be there, too, to hang out. That's a date. At least these days it is. It's a lot better than most so-called dates."

Why was Cathy pushing this? Jed Smith was Cathy's little boyfriend. The high school love people. What was she doing? Was this another scheme like Bianca's ploy to foist Scott onto her— the psycho thing girls did when they liked a guy, talk about him incessantly and try to trick their best friend or sister into liking him too? Convincing girl B he's hers for the taking, when all along, girl A likes him and ends up with him anyway. Ugh. Not again.

They continued the yard work until it was nearly dark.

"Where is Jed these days, anyway?"Cathy asked, resurrecting the subject of two hours previous. "He hardly talks to me at school lately. Did something happen between the two of you the night he came back from Lake Powell?"

Cathy knew. She absolutely knew. Julia desperately wanted to deny her treacherous act, but it was useless. The truth had to come from her own mouth eventually. She might as well admit it now, as she was being questioned point blank.

"Actually, something did happen." This was hard. How could she tell her sister that she'd smooched her boyfriend? "We were just sitting there, and I told him my good news about the composition, and, the next thing I knew, we kissed." Cathy's eyes grew wide—not with jealousy, more with revelation. "That was it—a short kiss, and that was the last time he talked to me or I to him. It never should have happened. I'm really sorry if I hurt you in any way."

"Me? What are you talking about?" Cathy looked shocked. "I told you last fall I didn't like Jed anymore. I found out he liked someone else and then realized I liked someone else, too. Don't you remember? Didn't you believe me?" Sure, Julia remembered, but she figured Cathy's fickleness matched her own. "Are you so thoroughly dense that you couldn't see who Jed liked?"

Was Cathy implying Jed liked her? Julia? No. Impossible. Absolutely and completely impossible. Julia rejected it out of hand. He had his high school things, his social stuff, his Student Body President super-busy popular life. She was just a friend's older sister he took pity on each Saturday afternoon, entertaining her for his charity service hours. One night things got out of perspective, and he slipped up and kissed her by accident. Then he was so grossly embarrassed he figured it was safer to drop her entirely. Now *that* was a more likely scenario.

"I judge by your silence you *are* that dense." Cathy tossed her gloves on the cement curbing next to the garage's back entrance and called to Julia over her shoulder as she went inside to wash up. "He's a good person. The first and only one so far who's been worthy of you. Don't blow it, Julia." Cathy let the door swing shut behind her, leaving Julia alone with her thoughts in the yard.

CHAPTER TWENTY-SIX

The dorm phone rang, breaking Julia's Music Theory concentration. It was the third time in the past hour. She went out and picked it up impatiently.

"Rory, she's not home yet. Just go over to the library and find her." She exhaled forcefully to show her displeasure.

"Who's Rory?" the female voice on the other end asked. "Is this Julia?" It was Bianca. The long lost sister. All those trips home and not one sighting of her in the past month. The hours at the mall must be extended for some big sale or something. She didn't even have time to help with the wedding prep.

"Hi, sis. What's up? I haven't seen you in a while."

"I know. It's been forever. Retail can be murder sometimes." She couldn't imagine a perfume counter as murder during any season, but everyone has his or her perception of stress in life. "So what I'm calling for is this. The plan is so fun I'm going to be totally bossy about it, okay? So, I want you to drop whatever plans you have for this weekend and come with me and Scott and maybe some others out on a little road trip. Friday night." Friday? That was the night before her students' piano recital. No way. She had way too much to do.

"Where are you going?"

"The funnest place." Most fun. "Wendover! And the drive is only about three hours, so we can go and come back in one night. We'll be back by dawn." An all night trip to, of all places, Wendover, Nevada? It just didn't sound all that fun to Julia. And the old question of transportation reared its ugly head. Julia refused to take the Century anywhere farther than Logan and Huntsville. Dad had grounded it to the Wasatch Front. So, what were they left with? Enviro-defying pollution machine truck belonging to Scott, or hurtling pink death trap tuna fish can of Bianca's? What a choice. But Bianca persisted.

"I hope you're not balking. Everyone wants you to come." She wondered who "everyone" meant and feared it only meant Bianca and excluded Scott and probably referred to no other people. "And I need a chaperone." That was the clincher. Bianca needed her. If Julia didn't go, Bianca couldn't go. Aha. Chaperone.

So, Julia agreed to meet them at Bianca's apartment at 5:30 Friday afternoon, "If," she made Bianca promise, "you guarantee we'll get back early. I have a ton of stuff this Saturday."

Sure. Bianca promised.

Friday was still two days away, and Julia had two mid-terms between now and then. She put it out of her mind and picked up her Music Theory notebook again. This quarter was the hardest yet in the series. They were finally covering information she didn't learn in high school. She actually had to study for this test. Hard.

The phone rang again. Apparently she was the only person home on the whole dorm floor. She stomped out into the hall and picked it up exasperatedly, breathing a sharp hello into the receiver.

"Um, Julia?"

"Yes."

"I'm downstairs at the dorm desk and wondered if you have a minute to come down." It was Jed! Four in the afternoon. Jed! Her heart did a round-off back handspring.

"Absolutely. I'll be right down." Her stomach followed with a flip and an aerial cartwheel. That was a lot of internal gymnastics for just Jed. Her old buddy Jed. Keep her in suspense for an entire month Jed. How did she look? She checked the mirror as she passed. Lip gloss. She needed it. Other than that, she noticed today was a high self-esteem appearance day. Hair curled just right, wearing a waistline-flattering shirt, and just the perfect line of eyeliner on her eyelids. She even felt thin. Ah, the benefits of having a roommate who never suggested a late-night frozen yogurt run. There was flavored lip gloss in her coat pocket, and she snatched it on her way out the door.

He stood nervously shifting his weight in the lobby below. She emerged from the elevator, and a smile spread across his face.

"Hi, stranger. Long time no see." Julia linked arms with him, and they walked out into the courtyard. "What brings you north?"

They walked past the tennis courts where spring training was in full swing.

"Just more paperwork. I already turned it in."

"Then you came to see me? I'm flattered." She was flattered, though she said it in a flirty, sarcastic tone. "What shall we do?"

"What about going to see that weeping lady?"

"Oh, that's only good at night—under a bright moon."

"There's one tonight." Really? She seldom paid attention to the phases of the moon. "So, okay. Until then, let's do something outdoors." He paused, thoughtfully. "Hey, Julia. Do you have time for this?"

She didn't really. Mid-terms were upon her. The recital was Saturday. Between now and then, there was Bianca's trip to Nevada. But somehow she found herself saying, "Heck, yeah. I always have time for you, Jed." He looked relieved. "I have an idea. Let me just go back to my apartment and grab something."

"What is it?"

"You'll see."

A few minutes later she emerged from Valley View Towers with a plastic bag holding some mysterious white disks.

"What's that?"

"Come with me. Are you up for a walk?"

"Always." His lean, youthful body looked well-exercised. Julia realized she'd never asked him about his interest or participation in sports. He could have been captain of the football team or a track star for all she knew. They headed east toward the Fine Arts building and the Golden Toaster.

"I thought I had some bread in my dorm room, but I must

have eaten more peanut butter sandwiches than I thought. This was all we had left." Julia held it up to reveal a label reading Quaker Rice Cakes, Apple Cinnamon. She held it closer to his eyes so he could see the expiration date: January 5.

"Appetizing. Can I have *two*?"

"You'll have to fight me for them."

"Those things are almost like styrofoam. Why did you buy them?"

"I didn't. True, my roommate, must have. I'm not sure if she was saving them for a special occasion, or what. I'll buy her another pack."

"Wait until she mentions it. She *might* not miss them."

"Good idea."

They were walking along at a good clip and continued their idle chatter. He told her today was the last day for another scholarship application, and being a great procrastinator, he was forced to bring it personally to the scholarship office to make the deadline.

"So, are you for sure coming to Utah State next year?"

"I hope so. It depends. My family is pretty big, and my folks can't afford to pay for all of our college tuition. They warned us a long time ago if we wanted a degree we'd have to get scholarships or good jobs to pay for school. Weber State already offered me a pretty good deal, but I like the campus up here better." *And some of the people*, she wished he would add. She still doubted Cathy's hinting. Other than the one display of affection, Jed showed her no signs of liking her. Sure, he spent quite a bit of time with her on weekends. Sure, he acted like he was interested in her general happiness and well being. But Jed was one of those people who's kind to everyone. She'd hate to drive him off by getting the wrong idea.

They passed the Golden Toaster and kept walking east toward the mouth of Logan Canyon. When the wind blew just right, she could hear the honking of the geese.

"So, then I asked my English teacher why it was that the word sub-par doesn't mean 'good.' Isn't the goal in golf to get a score lower than par? And my English teacher just smiled and went on with the lecture on Latin roots, and I gave myself five points, and bought myself an extra bag of Sugar Babies from the vending machine at lunch." Mmm. Sugar Babies. Julia loved how those little brown sugar drops stuck in her teeth so she could keep enjoying them for dozens of minutes after the bag was gone.

Julia also liked the way Jed started telling his stories as though he were continuing a topic, even if they'd never discussed the subject before, like they were already in the middle of a conversation. It was as though they'd been friends so long they'd discussed everything in the world already and any change of subject was simply a continuation of a long-ago story. The oldest of friends. Come to think of it, other than family members, Jed was swiftly becoming her oldest friend. He was certainly the easiest to talk to. And he understood her hopes and fears better than anyone else—and seemed to actually care about them.

What a good friend.

"So, while I was on a roll, later that same day I asked my Seminary teacher if the reason there were so many 'lost books' in the Bible was because Nephi stole the last copy. And he said he wasn't sure if 'stole' was the right word, and I said 'what would be a better word then,' and he couldn't really answer and went on with his lecture on the Apocrypha, and I gave myself ten more points for asking stumper questions that day."

"What's your stumper for me?" Julia asked.

"Okay. Um. What's your favorite color?"

"How on earth is that a *stumper*?"

"It's like this. Stay with me, okay? I think it's a totally unfair question. However, people ask it all the time—What's your favorite color? What's your favorite color? How can someone be expected to pinpoint a selection from an almost infinite range of hues? It poses an unfair expectation."

"What do you mean? Can't you just say blue?" Blue had always been Julia's answer to that question.

"Most do. Did you know that about fifty percent of people list blue as their favorite color?" That high, huh?

"Does that make me in with the in-crowd or a sheep?"

"That's a tough distinction." He raised his eyebrows and snickered. "But to continue. I don't think the answer 'blue' could be entirely correct. Be honest. If your favorite color is blue, aren't there some shades you *dislike*? Or some that just don't work in that context?"

"Sure. I almost always *dislike* teal blue. Unless it's on a living, crying peacock's feather. Then I like it for some reason, although peacocks sort of repulse me up close. They're a little dangerous."

"Exactly my point. The teal part."

"Well, fine then. Cornflower blue is my answer. So. Here I go with a stumper for you, Jedediah Smith. I bet, forming my deduction just by looking at the sea and the sky, that there's a chance that the Lord's favorite color is blue. Or a toss up between blue and green. Look how much of our lovely planet is blue or green."

"You may be right. But then again, Julia Cronquist, it could just be a natural phenomenon due to the color spectrum thing."

They made their way down the slope to the reservoir at First Dam. It was cooler in the shade of the hill, and Julia wished she'd brought her jacket.

"Brr." That was all she hinted of it, but almost immediately, Jed put an arm around her shoulder, warming her slightly with his side. A few people, not so many as at the first warmth of spring, were tossing offerings to the ducks and geese paddling in the water. Three or four cars were in the parking lot, including a sea green pickup truck with the Logan City Parks and Rec logo on the side.

"Now I get it." Jed pointed at the rice cakes. "Do you think they'll eat it?"

"I wouldn't, but ducks aren't the intellectual equals of you and me."

"We'll see."

They approached the water, and Julia dug down in the bag for a delicious disc for Jed and one for herself. "Here, ducky, ducky," he called as a small defection came their way from the main flock near the children throwing bread. "Come get this low-fat meal, little duckies. I like bread and butter, I like toast and jam, I don't know this song, but put Quaker rice cake in my hand." He improvised the jingle from the commercial. His singing voice wasn't bad either.

"The ducks appear to be smarter than we thought. Look, that one actually spat it out." All the crumbled white fragments they'd thrown still lay floating at the edge of the wall lining the pond. "Look. They're leaving."

"We don't need no stinking rice cakes."

Just then, Julia felt a tap on her shoulder.

"Excuse me." She turned around in surprise. "That is an express violation of State Fish and Wildlife code." A tall, brown-shirted male in a flat brimmed hat spoke to them. A badge glinted on his chest in the long rays of the setting sun. "If you don't cease and desist at once I will issue you a $75 ticket, and you will be banned from state fishing licence application for five years."

"I'm sorry, sir. What did I do wrong?" Jed spoke for them.

"You and this young lady should know better than to pollute our city's waters with trash. And in broad daylight! The wildlife can choke on styrofoam and die. I need not explain the dangers of your actions to you. They are self-evident." He pulled his ticket-pad from his chest pocket in a threatening gesture. "Now, do I need to write this up, or are you leaving the premises at once?"

"We will go, sir." Jed dropped his head in shame and took Julia by the arm. "We're truly sorry for our ignorance and thoughtless action."

"But—" Julia tried to explain to the officer his error.

"No, Rolanda. He's right. Let's go." Rolanda? A fake name? "We've been reckless."

Julia followed him away from the park, and when they were out of earshot the two of them burst into uncontrollable laughter.

"Just call me Reckless Rolanda." She dumped the remaining rice cakes from the package into the roadside ditch.

"Okay, Rolanda." He dragged her by the hand as they ran giggling up the hill. "And you can call me Theo. Thoughtless Theo." They reached the top of the hill, breathless, and sat down under the roof of the roadside picnic area overlooking the Country Club's golf course on the north and the Island on the south—a flat, suburban home area at the base of the campus's hill at the same elevation of the mouth of the canyon. It was a scenic spot to watch the sunset.

"I should stop going to that park."

"Why? Don't let Ranger Rick spoil it for you."

"It's not just that. Last time I was there I had an even more unfortunate incident," and she related to him the tragedy of the overloaded backpack.

"Maybe you're right. First Dam park doesn't seem to like you. But, hey. You seem to be walking fine now."

"Oh, three weeks and thirty muscle relaxants later." In truth, it only took two weeks to heal most of the way. "I followed the doctor's orders to wear the backpack on both shoulders, and I haven't had a problem since."

"Smart move." The sky was beginning to pink up as the sun dipped behind some mountains Julia didn't know the name of yet. "What were you doing hauling it around on one shoulder in the first place? Sounds uncomfortable."

"It was. But everybody does it anyway."

"That's ridiculous."

"I know that now." She rubbed her back in dramatic demonstration. He took her unintentional cue and scooted close to her to rub her shoulders. "Thanks. Yeah. Right there. Where were you when I needed you?"

He paused. "Sorry about that." She hadn't intended to accuse him of anything, but he went on explaining anyway. "It's just I guess I was a little ticked off." About what? When?

"What happened?" She tried to hide the concern in her voice. Did *she* make him mad? He stopped rubbing her shoulders, and she turned around to face him.

"Maybe it meant something different to you. I guess I read the situation wrong." He was staring at the wooden bench, then bent over and plucked a piece of grass from under the picnic table. He stuck it in his teeth.

"What do you mean?" Oh. Was he referring to the kiss? He was. Why did it tick him off? She *knew* she shouldn't have done it. Oh, shoot. Now what? She didn't want to discuss this topic. "Hey, I'm really sorry if I did something wrong. Never in a million years would I jeopardize our friendship." That was true. "If I promise never to let it happen again, will you forgive me?"

A look of earnest searching came over his face. She projected her most sincere countenance.

"Sure. Forgive me for staying away? What I should have done was come to you right away about it. Sorry."

"Friends?"

"Friends."

Sure, they were friends, but so much for her little hopes regarding the flavored lip gloss in her pocket and the moon's shadow on the weeping lady. She'd just promised never to let that happen again. What was she thinking? Maybe it wasn't true that she wouldn't jeopardize their friendship for anything. For another chance at a kiss from Jed, she'd put a lot on the line. Couldn't they be friends that kissed? Kissing friends? Weren't there such things?

The sun pulled its final beams beneath the horizon, leaving only a pale blue sky and one pink cumulus cloud. Venus sat low in the west, brilliant, crystalline. Julia and Jed pulled themselves to their feet and began walking back toward the campus.

"So, are you all set for the recital Saturday? It's this Saturday, isn't it?"

"Yeah. Not quite." The pressures of her actual life resurfaced in her mind. "The little programs are all printed up." They walked side by side, hands in their own pockets.

"What's left?"

"At the end of the recital I'm planning to play the piece I did for my final project last quarter. It's only a few minutes long, but I haven't practiced it *since* last quarter, so I need to go over it a few times."

"Can I hear it?"

She welcomed the chance to kill two birds. "My practice room is just over there in the Fine Arts building. If you don't mind, we could go in there, and I could run through it right now."

"Sounds good." Jed grabbed her hand and led her running across the highway. They ran the entire distance to the building and then all the way up the stairs to the third floor practice rooms. One was empty, and the schedule sheet on its door was unmarked. Heaving for breath, they entered the tiny soundproof room with the well-used baby grand piano, and both sat down on the bench. There was barely enough room for two people.

Julia played the Bach piece, roughly at first, but better with each successive run-through. Jed sat silently beside her. In her concentration she nearly forgot he was there. When she finally reviewed it to a point satisfactory to herself, she lifted her hands from the keys and set them in her lap. Jed offered enthusiastic applause.

"Magnificent-ent-ent." His voice reverberated a sedate Carnegie Hall announcer's tone. "The audience has just heard Miss Julia Cronquist at the piano, playing a selection from her *White* album, to be released this September." She laughed and pushed aside the creeping suspicion that entered her mind when she recalled his presence—the suspicion that he'd been sitting beside her with a critical ear for each of the many mistakes she made in the initial practices. "Miss Cronquist." Then he resumed his applause and made hollow bravo calls, as though from a crowded concert hall.

"Thank you. Thank you. And I'd like to thank the Academy." She stood to go, and he followed her out into the long, fluorescent-lit hallway.

"Check that one off your list. Anything else to get ready for the recital?"

"Not much. I ordered a sheet cake from Albertson's bakery." They exited the building and began walking across campus in the spring night air. Streetlamps lit their path down Seventh North toward the center of campus. "Mom's got little plates and stuff. She's too busy stressing about the wedding to do much else, so I'll set up the folding chairs myself. There are one or two students I hope will do some concentrated practice before Saturday, but most of them are ready to go." She stopped, looked over her shoulder and pointed to the moon, a sliver of the top of which came peeking from behind Mt. Logan. It was bright and silvery. He paused with her.

"Nice." Jed paused reverently until the full sphere rose above the peak. It looked so big and bright and near before it began its far ascent into the night sky. "It sounds like things are pretty under control. Do you want some help setting up chairs?" They were nearing the parking garage now.

"Sure, that would be great. Say, two o'clock? It starts at three."

"I'll be there."

Julia stood under the moon, watching him go.

To Julia's surprise, True was home when she entered their dorm room at eight or so.

"Lo the prodigal daughter returns!" Julia shut the door and hung up her windbreaker. Her Theory book beckoned to her from atop her pillow. Soon. She had to get back to studying soon. "Have you ever thought of this? Our dorm room, despite its cramped drawbacks, is probably a heckuva lot more comfy than a castle ever was." True waved a copy of her Western Civ history book at Julia. "Castles were so drafty, cold, dim, and lumpy and dank. Water dripping down the moldy walls, and all. So, next time you're thinking this is an icky place, remember, we have more electrical outlets than all the medieval castles combined. So. What brings you here at this odd hour?"

"Oh, nothing."

"You have to tell me, Julia. We're roomies."

"Out."

"With someone? Who?"

"A younger man. Jed. My sister Cathy's friend from school."

"Tell all!"

"It's nothing. He's still in high school."

"A senior?"

"Yeah. So?"

"So, he might not be that much younger."

"High school *is* younger. He's a friend."

"How good of a friend? Have you kissed him?"

"No!" But an irrepressible smile of the inexperienced liar spread across her face. She couldn't deny it. "Oh, okay. I did kiss him, but it was a while ago. Months." One month, but it felt like a year.

"I knew it." True was triumphant in her ferreting abilities. "And why was there no repeat tonight? Full moon . . . True Aggie opportunity . . ." Her voice rose at the end of each phrase, expectantly.

"It just didn't happen that way. We're friends."

"I can't believe you let a chance like this pass you by."

Why *did* she let the chance pass her by? Probably because she wasn't a True Aggie herself, so, according to legend, she wasn't authorized to make someone else a True Aggie. But that would have been a perfect excuse! Oh, how she would have liked to use that excuse. Why didn't she plan ahead and make sure she was a True Aggie as preparation for a contingency such as this? The watermelon lip gloss sat unused because of her social leprosy. So unkissable. That's what she was. So unkissable. She vowed not to let another month pass by her without preparing for such opportunities. Sadly, she could think of no one in her acquaintance who could remedy that for her. She was surrounded by social lepers. A social leper colony. What could she do? Dan was probably a True Aggie. Yeah, he was one for sure. Should she call him up? Tell him to meet her at the A at midnight? It would show bold initiative.

She decided to confide in True.

"True, I'm not a True Aggie. I couldn't have used that chance even *if* I'd wanted to."

"Well, that's a problem. Let's get it cured." True cast her Civ text aside, stood up, and headed for the hallway. "Get your jacket, girl. We're on a mission."

Julia grabbed her windbreaker once again, gave her Theory books a longing look and followed her enthusiastic roommate out the door.

Three hours and twenty-two doors later, True and Julia stood outside the Anderson Apartments in the cool air.

"That was fun. So, even if we never did find anyone to solve your problem, we met some cool guys, huh?"

"Sure." Some of them were fun. Most of them were weird, guitar playing, folk music freaks. Lots of Political Science majors with pictures of George Bush and Ronald Reagan in their rooms. Some non-students just working at Weslo, the exercise equipment factory south of town. Not a True Aggie in eighteen apartments. At least none who would admit to it when they heard the proposition and saw Julia's face. Why was she cursed with ugliness? Why couldn't she be blonde and buxom and bubbly like Bianca?

What would Bianca do in this situation?

She would take matters into her own hands.

Brimming with resolve, Julia said good night to her friend and set out to tackle Old Main Hill just as she heard the clock tower chiming 11:30. Good, it was enough ahead of time she could catch any early birds and put forth her case.

At the hill, she easily found the stone slab balanced atop the four white letter A's. The day began to wear on her, and she considered climbing up on the little table and curling up for a catnap until the kissers started to arrive, but she decided that might defile the sacred object. So, she sat down on the steps nearby to wait. Night birds sang in the trees, a car passed on Sixth East far below at the bottom of the hill. The hundreds of giant trees blocked her view of the lights of town, and the Old Main building behind her blocked the moon. She waited.

What would she say if someone came along? If they were mere passers-by, she'd just say hello. But if they were coming to imbibe in the monthly ritual she'd whisper, "Hey. Can you do me a favor?" Then, if someone took pity on her (even with the full moon, it was dark enough that no one could see well enough to refuse due to how unattractive she was), the guy in the group might lift her up on the table and give her a peck in the moonlight, bestowing on her the power of True Aggie-hood with all its privileges. She'd thank him, refuse to leave her name, and disappear into the night. No sweat.

She waited. The clock struck 11:45. No one passed, in car or on foot. She waited. No kissers came. The clock struck twelve. Still no one. She gave it five extra minutes. Nary a soul.

She trudged home.

In her room, True was already in bed with the lights out. Her breathing changed when Julia entered, and she awoke briefly.

"Julia. Hey. I'm really sorry."

"For what?"

"I told you wrong about the moon. I checked my calendar when I got in. The full moon was last night. Where've you been?"

"Nowhere." Julia dropped onto her bed, defeated, deflated, depressed. "True? I think I'm going for another little walk. Don't worry. I won't be long." But True wouldn't be worried. She was sleeping soundly again.

Julia clutched her mace and her flashlight buried in her coat pocket. She wasn't scared. If she are prepared she shall not fear, right? She strolled, teeth chattering, through the cemetery. The quartz in the granite twinkled like snowflakes in the moonlight. Tall monuments, short plaques, a few crosses, a marble sculpture carved into a little chair with baby booties on it, another made to look like a tree trunk with a scroll on the side. William Johnson 1881-1946. A whole life was in that dash.

Then she saw it.

It wasn't as tall as she'd expected, but it was there. Right next to the car lane on the west side of the cemetery. The older side. Clearly outlined by the silver light, it was the weeping lady. A shiver ran up her spine.

Julia approached it cautiously. She'd never been one to get superstitious about graves or ghosts. In fact, when she lived in Virginia, she'd spent quite a few thoughtful, solitary hours in Arlington National Cemetery. As her father's daughter, to her, they were much more sacred than scary. Nevertheless, she approached cautiously, looking all the time for a glint of a tear.

As she came near it, Julia realized the woman's eyes couldn't look teary. Her carved granite hands were covering them. And her head was bowed, not so much in sadness—well, maybe some sadness—but in prayer, too. It was a humble depiction of a woman who had known pain and perhaps joy. Who was she? Soon Julia came around to the inscription. There it was in huge raised letters: *Cronquist.*

Cronquist? The weeping lady was rumored to be Danish, but Julia never expected her to be a Cronquist. She circled the monument, looking for more of an inscription, but none appeared. Pulling her flashlight from her pocket, she attempted to shine it around on the low-lying stones that surrounded the taller marker, but the batteries failed. So much for preparedness.

A zillion questions ran through her mind. Was Julia related to these Cronquists? Did the weeping lady depict an actual woman? Was it carved to look like her? Was the headstone made in Denmark? Could it be her own ancestor? Her father's family did hail from this part of the country, although she knew very little of their heritage. She'd never really asked.

No more information could be gleaned in this pale light, so she finally gave up and tripped on home, much lighter of step than when she first began this midnight walk.

CHAPTER TWENTY-SEVEN

Julia packed a small duffel bag for the trip to Nevada and loaded it into the Century. It was time to get out of town. Logan was not her favorite place today. A crashing, burning failure of her Theory mid-term this morning and a major disappointment on her mid-term piano performance test made the entire Cache Valley appear hostile. She left it behind gladly.

She was anxious to talk to her dad about the weeping lady, but her mom and dad were up in Huntsville, and she was only meeting Bianca in Ogden. Plus, Rex and Jan had a big weekend planned meeting Becca's parents. It was not the day for a leisurely conversation about genealogy.

Slightly before 5:30, zero hour for the proposed whirlwind trip, she arrived at Bianca's apartment. No lights were on, and both the Karmann Ghia and Scott's rolling arsenal were missing from the parking lot. Gassing up, she guessed. Soon enough, both vehicles arrived, about fifteen minutes late.

"Hey, Jules. You're already here."

"I thought you said 5:30."

"Oh, yeah. You remember Scott." Duh. He was her most embarrassing moment, and possibly she was his. Why was Bianca making these awkward introductions? Wasn't she supposed to be the social goddess? No gaffes? No uncomfortable guests?

"Hi. Pleased to meet you." Julia overplayed it to sarcastically lighten the moment. He smiled briefly and extended his hand.

"I've never been to Nevada before. Where are we going again?"

"Oh, a sleepy little border town. The Utah border, that is. Wendover. Loose slots, friendly dealers. But we're only going to dance, right?" She looked at Scott, and he nodded dutifully. Something didn't seem quite right. What had Julia gotten herself into? Maybe she should back out. Call it off. No. She already promised Bianca she'd chaperone. Their family had a long-standing rule against too much alone time with a boy. It was a good rule, and Julia wanted to help Bianca keep it—and the trust of her parents.

"You ready to go?" Julia was anxious to get on the road and get back. Tomorrow was jam packed, and she didn't want to be driving through the Utah desert too late at night, especially in the Karmann Ghia, tonight's desert schooner.

"Just gotta grab one or two more things." Bianca zipped into her apartment, leaving Scott and Julia standing in the parking lot.

"Your sister is crazy." Scott's eyes followed Bianca to the door.

"I know." Why didn't Julia see it before? Long ago. Scott was completely gaga over Bianca. Not just a mild crush. This was a serious case of total submission. The guy even gave up his combat boots for a pair of loafers—with buckles. All the more reason Julia needed to be along on this trip with Bianca as her protector. Scott in his infatuation might get the wrong idea in the desert. The kissing photo finally made sense.

Bianca returned, carrying a plastic grocery sack full of music for the ancient stereo's tape deck and a box of Golden Grahams cereal, "In case we get stranded."

The three set off, singing to the stereo for the first hour until it overheated and melted a pirated copy of an oldie but a goodie: Alphaville—right in the middle of "Forever Young." Then, for the next hour, Bianca entertained them with her plans for the upcoming pageant. Scott sat in rapt attention in the passenger seat, while Julia sat in the back and caught snippets of the conversation over the clanging loose muffler, which was doing little to muffle the noise of the antique vehicle's engine. Words like "poise" and "sway the judges" wafted back to her, along with exhaust fumes seeping in through the floorboards. This thing ought to be dubbed the

Kevorkian. She coughed and asked Scott to crack his window.

For a while the universe aligned, and she heard an entire passage of conversation.

"I'm not a big reader, but I do know my labels." Bianca flipped her hair over her shoulder. Scott sighed heavily as he caught a whiff of her hair's perfume. "So, I think I've discovered that shampoos with tea laureth sulfate are better for my type of hair than shampoos with tea laurel sulfate."

"I never would have guessed." Scott soaked it up. It was almost sad to witness. "You sure know your chemistry, Bianca. Another of your many facets."

"Facets? Ha ha. Like a diamond, right? Could I somehow work that into my speech to the judges? Thanks for the idea, Scott."

"I'm your number one supporter, beauty queen." Bianca giggled and then shushed herself as she glanced up at Julia in the mirror. Julia shut her eyes and feigned sleep. Her stomach was starting to hurt. Bianca was acting like a totally different person lately, and Julia didn't like the new Bianca all that much. Why, oh why was Julia here?

An hour after sunset, the party reached Wendover, and Julia was unimpressed. It looked like a run-down, mini-Vegas, filled with cheap neon and drunken cowboys. They parked the Karmann Ghia outside a dive bar and got out. A rock from the dirt and gravel parking lot got in Julia's shoe.

"I can't go in there."

"Sure you can. They have the best music. Can you hear it?" Strains of some bass-heavy band escaped when a couple entered the door. So did billows of smoke.

"No. I can't. It's a bar, isn't it?"

"Everywhere in this town is."

"In case you haven't noticed, we're the under-twenty-one crowd here. You two may pass for old enough, but no one is going to believe I'm of age." Julia was getting uncomfortable as Scott began to sneer at her and shift his weight impatiently. Bianca bit her lip and looked around. A swell of annoyance surged in Julia's gut.

"Yeah, Scott and I know someone, so we can get through, but, hmm. Hey. I might have a solution." Bianca the problem solver. More the problem causer. "Scott and I will just pop in there for a sec, order a burger and pop back out. We'll eat in there real quick and bring you yours out here in the car, then we'll find something else to do." She sounded like she thought her idea was an answer to the problem. "I just have to go in for a speedy quick jot. I read in the paper they're doing an awesome Rage in the Cage thing." Julia noticed as Bianca gave Scott a sly wink. "And, uh, Tony the Smasher is going in at 9:30. That's, like, now! Come on, Scott." And they were off.

Great. Here she sat. In the grimy parking lot of a rat hole bar named Retread. On the hood of a near-defunct asphyxiation tool with Golden Grahams all over her sweater, while Bianca and Scott abandoned her in favor of a charred burger and a lungful of cigarette and fog machine smoke. Some friends. Some sister.

What was the point in bringing her along anyway? Obviously not for her conversation. They ignored her the whole trip. Not for her company. Here she sat alone, kicking gravel, and trying to look like a non-target for some deranged cowboy. Was it a gesture of kindness—to keep Julia from being lonely on a Friday night? No. None of those. It was just so Bianca could make some lame excuse to her parents to keep the letter of the Cronquist family law. So Mom and Dad would continue to pay her rent and gas money as a daughter obedient to the family code. Ugh. Julia was being used.

Forty-five minutes passed. It got colder, and the winds of Wendover began to blow. Julia got inside the Karmann Ghia. When the door to Retread opened, she tried to crane her neck and catch a glimpse of Bianca and Scott inside. Once she saw someone with Bianca's poofy platinum hairdo spinning on the dance floor. But Bianca said they were only going to grab a burger. The grill must be pretty slow. An hour and a half went by and still no Bianca, still no Scott. She couldn't take it any more. At this rate she'd freeze to death before they returned with her burger.

"Excuse me." She tapped the bouncer at the door. "I don't want to go in."

"Then wadda ya doing here?" His tattoo flexed in the blue glare of the neon sign.

"I just want to see if my sister is still here." Please, be kind. She made her most innocent face.

"What's she look like?"

Julia described Bianca and Scott.

"Sounds like about half the couples in the joint." His face softened. An old softy. "Okay, sweetie. I seen you sittin' there a while. You can check inside if you want. But no funny stuff. This could cost me my job." She thanked him and forged her way into the haze.

When her eyes adjusted to the even darker atmosphere, she began her search. The band now was a sorry boy-band imitation—there was even a girl in it—doing sorry covers of boy-band hits, though the crowd seemed to be enjoying them immensely. The dangers of alcohol: impairing judgment in so many ways. No sign of Bianca at the bar or on the half-filled dance floor. Not at the little tables. Not in the band. No Scott either. Then she saw a familiar face.

"Mi-shrill." Oops. Michelle. Thank goodness the music was loud enough to cover the faux pas. "Hey. It's me—Julia. Bianca Cronquist's little sister." Mi-shrill gave a nod of recognition. "Have you seen Bianca here?"

Mi-shrill shook her head. "A while back. But not for an hour or so. I bet they went upstairs." What was upstairs? Julia sort of didn't want to know. It was definitely off limits to Julia, and most likely to Bianca, too. That was it.

"Thanks. If you see her, tell her I went home." Mi-shrill said okay and waved good-bye.

Almost two hours had passed since Bianca promised to just bop into Retread for a jif. Who knew how much longer she'd be gone—upstairs? Visions of gangsters and smoky roulette tables and vice in general filled Julia's brain. A harmless night in a sleepy little border town. How was she going to get out of this?

"Hello, Ted? It's Julia."

"Julia. Where are you? Mom called to see if you were here." She did? Oh, no. She forgot to tell her parents about the road trip. She was always home by this time on Friday nights.

"You're not going to believe it. Or like it." She related the whole situation to him. "Can you help me?"

"Where are you exactly?" She didn't know the address but gave him the name of the bar. "I'll let Mom know you're okay, and I'll be there by 1:30. Sit tight."

Ted didn't come at 1:30. Nor at 2:30. Julia was afraid to fall asleep in the Karmann Ghia, as the locks were broken, and she was afraid she'd be robbed, or worse. But Bianca and Scott didn't show either.

Finally, at four, Ted rolled in, driving his MG. "Sorry. Bit of engine trouble outside Tremonton. British cars prefer to spend their lives on blocks."

"Good thing you knew what to do to fix it." She climbed in beside him, glad he'd thought to put the hardtop on, as she was already hypothermic, and they had a long, cold drive ahead of them.

"So many years working on this baby, I have the engine memorized." He pumped the gas pedal and let the cured engine rip. Then he cut it. "Just a minute. I need to leave something for Bianca." He climbed out and deposited an envelope on Bianca's driver's seat. Then he returned, and the siblings started the long journey home.

After a while, he spoke. "What made you choose Wendover?" Ted was seven years older than Julia, and she could hardly remember him ever living at home when they were growing up. He had the "big brother" aura in the supreme.

"I didn't. Bianca just asked me to come along." She didn't add the *to chaperone* part. She figured Bianca was in enough trouble already. She couldn't imagine what the envelope sitting in the Karmann Ghia contained, but she didn't think it was an extra fiver for the slots.

"Sure makes you think about who your friends are."

Huh. Yeah. Now that he mentioned it, it did. She didn't reply aloud, but her thoughts worked on the topic. Bianca always made overt gestures at friendship, offering to give her makeovers, set her up with good-looking guys, inviting her to parties. But in retrospect, they all felt hollow. Clothes were just clothes. The result of the handsome set-up was an evident bomb. At the parties Julia never seemed to do much more than serve hors d'oeuvres or do dishes.

But she *seemed* so sincere.

"Bianca's got so many friends, she hardly needs me."

"Does she?" Hmm. Good question. She was surrounded by people all the time. They all acted *friendly*—when they weren't gossiping about each other or griping about the mall.

"It seems like it. She's always been so popular. Cheerleader, and all." She shouldn't have reminded Ted about that part. He always frowned on Bianca's short cheer skirts and being gone so much for games, not devoting enough time to her studies. That was just the difference between Ted and Bianca, though. He was much more serious. Bianca did call him Ted-ious, i.e., boring.

"I don't know, sis. In the past ten years I've never found her anything but . . . well, dull." Ted thought *Bianca* was dull?

"Really?" Ironic. Truly. She thought about it for a couple of minutes and leaned her head against the British rattletrap's window to look at the winter starscape. There was Orion's Belt. Bianca thought Ted was boring. Ted thought Bianca was dull. Julia decided that it depended on *your* personality whether you thought someone was interesting or not. Adolf Hitler would probably find Saddam Hussein delightful and engaging.

"Look, I know you look up to Miss Narcissa as your older sister, and all, but I wish you'd think carefully about who it is you choose to emulate." Whom. Or was it who? No, Ted said it right. Or, rightly? Correctly. Or did he? She was getting too tired to think about grammar or anything else.

"So, are you getting excited for the wedding?"

"Oh, yeah. Well, honestly, not so much for the wedding itself. But for being married, yeah." Julia thought she knew what he meant and didn't want to press. But then he clarified. "I mean, I have been single for all eternity, you know? And it's not what's meant for man. Even the scriptures say that. It's so great that I've finally found someone who makes me feel *not* alone. Do you know what I mean?" She thought she really did, this time. And then he clarified some more.

"I think Mom and Dad were pretty scared that I'd never get married. No one to carry on the Cronquist family name, and all. You obviously know I never dated much, never had a bunch of girls swarming around me. I was too geeky. Too serious. Too . . . everything. Then I met Becca, and she was too everything, too. For the first time in my life I was desperate to be popular—with her. And she let me.

"She's been really kind to me. Blind to my faults and alive to all my strengths. And she's opened her heart to me as well. Did you know she even built me a model rocket for my birthday? We shot it off, and it landed in a tree." Didn't that always happen to model rockets? Julia suspected a model rocket could land in a tree on a treeless plain. "So, getting married is fantastic because it's to her. Sure, she's not like Mom. And she'll never iron my shirts. But Becca could design an iron. And I like that more. And she's beautiful, to boot. I'm the luckiest guy I know."

Julia never knew Ted could get on such a roll about a girl. But it was nice. Really nice to hear him on such a . . . nice roll. She was getting tired. She turned and looked out the window at the vast treeless plain that was western northern Utah and watched the sagebrush blur by in the moonlight. Becca was lucky, too, to be loved by someone who thought so well of her. And it didn't matter that Ted never dated much. He was still happy now. Maybe he just didn't waste his time on the wrong people, saved up all his energy—and money—for Becca. Julia thought about this for quite some time.

"Do you have any music?" She closed her eyes to block out the pinking horizon ahead of them. Dawn was less than two hours away. Ted put Tchaikovsky in the deck, the "1812 Overture."

"That's soothing."

"Hey, a guy's got to stay awake." The cannons blasted. Julia opened her eyes. The landscape was still the same flat desolation, and in the side view mirror she saw the moon set. "How are things going in school?" Weird. It seemed like she seldom got asked that question.

"It's good. I flunked a mid-term today, but most other things are good."

"I heard about your composition. That's great." Mom and Dad must have told him. "Becca and I were wondering if we could come to the performance."

"Really? Sure! I mean, that would be great. It's at the end of the quarter, right before your wedding. Do you think you'll have time?"

"We wouldn't miss it."

A few minutes later she was asleep.

At 1:00, Julia woke up with a start. She was sprawled on top of the covers of her bed in the Dream Home still wearing yesterday's clothes. Her brain was a fog. Fog. It all came floating back to her like the Retread fog machine and the Kevorkian's fumes. What a night!

But what day was it? Saturday. The recital! At three!

Her shirt and hair smelled stale and smoky. The mirror revealed huge sleep-deprivation bags under her eyes. She had to shower. But was there time?

A few minutes later, she emerged dripping in the steamy room.

Jed was arriving in forty minutes to help with chairs. Where were the programs? When would she have time to get the cake? This was a disaster. Her first student recital was going to flop. All because her sister dragged her to the Retread bar in Wendover, Nevada, and abandoned her. Some friend. Things were much clearer regarding Bianca this morning.

With no ado, she raced to her closet, donned her black concert dress and pearls, and hurried to dry her hair. Oh, the curse of thick hair. Never in her life had it dried in under fifteen minutes. Today it took twenty-two long minutes, with Julia doubled over upside down in an idle effort to speed it up. Then she had to curl the frizzy ends, put on her makeup, nylons, shoes. What song was she playing? Under this much chaotic pressure she hoped she could recall even the title of the piece. What a nightmare.

The doorbell rang. She pulled on her black slingback pumps, hopping clumsily down the hall as she tried to pull the strap over her left heel. It rang again. Was no one else at home? Where was Cathy when she needed her? As she entered the foyer, she saw the living room was a complete disaster. Throw pillows thrown, newspapers everywhere, not a folding chair in sight. Her mom promised to have the chairs out!

"Hi, Julia. You look stunning."

"What? I do? No. Hi, Jed. I'm in a panic."

"What's wrong?" He came right in, took a look at the living room, and set to work without a word. Together they made a whirlwind pass through it and had it all neat in no time. "Where do you keep the chairs?"

"I think they're in the shed out back. I'm not sure." Jed tramped out across the now self-sufficient sod on the back lawn and returned with four Samsonite metal beauties, two in each arm.

"Your heels will sink into the grass if you try it. I'll get these."

"Okay, I'll take them from here." From the kitchen sliding door, she hauled them into the living room and began arranging them in neat semi-circles. At their next meeting, she said, "I think I'll need twelve more." He nodded and continued his trek back and forth. It was 2:40 when the chairs were arranged and each had a program neatly placed on it.

"Thanks, Jed. I couldn't have done it without you."

"People will be getting here soon, I bet. Three, right? Some people around here show up early for stuff."

"The cake! I never picked it up from Albertson's!" Oh, dear. Thirty guests and no cake. Oh, well. Let them not eat cake, she decided.

"I hope it's okay, but I figured it was on my way, so I just picked it up when I was coming over. It's in the pantry with the plates and cups. I brought it in while you were setting out programs."

"What? Jed. You're a lifesaver. How do you do it?"

"How do I do what? Oh, I did forget a couple of things. They're out in my truck." He skipped out the front door, and Julia checked the cake in the pantry. Perfect. A purple frosting flower on each square. Pre-cut. Excellent.

She heard the door bang shut and left the pantry to greet Jed in the kitchen.

"This is for the piano." It was a vase full of daisies. Wow! Just the touch of class the recital needed. "And this is for you." A corsage! With a red rose flanked by two more daisies.

"Jed. You didn't have to do that."

"I know."

The doorbell rang, and he hurriedly pinned the corsage to her dress as the first guests and pianists arrived.

"It was really nice to meet you." Julia smiled, trying not to look weary. This day had taken a lot out of her, but it had turned out much better than it began. "Amanda is one of my best practicers. She's going to be a great pianist one of these days."

"If she can attain half your proficiency, we'll be proud." Mr. Smith put an arm around the nine year-old's shoulders and gave her an encouraging squeeze. Then he looked up at Julia again.

"You're as talented as Jed told us. We appreciate all the progress Amanda is making in your lessons." Julia smiled again, grateful for the compliment. They shook hands, and Jed's folks departed the Dream Home. They were the last parents to leave, and only Jed remained behind to help clean up.

"Well done, Miss Cronquist. Your piano school is a smashing success."

"All thanks go to you, Mr. Smith."

Jed smiled at this formality. "Just one more recital to go before your musical year is complete."

This reference to the choir's performance of her composition reminded Julia about the pressures of school, where she needed to do some serious buckling down before quarter's end to make up for her dismal showing at mid-terms. But she was too tired to study today anyway, so she avoided the subject.

"Your parents seem so nice. They really support you kids, don't they."

"Yeah." Jed's face showed a look of admiration. Rare for a teenage boy when it came to parents. He'd done that before. She still liked it. "There are a lot of us to support, but they try to keep up. They really want each of us to find something we can do well."

"Like what?"

"Oh, my oldest brother was a pianist. Two sisters sing pretty well and blend great. They won first prize at the state fair when they were in high school. Another sister sews. My younger brother Matt—you know him—raises dogs. Runs the whole gamut." Matt was Cathy's age at school and had been by once to pick up Cathy for a basketball game. He was Jed's practical twin but three inches taller.

"What's yours?"

"I think they're still wondering about me." Oh, sure. This was a kid who had so many talents he needn't focus on one. "You look tired. I'll finish up here, and you go get changed so you can relax." The offer was very generous, but she continued to help fold up the chairs, and they jointly returned them to the shed. She could clean the mud off her heels later. It was fun working side by side with him.

When they were finished, she sat down beside him on the sofa. She leaned her head back and closed her eyes.

"Too bad your family couldn't be here today to witness your grand success."

"Naw. It was the only Saturday between now and the wedding when they could meet Becca's parents. They're flying in from Oregon."

"I guess that's pretty important."

"Yeah, it doesn't bother me. They've heard a million piano recitals in their lives, and it doesn't hurt for them to miss one." Her mom and dad apologized sincerely for having to be absent from today's concert. Too bad she kept them up late last night worrying about her. Worse, too bad she kept Ted out all night rescuing her. She hoped he wouldn't say something weird to the Kenners and jeopardize the wedding because he was so tired. She failed to stifle a yawn.

"Why so sleepy? What time did you get up?" Jed gave her cheeks a little tap with his palm to wake her up. "I came by at eleven, and no one answered the door." Meaning her.

"Oh, I had a late night last night."

"Oh, yeah? How late?"

"I'm not really sure. I think I got in around seven."

"This morning?" Jed looked surprised. "Well, I better really let you get some sleep then. Congratulations on today. See you." He hurriedly got up and left. She tried to follow him to the door, but her body was glued to the squishy soft sofa, and she just offered a weak wave. *See you next Saturday,* she would have said if her lips worked.

CHAPTER TWENTY-EIGHT

As it turned out, she didn't make it home the following Saturday. Julia's piano students were given a much-deserved month-long hiatus, and Julia remained in Logan those four Saturdays during the month of May. May in Cache Valley is incomparable, and she took in the beauties of the green valley through window panes while she maximized her study opportunities. Keeping her scholarship was her job, and, if she didn't put in the hours, it was in jeopardy. It got to the point where she considered offering to move out of the dorm and begin paying rent at the Fine Arts building where she spent night and day.

It paid off. Her final projects rolled around and she received A's on all three of them, and she felt confident she could ace the Theory final coming up next Wednesday. Between now and then she had nothing to do but prepare for that test. Her first year of college was swiftly coming to a close. The evening of her last final was also the women's ensemble choir performance, where her first composition would debut. After one or two short conferences with the choir director, she was pleased with the way the practices were going, and the choir sounded nearly exactly as she heard it in her mind when she wrote the piece. She couldn't imagine a more satisfying feeling than hearing it performed so well.

She lay on her bunk with a box or two packed up here and there when True entered in the mid-afternoon.

"Hi friend. How's the library?"

"I don't know. I haven't been there lately." What? True not spend time at the library? How would she see Rory, the main attraction?

Come to think of it, he hadn't called much the last month. Julia figured they were together so many hours of the day he didn't need to call. But maybe not. With all her hours playing piano tunes in the Fine Arts building, she been mostly out of tune with what True was doing.

"True, is something going on? You don't need to pretend. It's me, Julia here." Julia's voice filled with sincerity and concern. "Something isn't right with you. Is it Rory?"

"Sort of." True's eyes welled up. Julia had never seen her cry before. "He broke up with me a while ago."

"What? What are you talking about? Broke up? But you two were the greatest couple! He was so gone over you. You looked so good together." They did look good together, both so bone-thin and pale. Two of a mold.

"I thought so, too." The tears spilled out silently. True sat down on her bed and hugged her pillow.

"What went wrong?"

"Oh, he just doesn't understand. He said I was being selfish and controlling."

"That doesn't sound a bit like you." No, it didn't sound like the True Julia knew at all. True was generous and helpful and outgoing. Always serving someone else. "How did he get such a mistaken idea?"

"I don't know. I guess he just didn't think I was taking care of myself right. Come on! I was just trying to look good for him. He's not a very big-statured guy, and I always felt like such a blimp around him. I just wanted to slim down a bit so I'd look more like his mate. After a while he noticed and said I was wasting away. Of course, I denied it, but he said I was being selfish—so worried about how I looked and what people thought that I didn't care about what was right or good for me."

Julia never thought of True as having a major problem, but now she looked at her and realized how much damage had been done. Her hair looked brittle, and her face was sunken in, especially around her eyes. Her wrists looked like pretzels, ready to snap at any moment. The change was so gradual, Julia didn't notice how severe things had become. But she should have! What a bad roommate!

"He said I was missing the whole point. That my body is my ticket to salvation and happiness, and that I'm chucking it over for some misguided fantasy. He said I wasn't applying myself to get a testimony of the gospel and where I fit in it. But I'm getting up like at five to read the scriptures before I run. Doesn't he understand?" Her breath caught in a hiccup in her throat.

"Now that I have a little distance from it," True continued, tears still quietly streaming, "I can see he has a point." She sniffled, and Julia handed her a Kleenex. It was the least she could do. "He said he wasn't going to see me anymore until I got some help."

"So, are you getting some help?"

"Yeah. I signed up with a counselor at the Student Health Center. We've met twice, and she's helping me see what's going on with me. From what she's taught me, Rory was right about the controlling part, too. I was trying to control everything, starting with food."

In a way, Rory was a little harsh, Julia thought. A lot harsh. Dumping her for dieting? Sheesh. But then again, in a way, he was as merciful as could be. At heart, he must really love True and want what was best for her. Of course, he didn't want to saddle himself with someone crazy, either. Breakup sounded like the only option for a loving, rational man.

"It sounds like maybe Rory did the right thing. Are you mad at him?"

"No. I mean, I wish he was here to stick by me through this, but I needed some distance from him to get myself healthy." She blew her nose again, and the tears slowed slightly. "The sad thing is, the day he took me out and dropped the I'm-dumping-you bomb, I actually thought he was going to propose. I mean, we'd already talked about our ideas for family and where we'd like to live and stuff. We both like the name Cormack for a boy."

Unless True got herself back in shape, there was no way her body would carry a pregnancy full term, and little Cormack would be out of the question. Rory was right in insisting she get well.

"Do you think there's still a chance for the two of you?"

"Probably not. He sounded pretty final. He's going on an internship this summer to California to do databases and microchips, so I don't know when I'll even see him again."

How could Julia have been so oblivious to her roommate's supreme heartache? They lived in the same room, for heaven's sake! She vowed to make it up to her.

"Let's get out of town, True. Do you have any finals tonight or tomorrow?"

"No. I have one more on Wednesday, but it's just Psychology 101. Multiple choice. Why? Where are we going?"

"You need a mountain retreat in the green hills of Huntsville, Utah."

"That sounds so good."

"This is a road trip. We need road trip music." She popped ABBA into the Century's tape deck. The two girls forgot all their troubles as they sang "Mama Mia" at the top of their lungs, flying down Interstate 15. "Mama Mia, here I go again, Ma-ma, just how much I missed ya." When they pulled in at the Dream Home, Cathy's face appeared through the curtains, and she bounced out to greet them.

"Hey, Jules. Hi—" she turned to True, "you must be True. Julia told me about you."

"True this is my sweet sister Cathy."

"You're here just in time."

"For what?"

"Mom just got back from Sam's Club with a smorgasbord of ideas for the reception. We're all sitting around in the kitchen taste testing." Julia looked at True hopefully. For a moment, True hesitated. Food was still not a friend to her, but she had to face it sometime.

"Let's go!" True smiled and put a spring in her step as they entered the beautiful home.

The four women sat around the bar in the kitchen, sampling different goodies from various platters. "I think I like these crab puffs the best."

"They'd go well with the little cheesecakes."

"Hey, you're completely overlooking my idea of little smokies and beans. That's much more Ted."

"But it's not reception-y."

"That's the problem with receptions. There's always receptiony stuff there, nothing actually good."

"Mmm. Did you taste the filled cream puffs?"

Julia watched True out of the corner of her eye. Initially she lifted items gingerly to her lips, barely nibbling a crumb from the sides of them. But eventually, in the jollity of the atmosphere, she relaxed and began to take an actual bite or two. At that rate, color would be back in her cheeks in just a few months' time.

"Mom, I can't believe you are just now deciding what to serve."

"Well, I always thought we were going to do it catered, but the Kenners seem like such relaxed people, we decided we should relax a little, too." She selected another jalapeño popper from the spicy foods tray. "Plus, this is a much less expensive way to go. We've already dropped a bundle on the yard." It was true. But the yard looked absolutely Eden-like. Julia stole a look at their flowerbed handiwork through the sliding glass door. Everything was in full bloom, just in time.

"So, how many more days? Twenty?"

"Nineteen."

"When is the final fitting on our ugly bridesmaid dresses?"

"They aren't ugly."

"They're white. I look like a heron."

"You look good in white. Everyone does. It's a universal color."

"You've been talking to Bianca too much."

The banter continued for another half hour until the tasters settled on a menu: little cheesecakes, crab puffs, little smokies in barbecue sauce, and ribbon sandwiches. Raspberry lemonade to drink. Something for everyone. True helped Jan Cronquist with the dishes.

"Are you all right, dear? Have you been ill?"

True answered, unoffended. "I'm doing better today, thanks."

Rex Cronquist strolled through the kitchen on his way into his den from the garden.

"It smells great in here. Can I have one?" He popped two leftover little smokies in his mouth at once. "These are delicious. Are they for the reception?"

"Bet your bottom dollar they are. Nothing but the best for our son, right?"

"Bottom dollar is right. Have you seen the price of geraniums this year? Outrageous." He headed for his study, and Julia saw her chance.

"Dad, are you busy for a second?" She trailed after him and motioned for True to follow.

"What's on your mind?" Her dad settled into his swivel chair and twirled to face his daughter and her friend. "Hello. True, is it? Nice to see you." True smiled back.

"Dad, do we have any Cronquist pioneer ancestors? Maybe that were buried in Logan?" Julia asked hopefully.

"I think so. There was the one family."

"Can you tell me about them?"

Her dad tilted back in his chair and laced his hands behind his head. He sighed deeply, in thought. "Let's see. I hope I remember this right. There was the Peter Cronquist family. That was your great-great grandfather. He and his wife Tena had six kids. They crossed the plains in a wagon, but not with the earliest saints. A few years later, after the ruts were almost roads."

"So, things were easier for them than for the first pioneers?"

"In a way, maybe. But not necessarily. From what I remember of the story, they shared a wagon and ox team with Peter's brother

Hans. Hans and his wife Sylvie lost all nine of their children to a fever during the trek west. The fever struck only their children—and none of Peter and Tena's. It was a terrible trial for both the fathers and both the mothers. The family lore is that Sylvie begged to be among the first to be sealed to her family in the Logan temple when it opened in 1884. In fact, I think she was one of the eleven Danish-born saints to receive their own endowments on the day the temple opened, although she wasn't sealed to her children until later."

Julia thought for a moment about the posture of the weeping lady. If that wasn't a direct depiction of Sylvie Cronquist, it certainly could have been, under the circumstances. Nine children lost? No other posterity? What an unbearable burden. But she bore it with faith, in prayer, faithfully waiting to enter the temple, and then entering with haste at the first opportunity. Sylvie Cronquist. The weeping lady? Maybe so—she'd have to check the name. How blessed she was to live to be sealed to those lost little ones. Was she weeping at her loss or her gain? Hmm. She glanced over at True. The story had affected her as well. She wiped a puddled tear from below her eye.

"Thanks, Dad."

"Sure. Anytime. I've got more stories, you know."

"Yeah. I'll ask you for some more soon."

Later, the three girls flipped through magazines in Cathy's room. True sat at the vanity, while the two Cronquist sisters sprawled on the fluffy bedspread.

"When does your school get out, Cathy?"

"On Thursday. I'm in charge of the senior party on Wednesday night. Don't ask me how that happened. I'm only a junior."

"Because they know you're the only one who will make it as fun as they want it to be."

"I don't know. But the bad thing is it means I can't come to your concert."

Oh, that was right. Wednesday. Julia couldn't conceal her disappointment.

"Darn. I really hoped you would be there."

"Me too. I was counting on it. Maybe I can swing something. Let me see. I mean, I'm not a senior. I can't actually be at the party as a guest. And I don't want to be the seniors' slave." Cathy was flipping through a magazine and pointed out a new hairstyle she wanted to try with a fancy clip.

"I have a clip like that, but it gives me a headache." True looked at her tragically damaged hair in Cathy's mirror. She frowned sadly and sighed. "Hey, Julia, what ever happened to that guy who came to visit you last month? You never told me the rest of the story on that."

"You had a guy come and visit you?"

"Just Jed. He was up there anyway and dropped in. We walked around campus some, and then he went home. Nothing to report."

"Why aren't you nicer to him? He likes you so much."

"No he doesn't."

"You must be blind."

"I'm telling you, he doesn't. When he came to visit he told me he was mad about what happened between us over spring break, and that's why he stayed away for a while. I promised it would never happen again, and he said we could be friends. That's that." Spelling it out so succinctly gave her a hopeless feeling for some reason. "End of story."

"Huh. Maybe I was wrong." Cathy picked up her magazine again. Her voice didn't sound convinced.

"So, what about Daniel?" True, in her loneliness, seemed to need to discuss someone else's love life as a form of comfort. "Are you going to invite him to the women's ensemble thing on Wednesday?"

Julia hadn't even considered that. Of course, she'd seen him hanging around after class a few more times lately. Maybe he was enchanted with the music. Maybe he would enjoy a personal invitation. Maybe this was the final nudging opportunity he needed to push him over the edge and into her arms.

"I hadn't thought about it," she replied noncommitally. "That might be an idea." Yes, it might. In her mind she was already designing a little card she could send.

CHAPTER TWENTY-NINE

"I had such a great time at your family's place last night. Thanks for the getaway. I needed it." True plunked her Chemistry books into a big cardboard box. "All done with these for a while, thank goodness." She was nearly packed, except for a few daily essentials. "I don't know why you don't like that house. It's gorgeous—everything I'd ever dream of."

"I don't know how I feel about it these days. Sure, I didn't like it when we first moved in. But I guess it's kind of grown on me." Julia was doing Theory flash cards for the final. "Like you said, home is where the family is."

"I wish my family were that close. My mom and dad divorced after mom got her stomach stapled when I was twelve." Julia never knew that. "She remarried and moved back East. I haven't seen much of her since then." Why did True allow her weight to become such an obsession then, when she saw the obvious dangers of it? Weird. "Your mom seems so great."

"Oh, she has her great mom moments. Quite a few great mom moments, actually. Yeah, we're all basically pretty close. Of course, Bianca hasn't shown her face much lately, but she's always been on her own page—in a different book from the rest of us."

In the past few weeks, no apology had issued forth from that lone apartment in Ogden. No phone call. No nothing. The seed of distrust Ted planted in Julia's head began to foster and grow, and soon it became clear what kind of a friend Bianca was. Or wasn't. Part of her was furious at Bianca, but part of her stood wide-eyed at Bianca's immaturity and shortcomings. Just because Bianca was *older* didn't mean she was *wiser*. Mom and Dad never gave Bianca's judgment much credence, but Julia could never understand why— until now.

"Are you still mad at her about the Wendover thing?"

"Not really." Sort of. Okay, yeah. Still mad. "What I wish is that I hadn't fallen into her little trap to get me to like"—code word: kiss—"that weirdo Scott, though. What a waste of perfectly good crush energy."

"Speaking of crushes, did you send that card to Danny Boy?"

Julia described her little idea for the concert invitation.

"Hey. That was a really cool story your dad told us about the pioneers and the lady who had all those children who died." True sat on her bunk and stared out their window at the mountain view. Snow still caked the northern slopes. "It made me think. A lot."

"Yeah?"

"Yeah. About the kids and the sickness and how the mom felt and about the temple. It made me think about how totally right Rory was about what's most important." If Julia craned her neck just right she could see one of the spires of the Logan temple through the trees of campus. It looked like the tops of the old New England-style churches she saw growing up. It felt comfortable. Home-like. Clean. "Why did you ask your dad about those people, anyway?"

"Oh, I just felt like I should."

"Well, I'm glad you did."

All day Thursday, Julia poured all her creative juices into making a pretty, formal card.

It Would be an Honor to Have You as my Guest
at The Women's Ensemble Choir Recital
Wednesday Next, 7:30 p.m.
Fine Arts Auditorium at Utah State University

She embossed it, used metallic pens, the whole nine yards. After laboring to make three of them, she could waste no more time on it. The first she mailed to her parents, and Cathy, of course. The second, she sent to Ted and Becca. The third, she hung onto. Sending it to Daniel might be a big mistake. He might not come. Then the card would be completely wasted. All that work. Or, he might come, and then what would she do? Have him as her honored guest, and what? Ask him to sit with her family?

She put it in an unaddressed envelope and carried around in her backpack for a day.

After twenty-four hours' rumination, she came to a decision. Dan liked the music so well, he would probably be there anyway, obviously, or else why would he hang around the classroom so often? Why waste her creative juices on that? A more appropriate waste of creative juices would be sending the card to Jed Smith. Even though she hadn't seen him for nearly a month, he deserved an invitation. Without him, she never would have taken the class, and she never, ever would have found the most excellent lyrics of "To Electra." Yes, Jed deserved the card. She addressed it and dropped it in the mail to him. Of course, she knew it was a waste. Wednesday was the night of the senior party, as Cathy told her, and he'd be too involved in that to come anyway. But not being invited is worse than being invited and unable to attend.

Wednesday came all too soon. Julia felt good about her Theory test. Good enough she thought it might salvage her grade—after the abysmal midterm—and her scholarship. Good enough she ran all the way back to her dorm in excitement. Good enough she offered to take True out to lunch for a thick slice of homemade bread at the Sweet Shop in the Student Center. Mmm. Hot bread with honeybutter and raspberry jam. Nothing more delicious. True accepted.

The two girls entered the Student Center on the ground level near the Hub. As they walked by, Julia tried to avert her eyes, so as not to be forced to recall her embarrassing experiences in there.

"I was eating lunch in there the other day," True commented nonchalantly as the scent of burnt chili filled their nostrils, "and met the most interesting person. He knew Rory and was a Computer Science major. We had a fun little talk." True went into the Hub? But she hated the Hub and everything it stood for. Huh. Maybe everyone can change their minds about what they despise and what they don't.

They sat together at the small round table in the Sweet Shop, vainly trying to keep honeybutter from dripping down their wrists. True ate just half of her bread and wrapped the rest of it up for later. Julia told herself yes to the whole thing. It was a celebration of the completion of a triumphant year.

"Have you already decided what you're going to do tonight?"

"I think so. If he's there, I have a little plan."

"What is it? Run up to the microphone and yell? Daniel Chitwood, take me, I'm yours!"

"Not exactly." But she laughed at the idea. At one point in her crush on him, the suggestion wouldn't have been out of the question. "The director mentioned at our last practice there's a tradition that after the recital people tend to loiter for a while to visit and get other students to autograph their programs."

"Like yearbook signing? How high school." Good old True. She'd always hold some things to be beneath her.

"It sounds like it, huh? So, anyway, if Dan's there, I'm going to ask him to sign my program."

"What do you think he'll write?"

"Only the Chitwood knows. I've been imagining it ever since I came up with my diabolical scheme."

Julia, I've seen you from afar. I want to see you from a-near. Love, Dan.

Julia, You've fallen for me time and again. Fall for me now. Love, Dan.

My Julia, Let me pour my soul into you. Love, Dan.

There were infinite possibilities.

"He has to know I like him. How could he not? And with all the time he spends outside my class, I'm getting the hint from him, too. It's kind of like payback time from when I waited around for him in the Business building during fall quarter." Finally she could give him the opportunity to declare his love. How grateful he would surely be. No more frightened waiting in the wings. He could come right out and tell her of his admiration and affection.

Dearest Julia, Come live with me and be my love. Your Dan. Ah.

CHAPTER THIRTY

The concert was a smashing success. The women's ensemble received a standing ovation and cries for an encore. The other choirs did well, too. An evening of high entertainment.

Though it wasn't announced aloud by the Master of Ceremonies, the fact of her authorship of "To Electra" was noted in the program. Stage lights blinded her, but from the audience she distinctly heard cries of "Author! Author!" coming from the general direction of her parents' seats. The hall was nearly two-thirds filled at curtain time, much better attended than Julia dared hope, and she felt so victorious at having her song debut before such a great crowd—and that it was well-received—that she didn't care a whit that she wasn't a soloist. Stringy Pout girl performed tolerably well; she didn't even get "pitchy," like the choir director warned her of in class occasionally.

When the lights came up after the final numbers, the audience began rising from their seats and heading for the exits. Julia frantically scanned the crowd. She had a mission to accomplish before the evening's end—something that was tonight do-or-die. She glimpsed her family in the lower west section but didn't waste time looking at them. Her family had agreed to meet her at Fredrico's Pizza after the show, a short walk away, and they planned to go right over to order. She'd talk to them about the concert there.

But where was he? She just knew he was here. She felt his presence, his love emanating from somewhere in the room. Her heart was attuned to receive it. It pulsed wildly in response.

Danny, my Danny. I'll find you.

For several minutes, she lost herself in a crowd of prattling students. They were all taller than she was, and she started to panic. Finally she emerged, took a deep breath, and forged her way up the aisle on the east side. Most of the audience was gone now. She wanted to get the director's signature, too, and Dr. Bailey's. She hoped they wouldn't leave before she found Dan. But her priority was clear: Dan first.

Out into the lobby. Down a dark hall to the backstage area. Across the stage. Past the risers to the other wings. No sign of him. Back out to stage front. Why didn't she think of that before? The height gave her an advantaged view. More students, males and females, exited the auditorium. One woman carrying a baby. An older couple hand in hand. A guy with a bouquet of flowers. All flowing out the door. She scanned the room again.

Aha! There, in the dim of the cheap seats at the back on the west side was the face she searched for! Longed for! She considered leaping from the stage and running up the aisle, but it was a long way down into the orchestra pit, and she was in her black concert dress and heels. No more falling. Not literal falls, anyway. Not tonight. Tonight she would be grace itself. Beauty incarnate. Spunk. Fun. L-o-v-e.

"Hi. Excuse me." He was talking to two guys and the Stringy Pout girl. She was out of breath from her speed walk up the aisle. At last. Unafraid, sure of his ardor, she confronted him. If only she'd been so confident nine months ago. But, no. Sometimes the best things take time. Like a fine cheese.

"Uh, huh?" He looked like he wasn't sure she was talking to him. Coy. Humble. So cute.

"Would you please sign my program?" She said it in a husky, out-of-breath voice and hoped it came across as alluring, but then it cracked from so much singing and running. Definitely more nerdy than sultry. Oh, well, he knew her heart well enough to know what she meant.

"Okay." She handed over the program and a pen. The

surrounding people backed away slightly. Yes, step aside for true love to take its course. Step aside. A long moment passed while Daniel Chitwood scrawled his love on the linen paper. She resisted all temptation to read over his shoulder, and instead stared at his strong hands. The hands that lifted her from peril that snowy morning. *Up you go.* Fresh and clear the words still rang in that great, kind voice.

"Thank you." She raised her eyebrows and considered a wink but decided against it. No use overdoing it on the first night of their true acquaintance; no point in using up her entire bag of tricks too soon. "Thanks a lot." She smiled and turned on her heel to leave. She didn't look back. That would get him.

"Who was that?" Julia recognized the Stringy Pout's voice, but knew it contained awe—a rhetorical question. Like when the Lone Ranger leaves a village, and the grateful pioneers ask breathlessly, *Who was that masked man?* She didn't listen for Daniel Chitwood's reply. All he needed to say was written on the paper now clutched to her heart.

She scuttled down the aisle, anxious to locate Dr. Bailey and Mr. Christensen, the choir director. Sadly, she missed that chance. No other girls from the women's ensemble were milling around either. Oh, well. The time was not squandered. Her true mission was complete.

Julia wanted to race into the ladies' room, lock herself in a stall and read the message immediately, but she needed to get over to Fredrico's. This was reading that needed savoring, savoring she had no time for now. She'd waited nearly nine months for this declaration. She could wait one more hour for when she could read it in the privacy of her own dorm room—at least hers for one last night.

"You've sure got perma-grin." Ted and Becca scooted over on the red vinyl booth bench to make way for the conquering hero. "I can see why. You're song was a complete hit!"

"We're so proud of you."

"Completely impressed."

"Where's Cathy?"

"She's heartbroken. She had that senior party responsibility and couldn't get out of it."

Oh. Darn. She'd really wished Cathy could be there. She and Jed were her two biggest supporters, and neither of them could attend. Darn.

"Where did you get your idea for lyrics?"

"Actually, Jed Smith helped me find them."

"Jed? He's such a nice boy. He hasn't been around as much lately. Is everything okay?"

Okay? Yes. Why were they asking? "He must be busy with graduation and stuff. He's the Student Body President, you know. Big shot guy. Lots of stuff at the end of the school year."

"I wish I could create something that beautiful, Julia," Becca said. "It touched our hearts. What a gift you have."

Their salads came, hers with Thousand Island dressing, her favorite. Mom remembered. Then garlic cheese bread and two pepperoni pizzas. Everyone talked and laughed and ate for an hour, and then her honored guests declared they needed to get going home for the long drive into the night. They offered to drive her back to the dorm, but she declined. It was such a nice night for a walk, and it was her last time to walk that familiar way for a while. They understood. Mom and Dad hugged her, Ted and Becca congratulated her once again, and they parted. "See you at the wedding."

"See you."

Back at her dorm, she took the stairs to burn off a few cheese bread calories. When she came to the third floor for her last time as a freshman she peered down the long hall. None of the dorm door decorations remained. Even the "Smile: It increases your face value" poster on door 312 that irritated her each time she passed was gone now. All bad things must come to an end, too.

As she rounded the corner for her room, she spied a bundle on the floor beside her door. Had she inadvertently dropped something on her way out? How embarrassing. But, no. What was that? It looked like cellophane. It was—a bouquet of spring flowers with daisies, tulips, lilacs, irises, wrapped in cellophane, tied in yellow florist's ribbon.

Her first thought was it was an apology from Rory to True. A belated apology, since True left for Wyoming earlier that evening. You're too late, Rory. She's gone. Julia decided to snoop at the card.

"To Julia—Glittering. Smashing. Absolutely smashing. So was the concert."

No signature, but the handwriting she knew: Jedediah Smith's. But, how—? Was he there at the concert tonight? Where was he? Why didn't he come and talk to her when it was over? Oh, she'd been too busy searching out Daniel Chitwood. Daniel Chitwood, whose love declaration lay hidden in the pocket in the recessed folds of her black taffeta concert skirt. Daniel Chitwood whose face made her heart go pitter-pat. Whose love was now within her grasp. Why, oh why didn't she think to offer to sign *his* program tonight—and add her phone number so he could keep in touch over the summer? Darn. Well, surely he was astute enough to locate her if he wanted to. And he would. She was confident. She fumbled in that same pocket for the key to her door.

Inside, she pulled the blinds down in the half-empty room, feeling anxiously alone for the first time. It was really weird to have True's stuff all gone. She wondered how True must have felt all alone in here for the first two or three weeks of fall. Probably not this alone—with a void due to the absence of a regular presence. The overhead light made a strange glare off the blank facing wall, and everything seemed to create a hollow echo. Good thing she was leaving first thing in the morning. Too creepy here.

She pushed spooky thoughts aside and refocused on the delightsome task at hand. With a trembling grasp she gently opened the program to read the single autograph inside. Before deciphering any of the scrawled words, she assessed the handwriting. Messier than she expected. But masculine. His signature slanted backwards. What did experts say about that? A backwards slant did not bode well, as she recalled. Never mind. The message, the message!

"Hello." Nice greeting. Very formal. Didn't use her name. Why? Hmm. "I liked the concert tonight." He did! He really liked it! "I'm sorry I don't really know who you are," No, we haven't been formally acquainted . . . "but have a nice summer. Dan Chitwood."

Huh. It seemed a little flat on first read.

She re-read it. *Have a nice summer.* As True might note, very high school yearbook-y. How many times had she written that herself? Mostly to people she shared no experience with. *I'm sorry I don't really know who you are.* He's s-o-r-r-y he doesn't know me. That implies he'd like to know me. It grieves him greatly to be unacquainted with me.

Perhaps that could be stretching the implication there. She refocused on a different possible interpretation. Oh. Bad. He apologizes for the fact that not only does he not know me, he doesn't know *who I am!* This was far worse. Far, far worse.

She flung the program aside, but not before noticing his signature smudged over the line crediting her with authorship of "To Electra." Argh! Not only did he fail to declare love, he paid her a great disrespect by deleting her fame and glory *in her very own souvenir program!*

Worse and worse.

She stomped angrily around the room, trying to get ready for bed. Have a fun summer. Ha. Some consolation prize. She shoved the piles of rustling taffeta into its hanging bag. How was it possible? It had to be an exaggeration. *Was* it possible that he simply didn't know who she was? After all that passed between them? The falls, the dance card, the daily vigil, the Hub, the doctor's office, the hallway collision in Fine Arts—all unnoticed by him? How could that be?

Simple. It couldn't be. He was lying. Teasing her. Leading her on. The message he wrote was a gag message, a red herring, and the real note was on the back somewhere. Code, maybe.

She plucked it from the floor and flipped it over expectantly. Nothing.

All the while she knew she was deluding herself. No secret message. No love declaration. No . . . love. Really and truly he had no idea who she was.

She just spent the past nine months of her life chasing a dream that had no substance. Smoke and mirrors. Illusion alone.

And she'd been the most deluded of all.

She stood in the center of the room in just her black nylons and full slip and let the tears of hurt and anger roll down her face. Hurt that he didn't care, hurt that he never noticed her, hurt that he never would. Anger that he was so oblivious to her ardor, anger that he brushed her off pitilessly, anger at herself for opening her heart enough to have it stomped on by an unfeeling stranger. Why, oh, why?

There was a reason they were called crushes: they hurt.

When she'd exhausted her strength for drama, she finished changing into her pajamas and climbed into her spring-loaded dorm bed for the last time. Old Main struck one. The sound of the faraway chimes lulled her into much-needed sleep.

SEASON FOUR: SUMMER

CHAPTER THIRTY-ONE

When she awoke the next morning, the sun shone bright and warm, even through the pulled shades. Summer was nearly here, seasonally, although it officially began today for Julia: a whole new season with no horrific crush incidents in it—she hoped. As usual, a good night's rest seemed to put things into perspective. Yeah, the whole year of wasted energy wasted on a waste of a guy who didn't know she was alive made her eyes drop in shame, and a sharp twinge of pain raced through her heart. How could she have been so blind? It was embarrassing.

But where she was going, Huntsville, no one knew about him or all the stalking of him or all the talking about him she'd done. She could—and would—pretend it had never happened. Besides, ha, she had the solace of realizing that Daniel Chitwood himself never knew it had happened.

As she arose and began packing her final belongings to take them down to the Century and head for home, she noticed an envelope near the base of her dorm room door. It was shoved to the side, but she still couldn't imagine how she missed it last night. Picking it up from the floor, she recognized the handwriting on the front right away. Jed. Jed! Jed's flowers! She never put them in water! Hurriedly she filled her sink with water and set the bouquet in it. Darn. Some were already wilting, especially the lilacs. Shriveled and closed. Maybe they would revive? Oh.

That task completed, she turned to the interesting envelope. What more did he have to say beyond the friendly note attached to the flowers? She ripped it open to see.

Dear Julia,

So, there I was in the concert, just minding my own business when, suddenly, a bright glint flashed, blinding me. I shielded my eyes—for ocular safety—and tried my best to discover the source of the light. Eventually my eyes adjusted, and then I saw: the shimmering, sparkling, dazzling glow came directly from your beautiful countenance. It filled my eyes, then my heart, my soul with warmth and satisfaction. There she is, my heart sang, there is my spectacular, shining friend. The wellspring of my heart's great happiness.

Thank you for filling my life with light.

Jed

Wow. Wow! A good letter. A very good letter, indeed. Impressive, especially coming from a high school boy. But her heart knew Jed certainly didn't fit the classic definition of the high school boy. He missed it by a mile.

She re-read it. Very nice. Neat handwriting, too. Not feminine neat, just precise. Profound. Poetic. It struck her even more deeply than the Robert Herrick poems to Julia—perhaps because this poem was written directly to her.

She re-read it, imagining Jed's pen as he wrote. Jed's hand as he held the pen. Jed's face as his mind calculated to compose the letter. Jed's lips as he mouthed the rhythms of the sentences. A warm wave rushed into her, and suddenly she felt filled, from bottom to top.

She stuffed the letter back into the envelope. As she did so, she flipped it over. There, scrawled on the back in a hurried hand, were these words:

Tried to catch you after the concert. You looked busy. Stopped by to say good-bye. Must have missed you. Hope you get this. Have a nice summer. J.S.

Have a nice summer?

CHAPTER THIRTY-TWO

The Cronquist family sat together around the dinner table, minus only Bianca. Ted and Becca made a special trip to Huntsville for the weeknight feast. Two days out from the wedding, and final preparations loomed. Everyone grabbed a few minutes of non-stressful time together before Cathy dashed off to graduation, and Ted and Dad set to work on the yard again. Jan, Becca, and Julia planned to finish winding the final strips of heavy white satin into rosettes to place on the tables, and Julia had her final fitting for the bridesmaid dress—a busy night for everyone.

After dinner, Julia followed Cathy to her room for a brief chat.

"I'm sorry you got roped into that thing and couldn't come last night. We missed you, especially at dinner. It was weird without you there." Julia did up the back buttons for Cathy as she put on the red dress she wore to the Christmas dance. It looked nice, even for spring. "I don't always know what to say to Ted and Dad. They're always thinking up something smart, and I can't keep up."

"Me, too. Sorry I missed it, I mean." Cathy pulled her hair up in a twist, securing it with several bobby pins. "But I knew someone else deserved to be there more than I did."

"Who? You're my support—my helping hand great sister! Who deserved to be there more than you?"

"Didn't he tell you? No, I guess he wouldn't." What was Cathy going on about?

He who? Did she mean Jed? But he was there. Oh, yeah. Jed

207

was in Logan last night, not at his senior party. Not taking charge as S.B.P. there. It all crystallized.

"Cathy, did you take over for Jed at the senior party so he could go to my concert?"

"I guess you could put it that way."

"Wow. I can't believe you did that. I mean, it's really nice. *Really* nice. But why? You didn't have to do that for me."

"I didn't do it for you."

Oh. Cathy didn't do it for Julia. She did it for Jed. More of the implications of this conversation began to set in. Jed skipped his senior party, a once in a lifetime event, to attend her concert. Cathy sacrificed, too—in several ways. Jed made a special trip to Logan, flowers and letter in hand, just for Julia.

And Julia didn't even say hello to him after the concert.

Her heart started pounding with anxiety and guilt. What had she done?

"Cathy, I haven't talked to Jed for a while."

"I know." She did?

"But, anyway, he left me this nice letter last night—" Did Cathy know that too? "—and in it he told me to have a nice summer. Is he going somewhere? Do you know?"

Cathy dropped her arms from working on the twist and turned around with an irritated look on her face. It was only the second time in her life Julia had seen Cathy look so accusatory.

"Don't you pay attention to anything?" What? Of course she did. "Jed is leaving this weekend for basic training. He joined the ROTC—the unit at Utah State gave him an Air Force scholarship, and he's leaving for ten weeks of basic in Texas." What? Ten weeks? Military? "You know all those trips he made to Logan? He was applying and interviewing for the scholarship. Weber State offered him a much better deal than USU did for a straight academic scholarship, but he worked out a deal with the Air Force so he could go up there next year. He takes off Sunday morning."

In three days? Less!

Julia thought fast.

"If I give you something, would you take it to Jed tonight at graduation?"

Cathy's disgusted look faded slightly. "What is it?"

"I have it in my room—but I need to finish it. What time are you leaving?"

"I'm an usher, so I have to be there in twenty-five minutes."

"Don't leave without this, okay? Promise?"

Cathy promised.

What was she going to do? Tonight was his graduation. Tickets for Huntsville High's graduation ran out weeks in advance. In fact, some students could only invite one parent. She couldn't get in now if she wanted to. And graduation was a family thing. Plus, she had her own family things to attend to. She and her mom were getting everything ready for Becca's last minute bridal shower tonight. Plus she had to finish Ted and Becca's wedding present. It was almost ready but still needed an hour or two to be finished. No, seeing him tonight was out.

Friday wouldn't work, either. That crazy last minute bridal shower would take most of the afternoon. Grandma Cronquist and all the aunts from Wyoming were coming a day early for the wedding so they could meet Becca while her parents were here. Julia was in charge of cleaning the gargantuan house—all the while making notes to herself never to buy a home larger than she could stand to vacuum—while her mother did the baking for the shower. Plus, Julia and Cathy had been put in charge of all child care during the wedding. Since Julia was done with school, she offered to get the kid-entertainment items prepared.

And Saturday was the wedding itself, along with the wedding breakfast and the reception in the Cronquist yard and cleanup and everything that entailed.

No, there seemed to be no hours of daylight or otherwise left to see Jed before Sunday morning. Unless—

Her mind began devising a little poem. It stunk, but it worked for now.

Saturday night
Meet me at eight.
The moon will shine bright
And work tricks of fate.
Under the gazebo
I will wait.
Please tell me, my darling,
That it's a date.

Hmm. No wonder she only pulled a B minus in her poetry class. But there wasn't time to worry about that now. She stuffed it in an envelope, gave it a squirt of her favorite perfume tester from Bianca and hustled it into Cathy's room. Jed and Julia. Jules and Jed. Julia and Jedediah.

"Cathy, uh, thank you for doing this." Julia suddenly felt sheepish. Several situations were coming clear to Julia, but she couldn't take time to consciously define them just now. "You're a really great friend. You know that, don't you?"

"Yeah. I know."

"Do you think Jed will forgive me?"

"For what?" Cathy's tone implied that she wondered for which of the many, many things Julia hoped to be forgiven.

"For being so stupid."

Cathy paused for a minute. Then, with a kindly, warm smile she replied, "For your sake, sis, I hope so."

CHAPTER THIRTY-THREE

Saturday dawned bright and sunny. A perfect day for a wedding. Julia lingered in her room, applying makeup and adjusting dangling ringlets. The french braids were the perfect solution for hiding her brassy coloring mistake. Pretty? Could it be? From the kitchen she overheard her parents' talking.

"Rex, honey, I just don't know what to do with her. She didn't even come to the bridal shower with Grandma Cronquist. Everyone asked where she was, and, frankly, I didn't know what to say. She hasn't been here in weeks, Rex. This family counts on each member. Besides, I fear we're supporting this irresponsible lifestyle." After the shower, Jan had called and left Bianca a stern message. Bianca called back with a perfunctory apology and a promise to be at the wedding for sure, but to Julia listening now, their parents sounded unimpressed with small efforts.

"Try not to let this get to you this morning. There are more pressing matters."

"More pressing than the welfare of our oldest daughter? She is setting an example for the younger two, whether we like it or not."

"I only wish our little experiment had worked better last summer. I know she's younger than Bianca, but I thought for sure some of Julia's maturity and soberness would have rubbed off on her."

"Honey. How do we know it didn't? It might have had more of an effect than we know." Dad's voice softened. Julia heard the clank of forks on stoneware. She felt bad eavesdropping this way, but the information was too important for her to quit now. Besides—her parents had been counting on *her* to be the example for Bianca? Wait a minute! What universe had she entered? Julia had nothing to offer that Bianca would want. Hmm. She needed to mull that one over in her mind for a while.

"Look, Jan. We both know the situation, and if we factor in what Ted told us last night, the discipline is clear. Our Smurfette's wings are clipped for a while. She'll fly straight soon enough. We trust that she'll mature eventually, don't we?" Smurfette? Didn't they mean Barbie?

Then the realization hit her that the *reverse* of her parents' wish had come true. Instead of Julia's being the example, she'd made herself into Bianca's little protegé, rhinestone-studded shirts and all. She had fallen into that awful Venus's icky trap. What business did she, Julia Cronquist, have trying to be anything like her older sister? None. None at all.

"She isn't going to like living at home for the summer, without a car, riding your old ten-speed. And she'll like working for you even less." At their dad's office? The only possible job there was night janitor. No, not Bianca's style. Unless it wasn't at his office. He did manage all those funeral homes. What were they going to make her do? "After all, she's nearly twenty-one." And the thought of Bianca on a ten-speed. Why, it was ludicrous! Could a bike conceivably be pedaled by legs in pants that tight?

"No matter what her age, we are her parents. We can't support her bad decisions. We have to do what's necessary and in her best interest." Rex Cronquist laid down the law. After that, no discussion made a dent in it. "Jan. Underage gambling is serious business."

"You're right. Oh, I wish poker weren't so generally accepted these days. The kids start thinking that Texas Hold-'Em is an unobjectionable party game. It disturbs me."

"It's a good thing Ted left her that check made out explicitly to the gas station on the seat of her car. She wouldn't have even made it home. She might still be in Wendover doing who knows what. I can't believe she wasted her entire paycheck! Haven't we taught her anything?" So, that's what she and Scott were doing all that time while she waited outside of that dive Retread—playing poker. What a nightmare night.

"But don't you think her being excluded from Miss Weber County is punishment enough?" Out of Miss Weber County? But Bianca lived for that! "The directors called to say her entry form and fee refund were in the mail. Underage gambling is not a value the Miss America organization wants to promote. They're very strict."

"And we should be, too." Dad sounded like he wasn't afraid to err on the side of too strict. "I really like your idea of the two jobs. Daytime flower arranger at the funeral home and nighttime janitor at my office will keep her busy doing something productive." Oh! It *was* the funeral home! Julia didn't want to be there when Bianca heard about her fate. There would probably be radioactive fallout.

"And, as her chief laundry-doer, I'll make certain her wardrobe becomes much more appropriate—in modesty and in scope. The D.I. truck will be in the church parking lot next week, and that's when her rent will be due, and she'll have to move home. I'll start taking care of closet weeding then." Julia heard her mother rinse the dishes in the sink.

"This wing-clipping sounds like it's starting to take shape."

"It gives me some hope."

"Me, too. Some people just mature later than others. It appears our Bianca needs some serious structure to get her back on track here. I'll talk to her right after the wedding breakfast." Rex sounded grave. "There's no time before that."

"The sooner the better, dear. I hope this works."

"Me, too." He sighed audibly. "I'm going to miss Cathy this summer." Cathy was Rex's little princess. She was going to that troubled teen camp for two months—as a counselor, of course. Julia was going to miss her possibly more than her dad would. A summer with just her and wing-clipped (and probably pouting) Bianca was not much to look forward to.

"But Julia will be here. It's going to be fine." Mom started the dishwasher, and Julia put the final touches on her makeup and put the last curl in place. "Come on, Rex. Let me straighten your collar. Call the girls. We need to leave, or we'll be late."

An hour later, just as the Cronquist family was loading into the car for the temple, a familiar rumble echoed against the mountain walls, and a pink Karmann Ghia tore into the gravel drive.

"Sorry I'm late." Bianca looked frazzled but gathered up the masses of skirts on her heavy dress and mashed herself into the back seat of the Lincoln Town Car. "Did I miss anything?" No, Bianca's excitement still lay ahead.

Their mom dashed back inside to get her temple bag and camera and six other items she forgot, and their dad, anxious, worked off some nervous energy by pulling a few weed sprouts that had sprung up overnight. Up drove a familiar vehicle with a familiar face.

"True, what are you doing here?" True climbed out of her beat up Nissan truck and smiled at Julia, running over her with an approving eye.

"I tried to call you at home, but it was busy all morning." Ah. Jan Cronquist had been giving the cello ensemble last minute instructions. "I knew you would be here at some point this morning, so I dropped in. Do you have a sec?"

"It looks like it. But, hey, what are you doing in Huntsville?"

"Didn't I ever tell you? Rory's family lives here." They did? Weird. Maybe that was why True mentioned possibly running into her in Huntsville over spring break.

"But—wow. Okay, so, why are you here? Last week Rory was public enemy number one."

"No, he was never on my bad list." Oh, yeah. True was just on his. "After USU graduation yesterday, I ran into him. Okay, I meant to. But I just had to see him again before he left for California." Dad trundled past them to the garbage can with a small handful of weeds. He checked his watch, looked nervously toward the house, then went back to his petunia beds. Cathy and

Bianca sat in the back seat of the car. Cathy was doing up Bianca's satin-covered buttons that extended from the elbow to the wrist of her bridesmaid dress.

"What did he say?"

"Oh, Julia, you won't believe it. He looked so happy to see me. He came and hugged me and whisked me off to meet his parents. When he introduced me he said, 'Mom, Dad, this is True, the girl I told you about—the one I want to marry.'"

"What!"

"Yes! To marry!" True flushed with excitement. Mom emerged from the house and headed for the car. Julia gave her the 'one minute' finger. "He told me I was looking great—I've gained ten of my thirty pounds back—and he said if I promised to keep on track with myself, he promised to keep on track with me, for always."

"Wow. I'm so—surprised. And happy for you!"

"I know. Me too. And so, we're getting married in August—the week he gets back from California, the week before he starts his full time job with the county here. Can you believe it?"

Julia took a moment and tried to force it to sink in. True and Rory, getting married. Of course! They made a great couple. And Rory was really good for her.

"We'll live in Ogden for a while, and I can commute up to school—or just finish at Weber. I'm in the Weber State cooperative nursing program anyway. When I started out I had a feeling I should go to the USU campus for classes. And now I know why!" Her friend's ecstatic face beamed, lighting the dimness under the shade tree where they stood.

"I'm so happy for you. Do you have a ring?"

"Not yet. We want to wait a month or two to get it, so I can size it right. His family is so nice. And I just love Huntsville. We even talked about living here, too. To raise our family."

True sounded so grown up. Raising a family. It all sounded so distant for Julia.

"Congratulations, True. I wish you all the best. If there's anything I can do to help, please tell me."

"Will you play the piano at our reception?"

"Of course. I'd love to. Oh. Hey, I'd better get going. Are you staying around? Can you come to the reception tonight? It's here. In the garden."

"I can't. Rory's folks are waiting to take me to his grandma's house. Meeting grandma is a requirement. Hope I pass muster."

"Good luck." And with that, True gave Julia a hug and wafted back to her car, light as a feather, or maybe just slightly heavier. Julia congratulated her again warmly in her heart then rushed to where her family was waiting in the car.

"Who was *that*?" Bianca elbowed Julia when she squished into the back seat of the family's Lincoln Town Car beside the girls and their enormous masses of skirts. Bianca continued arranging the baby's breath sprigs in her blonde poof. "Did you see her hair? What a mess. Looked like she got it caught in her blow dryer and had to cut it off." Mom and Dad climbed aboard, and they sped away. Julia was too horrified to even answer this cruel taunt. She had no words specific enough to reply appropriately and still be standing on the temple grounds in a few moments. But Bianca's moment was at hand.

While Julia tended five children under nine with Cathy in the gardens on the grounds of the Ogden Temple, she let her mind be occupied with thoughts of what was about to go down in Bianca's life. A vengeful "bwah-ha-ha-ha" gurgled up in her throat. No car. No clothes. No Dillard's. No social life. Worst of all, no pageant. It was exactly what she deserved. When she reflected on the multiple humiliations Bianca inflicted on her throughout the year, torrents of anger flooded her mind. Every time she came into contact with that sister it ended badly for Julia! A flush rose to her cheeks. How could someone be so false? So fake? Bianca pretended to be her friend, but everything she did was for her own glorification. Julia was merely her pet project. Bianca deserved every punishment her parents had in store for her.

She looked over. Bianca was flirting with the photographer near a stand of hydrangeas, trying to get him to take her picture. He seemed extremely uninterested.

"Julia!" Cathy called from the other side of the fountain where she was taking care of Aunt Heather's baby Emma. "Look at this!"

As Julia came around the fountain, still keeping one eye on the kids who were on the bench in the shade, Cathy let go of Emma's hands. Emma took two steps in her little white leather shoes and tumbled onto the grass. "Heather said Emma might take her first steps today, and look! Look-y here!" Cathy swept the baby up and set her on her feet again. "Isn't it amazing? And we got to see it. How neat that her first steps were toward the temple. I can't wait to tell her mom." Julia took Emma's fingers and walked her around a little then sent her back to Cathy who ruffled her little curls and straightened her dress. "I wonder what she'll be like when she's grown up. Don't you?"

"Yeah."

Julia glanced at the baby and then sucked in a deep breath of the fragrant springtime air. She glanced up at the stark, rock-laden mountains to the east and then turned back to look at the temple. It was a neat shape—like an art deco mushroom or a really cool upside down stone cupcake. At first the Ogden temple wasn't her favorite, but with its grounds and fountains and view of the peaks, it was starting to grow on her. Its whiteness made it even more endearing. And the steeple, or whatever it was Moroni was standing on, pointed directly heavenward. It didn't lean to the right or to the left. It got her thinking about Big Things.

Big Things. Like going back to live with God again someday. Like families. And togetherness. And love. What was it Ted said the other night? About being single for eternity up until now? Well, probably by now his alone-phase was over. He was on his way to starting a new family. With togetherness. And love. Whew. Julia hoped for his sake he didn't end up with a daughter like Bianca to plague him. It did seem genetically impossible for Ted and Becca to produce such a child, but there were odd things in nature and in the Lord's plan. Lehi and Sariah had Laman, right?

But they also had Lemuel.

Lemuel, the follower.

Lemuel, that rotten Laman's rotten little tagalong yes-man. His protegé.

Couldn't Lemuel just as easily have followed Nephi? Sure, he didn't have enough substance or charisma on his own to be a leader, but he definitely possessed the power of free choice regarding whose example he was going to follow. Sam, the other brother, proved that. He followed Nephi so closely that his posterity got swallowed up under the title of Nephites entirely. They never mention Samites in the Book of Mormon, do they? But that was Sam's choice—even as an older brother. He picked Nephi to emulate. Huh.

She couldn't help but notice her own family. There was Bianca with her bevy of boys and her insulting remarks and her own idea of what was "fun." Of course she wasn't plotting their father and brother's death or anything, but she certainly wasn't doing much to add to the family glue. Then there was Julia. With . . . what? She wasn't sure yet. Then there was Cathy, with all her obvious strengths. She was large in stature in a lot of ways that had nothing to do with her skinny little frame.

"Oh, look, Jules. They're coming out." Julia looked over at the wedding party emerging from the temple doors. Ted held Becca with one arm and raised the other in triumph. "Let's gather up these kiddos and head over there for pictures." Julia shepherded the remaining kids and followed Cathy over to give their new sister-in-law a welcoming hug.

"Bianca, would you please ride over to the wedding breakfast with me?" Rex Cronquist took his oldest daughter by the arm and led her out to the Lincoln. "Jan, would you and the girls ride with the Kenners?" Uh oh. The oldest Cronquist girl was in for the complete Dad Treatment. A drive in the car and everything. Both

Julia and Cathy were fully aware of the implications there.

"Hasn't it been a lovely day so far?" Mrs. Cronquist addressed the Kenners as she and her two daughters climbed aboard the rented Jeep Cherokee and headed for the restaurant.

"It certainly has." The Kenners beamed. "We're so glad you raised a fine boy like Ted to be our son-in-law." This pleased Jan Cronquist to no end.

"We're so glad to be getting Becca as part of our family." It was a pleased-fest all around. At least in this vehicle.

Later, sitting at the head table in the restaurant's conference room, Julia checked her watch again. The wedding breakfast officially started sixteen minutes ago, and still Dad and Bianca failed to appear. Physical and emotional torment set in. Julia was starving. When were they going to serve the food? The bread basket taunted her! Worse, she was worried for her older sister. Well, part of her was worried. The other part of her wanted to know exactly what was going down between Bianca and their dad.

"What do you think Dad's saying to Bianca?" Julia whispered as she poured herself and Cathy their fourth glasses of ice water. It took all her willpower not to take a second piece of bread. Why did they call it a wedding *breakfast* when it was at 2:30 in the afternoon?

"I don't know. But I know he and Mom have been pretty upset with her. I heard them a few days ago."

"I heard them this morning. They devised quite a plan for her." Ten speed bike and everything. Boy, the Karmann Ghia would never look so good. Ha ha. A smile tugged at Julia's lips.

"Yeah. I hope for her sake it works." Cathy went ahead and took another roll. Julia decided to follow suit. After all, the meal was paid for, right? Food was for eating, right? She only had to think of True for a split second, and she told herself yes to a little square of butter as well. She dug in.

"I've been so worried about her, Julia. She's never really had her head on straight. Mom and I fasted for her a few weeks ago, but things seemed to go from bad to worse. It was before your little night journey into the desert. Ted told me about it. Don't worry. No one's mad at you. You couldn't control what she did. If anything, Mom and Dad felt bad for you."

Julia wasn't worried about that. She hadn't done anything wrong. At least not that night. But a different worry crossed her mind—Cathy's worry. Their younger sister was that concerned about Bianca? Concerned enough to fast for her? That probably most likely included praying, too. Fasting and praying for Bianca? Oh. Julia took a little nibble of her bread and chewed it a bit. It seemed dry, even with the butter.

Big Things like family and togetherness and love came into her mind all over again. Then another Big Thing called forgiveness passed through. The torrents of anger and shame she felt when she thought of all the humiliations Bianca had caused her to endure made a last roaring pass through her mind before the word forgiveness could come ashore to rest there.

Forgiveness. It was a big word. Bigger than it sounded. It seemed she'd used it herself recently. In fact, she did use it the other night, in passing to Cathy. *Do you think Jed will forgive me?* Jed. His heart was so big. Of course he'd forgive, wouldn't he? Plus, Julia's own trespasses against him were so minor compared with Bianca's against Julia, right?

Or, were they?

Just then, Bianca and her father emerged through the double french doors. Bianca took her place beside her sisters, and Rex sat down next to Jan whose face unwrinkled in relief. Out of the corner of her eye Julia saw her mother whisper in her dad's ear and her dad nod toward his wife reassuringly. The deed had been done. Julia glanced at Bianca, whose brows were knit in anger and whose arms were crossed over her chest defiantly. Now was not the time to ask. The dinner began.

While everyone was eating, Cathy talked to Becca The Radiant Bride who sat on the other side of her. Julia had some time to think, and she peered into her mental backpack that carried all the books of her memories of the past year. One by one she fingered through, pulling out the offenses against Julia perpetrated by Bianca and those inflicted on Jed by Julia herself.

She stacked them up side by side. One in Bianca's pile: *Heat of the Moment*, the tale of the fisherman knit sweater in Indian summer; one for herself: *The Brush Off*, wherein Julia shot down Jed's New Year's Eve invitation. Another in Bianca's pile: *The Mistletoe Misfire*, her embarrassing and oh-so-public first kiss; another for her own pile: *Younger Man*, treating Jed like a non-person for such a shallow reason. A big, thick, heavy one for Bianca: *The Desert Drive to Abandonment*; then, an equally big, thick, heavy one for herself: *The Invisible Super-Guy*, ignoring Jed at the choir performance when he alone made her triumph possible and made such a sacrifice to be there.

Gee. The bad memory books were stacking up pretty evenly— two here, three there, and so forth.

There was an entire *Encyclopedia of Crimes of Bad Advice* to place in Bianca's stack. Where to live, how to dress, with whom to be friends. Grr. Reviewing them mentally sent anger through her all over again. How could she? The anger gave Julia a twinge of satisfaction.

But that *Bad Advice* book was suddenly counterbalanced by the volume of *Simple But Egregious Insensitivity Toward Jed*. Shoot. For a second here her own pile looked bigger than Bianca's. It was so tall and menacing. Oh, how she wished it would just go away. All that righteous indignation she'd built up against Bianca now felt hollow, hypocritical.

She reloaded the piles back into that imaginary backpack and slung it over her spiritual shoulder. Chuh! It weighed a ton. It was definitely a two-strap pack burden, and sciatica was imminent.

At the word *burden*, an imaginary triangle pinged in her mind, *Ping!*, following which, her dad's voice rang true and resonant in her memory.

"Sin is definitely one of the heaviest burdens we will ever carry."

Suddenly it came to her—the answer to his Sunday School

lesson question of how to bear another's burden of sin. *Forgive.* The only way to get rid of all these offenses that were laden upon her was to forgive. The only way to feel relief and peace and healing was to forgive Bianca because Bianca bore these offenses, too, and for Jed to forgive Julia of all those things she'd done to wrong him because they weighted her down so.

But how? She asked herself silently, how could she let all that go?

And a whispering of the Spirit came, "You can. Give it to Me. You'll know when it happens."

A sense of peace, the first hint of it she'd felt in days and weeks, washed over her. She could really forgive? The hope of it caused an infinitesimal lightening of her spirit's load, and she knew she must. And she somehow knew the Lord would help her—because He wanted her to forgive, too. It was possible to let it all go, to hand it over to Him. Let Him take care of all those grudges she held against Bianca for the wrongs she'd done, intentionally or not. She wanted to give it up. A little prayer formed in her soul, *"Help me to let go."*

The room and reality came rushing back to her. It was Julia's turn to salute the bride and groom.

"I want to tell Ted and Becca how happy I am for them." Julia raised her water glass in the direction of the happy couple. "And I'd like to play them a song, if that's okay." Everyone clapped graciously, and Julia made her way over to the piano. It had taken many of her spare hours, but she'd prepared a short piece for them, a love song from Tchaikovsky's *Sleeping Beauty* that she thought everyone would recognize. "I know you, I walked with you once upon a dream." She knew Ted was a sucker for Tchaikovsky. At least one good thing came out of her trip to the desert.

CHAPTER THIRTY-FOUR

The backyard looked perfect. From the white satin rosettes to the bunting to the gazebo to the masses of floral rapture that lined the walks and exploded all over the yard, it was perfectly gorgeous. Julia felt a twinge of pride knowing she'd had a hand in making it so. The luminaries along the sidewalk were set up, ready to be lit when the reception began tonight. Julia and Cathy took this little stroll to get the full effect in daylight. The Kenners had dropped off the two girls and their mom at home so Bianca could help their dad do some errands before the reception. The crackdown had begun.

They hoisted up their skirts and stepped into the Dream Home where they found their mother standing in the kitchen without shoes.

"You girls better get some rest. I'm going to need you at five." That was in two hours. "Try not to muss your hair or wrinkle those dresses."

"Okay, Mom." Mom disappeared into her room. Probably to take eight Tylenol.

"Hey, Cathy." Julia followed her younger sister down the hall. "Can I come and talk to you? I'm not all that tired."

"Okay."

The first order of business was kicking off their satin shoes. Oh, what pain we recognize has been with us when it is suddenly removed! Then the sisters took off their satin gowns, hung them on Cathy's closet door, and poofed down on opposite ends of the bed. Julia could contain her question no longer.

"Well, what did he say when you gave him the letter?"

"Nothing. I'm not sure he knew what it was at first. Not that I knew what it was, but I have my guesses." Cathy smiled. "Lots of people give cards at graduation. He had a regular stack of them inside his suit jacket. I saw them." A lot of cards? Oh, dear. Maybe he thought they were all boring Aunt Martha cards with a dollar bill inside and a contrived poem. Wait, hers had a contrived poem. And no cash to recommend itself. What if he didn't even read it?

"Well, what did he *look* like when you gave it to him?"

"I told him it was from you, and he lit up." Cathy massaged the arch of her left foot.

Still, something bothered Julia. Not so much about Jed anymore. Sure, she had her serious misgivings about whether he might forgive her. But, as much as she cared for him, there was something of even greater weight on her mind. If she didn't take care of it right away, she could never even begin to enjoy being with Jed—if that ever came about.

"Cathy? I have to ask you something." Julia sat up in earnest. "And I need you to answer me in full honesty."

"A scout is honest, loyal, trustworthy, brave—I'm always honest, Julia." She said it jokingly, but Julia thought that it might actually be true, coming from Cathy.

"Okay. Well, a few months ago you told me you liked Jed."

"I don't think I actually said that." But she did say that. Julia needed not to argue this point but to press forward with the gist of her questioning.

"That's how I remember it, anyway. Later you said you didn't like him." She ought to choose her words carefully, but it was hard on the spot. "So, anyway, all this time has passed, and now I think I like him, and I'm wondering where you are, and what you must think of me. Your friendship—I value it so much. If anyone or anything got in the way, I'd gladly sacrifice it to preserve your trust. Including Jed." It was true. Harsh, but true. She needed to ask the clincher. "Tell me honestly, do you still like Jed Smith?"

Cathy paused, set her sore foot down and bit her lower lip.

"There was a time, a brief time more than a year ago, when I thought I liked Jed. When we first moved in." Not even last fall? Oh. "He's a really great guy. We became friends pretty fast, and he showed me around school and stuff, helped me with my campaign. I saw all his finer qualities, and they drew me in." Oh, dear. This was not sounding good.

"I didn't know he helped you with your campaign." Julia had been too busy moping about the move to help Cathy herself. That was a dark time.

"It's the only way I won. I rode in on his coattails." She paused again, reflecting on the year gone by. "So, we did a few things last summer to get ready for the school year—when you were living in Ogden with Bianca." Yes, last summer was all Bianca and Ogden and Texaco in her memory. "After school started, we didn't do as much together. I got busy with stuff, and he was spending a lot of time with you." He was? "My feelings for him sort of faded out slowly."

"But what about the Halloween dance? The Christmas dance?"

"What about them? At Halloween I probably still had some residual feelings going on. But that was the last time. And, oh, yeah, I did ask him to the Christmas dance. Not that I still liked him, but I couldn't think of anyone else to ask. We were friends. But he already had a date. Or at least he said he did. I don't think the girl asked him until after he said no to me."

"Why did he tell you no, then? What? Did he like some other girl and expect her to ask him?" That sounded so un-nice—so un-Jeddish.

"Nothing of the sort. The problem, like I think I told you—I figured out he liked someone else by then, and so did I."

"Who did you like?"

"That isn't the right question."

"What do you mean?" He liked the chicky who asked him to Christmas dance. Duh.

"The question is who Jed liked." Duh, duh.

"Who?" Julia asked it under duress.

"You. He liked you, Julia. He didn't go with me to the dance because he couldn't date the sister of the girl he liked."

He liked Julia? All that time? And wouldn't date Cathy because . . . Oh, how steadfast he was! How true, and how loyal, and—and how steadfast and true and loyal Julia wasn't. Please, she prayed, let him forgive me.

"So, Julia. You see, I fully relinquish any claim I might have on him for seeing him first. The last thing I need in high school is a boyfriend." Cathy rolled her eyes at the idea, and Julia thought how wise this younger sister was, once again.

The front double doors banged open, and Bianca stomped toward her designated bedroom.

Julia returned to her own bedroom, letting Cathy get a little rest before the day's events resumed. Plus, she wanted to think about what just happened, besides making herself available for Bianca whenever she needed to talk. She rehearsed the inevitable conversation in her mind.

Jules, can you ever forgive me? Bianca's eyes fill with tears of sincerity, remorse.

Bee, you know, of course, it's already done. Forgotten. Forgiven.

Oh, thank you, sweet sister.

How could I hold a grudge? Julia's speculative magnanimity warmed her own heart considerably. It waxed eloquent. *Sure, we had our bad times—*

Like my complete disregard for your safety and comfort when I dragged you to an unknown city and abandoned you, for instance—

Let's just leave that in the past, Bianca. I'm beyond it. Besides, you've taught me so many good things in the process.

Bianca's tears might overflow at this point. *Like what?* in a tone at once doubtful, yet hopeful. *All the things not to do in life, I'm sure.*

No. Lots of good things, too. Like, don't get an eating disorder. Like discover your hidden talents. Bianca's eyes brighten with recognition of her own little wisdoms. *And be a real woman. Look for the fun side of life. Have confidence in relationships. You taught by example.* The two sisters embrace in reconciliation and plan fun activities to do together as they live at the Dream Home for the summer.

Ah, forgiveness was sweet. Julia shivered a bit and got goose bumps. She repaired a chip in her frost pink nail polish until the expected knock came on her door. Bianca tramped in and slammed the door, then threw herself angrily onto the bottom of Julia's bed. She was still in her satin dress, and her eyes were mascara-streaked and her lipstick gone. The demeanor didn't exactly match Julia's expectations for this apology, but she'd take it however it came.

"Can you believe it?" Bianca's voice huffed angrily. "After all the work I've done to get ready for this thing, and *now* they tell me I'm *disqualified?*" Her shoes clunked noisily to the floor.

"You might want to hang the dress up for a while if you're going to lie down like that."

"Ugh! I don't care what happens to this awful thing!"

"But I thought you were going to use it for your evening gown." Then Julia realized what she'd said. It was hard to imagine Bianca's life without the pageant aspect. "Oh, sorry. Um, I overheard about Miss Weber County. You must be pretty upset."

"Upset? You bet I'm upset. I paid for dancing lessons and everything. Tanning passes, clear plastic high heels to wear with my swimsuit. Now what am I going to do with those?" Julia certainly couldn't answer that. "And the rolls of duct tape and ballet slippers? I am out so much cash."

Cathy peeked her head in and came to sit beside her sisters on the bed.

"You don't think they'll let you do it next year?" Cathy asked.

"Wait a whole 'nother year? Ha. Not likely." A year didn't seem that long. "Plus, I'll be so old by then." Twenty-one didn't seem that old. But, then again, maybe pageant years were like dog years: seven to one or something. No. There must be another reason Bianca was so upset. "I'm going to have to move to another county." Oh. Aha.

Someplace they didn't have a record of her offense. Hmm. Julia started to feel sorry for Bianca as her dream came crashing down before her eyes.

"It's so unfair. I hate this day." A pout formed on her lower lip, and tears welled in her lower lids. One spilled over and rolled down her cheek. "And Scott dumped me last night."

"Oh, no. Why?" That came as a shock. He seemed so totally gone over her just days ago.

"I don't know. He just said it was over so . . . 'Later, girl.' That was all he said. Can you believe it? Oh, well. It was probably for the best. Believe me, I am so done with playing cards. What a waste of time—time I could have spent perfecting my stage eyeliner and blush." Then she started to cry in earnest. Big tears wet both of Bianca's cheeks thoroughly and smeared all the colors of her makeup. Midnight Black mascara and Blueberry eyeliner mixed with Party Punch blusher and Ivory Beige foundation. She blew her nose several times and let more and more tears fall. Sobs joined the tears, and Cathy offered Bianca a washcloth to sop up all the various moistures involved. Julia put her arm around Bianca's shoulders.

"It's just not fair. You guys would never understand. I mean—" a breath caught in her throat like a little hiccup—"I mean, okay. We all know Ted's the smart one. And Cathy's the kind one. And Julia, you're the talented one." She was? They were? Julia had never exactly broken it down that way. At least never including herself. "How come you got all the talent? I wished every single day and every single night that I could play the piano like you. If only! If only! Then I could have shown those judges. Then they would have seen!

"But me, what am I? I've always been the 'popular' one. Which would be fine, except when you realize that when I'm alone—which I am now for, like, for as long as Dad makes me live here in solitary confinement—that when I'm alone, I'm not really anything. I don't have anything smart or kind or talented left over in me to show for it. And you guys couldn't ever understand that. And it's not fair." Bianca wiped a tear that was about to drip off her jaw with the washcloth. It left another darkish blot on the white terrycloth. "When I'm just by myself, I'm basically *nothing*. Without someone else thinking I'm so fun, I don't have *anything*. It's so awful to realize how empty you are. So awful."

The sobs came full and free. Julia and Cathy exchanged helpless, sorry looks. There was nothing they could say to counter Bianca's points. What she said was true—to a degree. And for the first time, Julia looked at Bianca in that light. How sad for her to think of herself as a vapid, shallow, intellectually inferior, talent-devoid, self-absorbed person. How utterly sad.

A crack formed in Julia's heart for Bianca. The angry torrents of earlier that day became tides of pity. She saw Bianca's weakness— her true weakness and humanity—for the first time. She was just a girl who was trying desperately to make up for her inner failings by accentuating her surface gifts. And in doing so, she was failing to notice what her true inner gifts were. No, she'd never be the family brain or the concert pianist or the recycling drive organizer. But there were things she *could* do. She just needed to discover who she really was and go for those things.

"And now Dad's going to make me work at the funeral home! The mort-u-ar-y! Why Dad ever thought of becoming a mortician I'll never understand. Besides, I only know how to arrange flowers because they're pretty. I never wanted to do it as a job. And now he's making me. And I have to quit Dillard's! That's my employee discount! My life, basically. What is everyone going to think of me? All my friends are there. Well, they were. Everyone's leaving, it seems. But it was so fun!"

She went on babbling and blubbering. Julia gave her a full hug. Bianca's shoulders shook as she gulped the air and told her sad tale.

"And I was going to move up to the cosmetics counter soon. I've been working on my foundation application skills." She sniffled. "It's so important, you know." Her tears dried a bit.

"Bianca, I'm sure you will figure out something—something

else exciting and fun. Like Miss Weber County USA." Julia suggested it in all sincerity. The Miss USA pageant didn't take the scholarship tack like Miss America. Their judging was much more up Bianca's alley.

Bianca's eyes brightened. She sniffed one more time.

"Hey, sister. You might just have an idea there." She sat sniffling and let that idea germinate. "Miss Weber County USA. I might still get my own float. Maybe I could really do it." Her eyes, red around the edges, sparkled blue in contrast. It was pretty to see. Something inside her—a light—seemed to be turning on. "And, you know girls, if I'm lucky, there *might* be a way to use my unique skills at my new job. Mortuaries have need of cosmetologists. I hear you can really make some money at it, too. Way better than at a salon." She seemed to be counting the cash already. "And I have always suspected I have a knack for it."

"I'm sure you do." Julia gave her another side hug.

"And it's such a service for the families, Bianca. You could make some people really happy." Cathy nodded approvingly.

"You think?" Bianca's face, cleared of all residual makeup by its generous salt-water bath, had a certain brightness. She looked at Julia and smiled, not a beauty pageant smile like she'd been practicing in the mirror for months, but a beaming from within that couldn't be contained. "You guys are good sisters. I'd invite you to my place for the weekend for some girls'-time fun, but it looks like *su casa es mi casa* for the summer, *no?*"

The apology didn't come exactly the way Julia expected, but the reconciliation felt just as refreshing. And unburdening. It felt light.

My burden is light.

The words just floated into her mind, and she believed them as she felt her lungs and her soul expand, and she knew she had let it go.

CHAPTER THIRTY-FIVE

The party was winding down at the reception. The luminaries lining the edges of Rex's prize lawn and the floating candles on tabletops provided the principle light now. The cello ensemble started playing "Jesu, Joy of Man's Desiring" for the third time. Local ensemble. Small repertoire. Small booking fee. Nice touch anyway. The night birds commenced their evening serenade.

Julia asked to be excused from her spot at the guest book. She threaded her way through the satin-topped round tables and found an empty chair away from the main group, near the southeast corner of the house.

She sipped the raspberry lemonade with floating raspberries and tugged at the bodice of her bridesmaid dress, wondering if the baby's breath in her hair were wilted yet. Does baby's breath wilt? It looked so pretty that morning before the ceremony, where she felt almost like a princess, until she saw Becca in her spectacular white gown, sparkling in sequins and pearls. Gorgeous. But Becca made Julia feel lovely by association.

Underneath the table she covertly slipped off her shoes. Never buy the half-size down for an occasion like this. Note to self. Completely unwise. She should start her own advice box. She could call it Julia's Rules of Common Sense. Ouch. What color might her feet be by now? Black, blue, red? All bruised, certainly. She hunched over and peeked under the table for an advance look at the bad news. She had to be cautious because when she bent over the front of the dress gaped open. She held the bodice shut and maneuvered herself under the table just right, though it was uncomfortable. There. Oh, dear. Blue! Dark blue! Oh, as bad as expected! But—no. Wait. The blue came not from blood from her feet, but from the bleeding of the blue dye from the lining of the satin shoes. Sweat-induced, not actual damage to her vessels and veins. Whew.

As she attempted to extract her head from under the table, a bobby pin snagged in the lace overlay atop the satin tablecloth. Doubled over, Julia could not reach behind her head to free her hair from the cloth. This was exacerbated by the fact that the long satin sleeves of her bridesmaid dress were a smidge too tight. If she just yanked herself up, the candle centerpiece could catch the whole party on fire. What a way to end a wedding. Not an option. If she slid off her chair onto the ground, she might grass stain the dress. There was an open house in Oregon next week and no time to dry clean in the meantime. Not an option. Time went by. No solution came. Breathing the same stale air through the folds of her dress for three minutes, suddenly she experienced a flash of claustrophobia. She had to get out. No air! No air!

As a last resort, she tried calling for help.

"Cathy!" She had no idea where Cathy was—near or far. Inside or out. "Cathy!" The cello ensemble was at a loud part of its rendition of "Eine Kleine Nachtmusik."

"Cathy!" She was going to pass out soon. Then she'd grass stain her dress *and* burn down the party. "Cathy!" She now truly understood the urgency of Heathcliff's wailing that name on the moors of Wuthering Heights. "Cathy!"

In a moment, someone was fiddling with her hair, *ouch!*, pulling ungently, and she heard a slight ripping sound. The lace. Someone was kneeling beside her. She clutched the bodice of her dress instinctively. Soon, she felt her head freed and sat up, filling her lungs with life-giving air.

"Jed. Was that you?"

There, in full uniform before her stood her friend—vainly attempting to squelch a smile. Oh, that dumb damsel in distress thing struck again.

"I was afraid you might miss the gazebo if I didn't help you out of there."

The gazebo. Jed. Oh! What time was it? She checked her watch. One minute to eight. Well, here was Mr. Punctuality—sporting a very nice military look this evening. She stood up straight and took his arm to steady herself after the long lack of oxygen.

"Thank you for saving me from my own ridiculous self." She felt the back of her hair and found three fallen locks trickling down the back of her neck. Fingering them, she discovered they were in near-perfect ringlets. Oh, well. Things could be worse.

"Sure thing."

The two began weaving their way across the back yard to the gazebo. The window boxes around the outside of the lattice structure spilled over with salmon pink geraniums. The scent was lovely.

"Why so snazzy tonight?"

"We got a family picture snapped tonight, and three of us wore our uniforms. Family tradition."

"Who all is in the military?"

"My dad and my older sister."

"Really? A sister? Wow." They sat down in the south corner of the gazebo, Rex Cronquist's own creation. The bench seat creaked under their weight, but Julia knew it was sturdy enough for the two of them.

"So, you're going tomorrow."

"Yeah. Did Cathy tell you?"

"Yeah. Are you nervous?"

"Not really. My dad and sister told me all about it. I think I can handle it. I hope." He chuckled a little. He'd be all right. Keeping a sense of humor would make it all right. She sucked in her breath and knew it was time to do what she needed to do.

"So, um, Jed. I have to apologize for about a million things."

"You do?" He looked surprised.

"Yeah. I'm sorry I missed you at the concert the other night, for one. I sure loved the flowers you left me. And the note. Especially the note." She hoped her tone of voice was conveying what her words weren't. What she meant was she was sorry for missing him for the whole last year. Missing what he meant to her. Missing the whole big picture.

"You looked so beautiful up there, singing. And the music was just the best. It was a great night. You don't have anything to apologize for." Yes, she did. But did he need to know the particulars? Probably not. "You look beautiful tonight, too. Glittering." She glanced down at her bridesmaid dress. It did glint somewhat in the light of the luminaries. Glittering—there was that word from the Herrick poem and Jed's letter.

The night birds sang, even over the orchestra.

"So, you take off tomorrow? Morning?"

"Right. Texas in the summer. How about that? Think of me whenever you think you're hot in Utah and remember . . . I'm hotter. Hotter by far." Yes, he'd be very hot in that uniform in the Texas heat.

"I'll do that, Jed. When will you be back?"

"At the end of August. Just in time for school. On my birthday, in fact."

"Your birthday?"

"Yeah, I'll be nineteen at the end of August. But I've got to go to one quarter of school before I leave on my mission. Scholarship requirement for ROTC. I hate to wait, but that's how it goes."

They were quiet for a moment, listening to the music in the evening breezes and watching the flickering luminaries. Summer was here. Something was working on Julia. Maybe it was the summer. Maybe it was the uniform. Maybe it was the first time she'd ever felt what she suspected might be a glimmer of actual love. Was this what it felt like to love someone for who they were, and not who she thought they were? Was this—

Hey, her thoughts interrupted her.

"So, you'll be nineteen in August?" He was a month older than she was!

"Yeah, my folks decided to start me a year later in school so my younger brother Matt and I would only be a year apart. They thought that might help us be closer friends." He took her hand. "And it worked. We're really close."

She felt herself inching closer to him herself. His hand was warm in the cool night air.

"I saved the program from the recital for you—in case you didn't save one."

"Thanks! I didn't," she admitted. "How thoughtful." The program she picked up that night now lay somewhere deep in the piles of garbage at the Logan land-fill.

The orchestra switched to Verdi, and Jed's voice got whispery and his face a little serious.

"I know you can tell, and I know I've made a fool of myself a thousand times, pining after you the way I do. But I've liked you so much, Julia. Ever since we first met. The beauty of your heart was even greater than the beauty of your face, and *even* greater than the beauty of your talents. I see so much in you—so much more than maybe even you can see."

He tipped her chin up to look straight at her face. She lowered her eyes. How could he think her beautiful with this mess of red hair, this imperfect face, this severe lack of confidence? How could he think her talent beautiful when she was so far from the level where she wanted to be? How could he believe her heart beautiful when all it ever did was flutter from one vain pursuit to the next, hardly glancing at anyone around her? What did he see in her she missed? Maybe it was in his eyes. She lifted her own to see if it were reflected in them, and, as she did, he bent to kiss her. It was different from that first kiss a month ago—tender again but somehow significant and filling, though it lasted only a brief moment. But for that moment, Julia felt so unalone. Her soul. His. It was like he'd poured his soul into hers. Finally she understood.

"Julia." He spoke softly. Shadows concealed them from the eyes of the seated guests visiting at the tables. "I've wanted to do that ever since you first let me kiss you in the spring." Really? He had? "I got pretty discontent only 'kissing the air that lately kissed you.'

You know—like the poem? From your composition." She knew. She knew just what he meant.

"But why didn't you come for our date the next week?" She knit her brows, baffled. "I thought you were mad at me—for kissing you."

"What? But I did come." His mouth pulled into a perplexed frown. "You weren't here."

"But I *was* here." Then it came back to her. She was *here*. In the back yard. Building the gazebo with her dad and planting flowers with Cathy. "I waited for you all day." She had to explain it to him, but maybe he needed a little teasing. She arched her brow and got a faraway look in her eye. "I stood on my front porch, calling after you. 'Jed! Jed! Where are you? Here I am! Come and take me away!'"

"No you didn't." He cocked his head and arched his own brow. "I know so because I was standing on that front porch ringing the doorbell. I'd have heard you for sure."

"Okay, okay. Now that I think about it, we must have been out back here working on the yard for this unprecedented outdoor extravaganza. Slave labor. I really did want you to take me away."

"You could've used my help out here, I bet."

"Yes, sir."

"That's yes, Airman Smith, sir, to you, ma'am." She giggled and ran her finger along his uniform's shoulder buttons. The stiff collar looked so sharp. The crease down the front of his navy blue pants and the high gloss shine on his black shoes, so smashing.

"Okay, soldier boy. Airman Smith, sir." She rested the palm of her hand on his smoothly shaven cheek, then patted it. What a kind face Airman Smith had. So kind to her, particularly. "I am sorry about the mix-up. I would never make you mad for all the ebony in the Steinway factory."

At this moment, it was true. Nothing in the world could induce her to hurt her dear friend Jed. She didn't delude herself into thinking she had never hurt him, though. The night of the recital loomed large in her memory. If only he would forgive her.

"Jed. I have something to ask you."

"Shoot." His voice rose a notch in volume.

"About last week. The recital at school. I, uh—" How in the world could she ask him this? It was completely unrehearsed, and she was the overkill-rehearsal queen. "I made a mistake."

"I didn't hear a single mistake. Every note rang true."

"Not that, exactly." Difficult. Very difficult. "You see, when it was over, I was busy, as you saw." He'd mentioned that on the back of the envelope he left with the flowers. "But what I was doing was so much less important than finding you—than thanking you for your support. For a few minutes I lost my head. You made a real sacrifice that night for me, and I made you regret it." Did he understand? "What I'm asking for is forgiveness."

His face softened. She knew she had it. Hooray! How good he was. Jed smiled and took both her hands. She smiled back, a smile of gratitude and relief.

"I'm glad you'll be up at school with me, at least for the fall quarter. Utah State is a pretty fun place to be." She was going to miss him tons over the summer, though. She hadn't spent time in Huntsville without him for so long. He *was* Huntsville to her. He was part of home.

"Yeah. College. You'd think I would be kind of nervous, but I'm not."

"Really? Why's that?"

"Well, Julia, because I already know all the right people." He winked at her and gave her one more kiss. The orchestra's Verdi swelled in the starlight. They were playing "Summer." Have a nice summer, it seemed to say.

A nice summer? She fully intended to.

ABOUT THE AUTHOR

Photo by Andrea Stanley

Jennifer Stewart Griffith was born in Logan, Utah, and grew up in Weston, Idaho, where she hardly ever practiced the piano but nevertheless wondered why she couldn't play very well. She studied English at Utah State, and no matter what anyone says, she insists that the white Smarties taste the best.

Jennifer and her husband Gary live in Arizona, where they're raising four little kids. She is also the author of *Choosing Mr. Right*.

Also by Jennifer Stewart Griffith

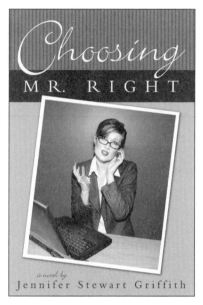

Kate has always believed there was just one right man for her. This hope has taken her through her youth, college days, mission, grad school, and still sustains her as she dedicates all her time to her job as executive assistant to the governor. She's now 28, and she feels like she has dated every available man. The "Why aren't you married yet?" question is getting pretty old.

After one unbelievably bad charity date finally pushes her over the edge, Kate is ready to clean her slate of all the men she's ever met. That very night, she receives an invitation to a reunion with her roommates from summer camp many years earlier. The other women are eager to share how they each met their Mr. Right, which would leave Kate as the odd one out. Should she go? If she does, what can she tell them?

Join the girls from the "Baby Bear Bungalow" in several fun and hilarious short love stories in one, with five unique girlfriends who meet, go different directions, and then reunite with an unforgettable outcome. An ideal read for anyone who believes in true love.

"A great read! Keep your eyes on Jennifer Griffith. She is definitely a rising star in LDS fiction."

— Chris Stewart, author of *The Great and the Terrible* series

ISBN 10: 1-932898-22-0   ISBN 13: 978-1-932898-22-4
6"x9" paperback   236 pages $14.95